Nonprofit Chronowar

Book Three
of the Jack Commer Series

Michael D. Smith

Sortmind Press, 2020
press.sortmind.com

For my wife Nancy

CHAPTER ONE
The Committee
Friday, May 5, 2028

Joe Commer lurched into hard wood, legs buckling.

"Jackie! God, *Jackie!*" He clutched at the angled wood and it was like sliding off a roof. Why was he falling? Was he going to throw up? No, that was shameful, this woman was *giving* herself to him, he had to steady himself, had to get *control.*

He fought for air. His mouth fell open. His fingers dug into polished wood. Why was he on his feet? How did he get so heavy? Had Jackie fallen off the bed? He had to be out of his mind.

Joe focused on a vast auditorium of expectant, puzzled faces. Midday sun surged through tall arched windows. Beyond, expanses of empty prairie. Blue sky.

"*Oh my God!*" His heart shot to six hundred beats a minute. "*What's going on?*"

"How'd that clown get in here?"

"I don't know! I just looked up, and he was *there!*"

"Are you--are you talking about *me?*" Joe said. He grasped the sides of a *lectern*. He stood at a *lectern*. He could hardly move. His fingers were weak. His legs were wobbly chunks of cement.

"Excuse me, sir, you'll have to take your seat in the audience," said a young man in a green polo shirt striding up the stairs to the wide podium, where Joe stood in front of hundreds of people.

"*No!*" Joe shouted, waving him off. "Where's *Jackie?*"

"Where'd he get that silly red costume?" someone snickered.

"Uh, sir? We're set to start with our first speaker," Polo Shirt said.

"*I'm in USSF uniform!*" Joe cried. "I swear to God a second ago I was completely naked!"

This got a laugh from the audience. How could there be an *audience?* Joe raised a fist. "Get back! Or so help me God! I

1

must be *insane!* She was *with* me! God, if you only knew how impossible I always thought that would be!" More laughter. An entire auditorium *laughing.* Joe caught sight of a sign at the far end of the hall: CTESOPE. "Oh, my God, this can't be true! This can't be happening!"

"Sir ..." pleaded Polo Shirt.

"Because if this is what I think it is--"

"He's drunk!" someone cried.

"Ranna, we may need to call the police," Polo Shirt quavered.

"Nonsense!" a voluptuous woman with brick-red hair called up from below as she passed out papers. "Just get a couple guys up there and toss him out. He doesn't even have a name badge. How'd he get in here?"

"I don't know, Ranna!"

Joe sized up Polo Shirt. Maybe the same age as Joe. Redhaired like the woman, but strawberry blond, and slender and fragile. No threat to Joe, who at thirty-one was in peak physical condition. But where were these jerks this Ranna woman seemed to think would take care of him? Instinctively he felt for the pistol in his holster: standard-issue Martian shattergun. Polo Shirt blanched.

"Look, it's okay!" Joe said. "I don't know how it got there either! I don't know what's going on! I had to turn in my gun when I quit the USSF. But somehow I'm wearing the uniform again!"

"Sir, it really is time to take your seat," the Ranna woman said. Joe met her brown eyes. She was older than he'd first thought, a mature woman, in command. Joe instinctively distrusted her. "Urside, just come on down," she ordered. "He'll leave in a second."

"Ranna, he's got a *gun,*" Urside squeaked. The audience gasped.

"Hey, look! It's all right!" Joe said. "It's okay! I won't shatter anybody!" He drew the weapon. "See? It's just a Martian shattergun. No big deal."

"God, someone call the police," Ranna whispered as the

first few rows of people began spilling out of their chairs.

"No, I can explain! I can see you're freaked out! But look at me! A second ago I was--" At this point Joe decided he didn't need to share the story of how he and Jackie had finally come to bed. He peered at the CTESOPE sign. "God, maybe it's true. Maybe I really *did* it." He turned to Polo Shirt on his way down the stairs. "Don't be afraid. Your name's Urside?"

"Uh, yeah."

"I think I have an explanation. Maybe. This auditorium--is this the 2028 CTESOPE conference? Really? Could it be? Am I pronouncing it correctly? Suh-TESS-ope?"

"Of course this is the CTESOPE conference!" Ranna snapped. "And you're wrecking our schedule! Dr. Norsen is supposed to talk about the animal disturbances."

"The animal disturbances! I was reading about them! And would that explain why this cat is up here with me?" Joe pointed to a Russian Blue jumping onto the lectern and trotting across a manuscript titled *Animal Disturbances and Their Effect upon the TropoEcoMind.* Blue cat eyes peered deeply into Joe.

"Churchill, get down from there! He has nothing to do with anything! Why are you here, why are you armed, and why are you disturbing our conference?"

"You! You're the organizer of CTESOPE! I read about that!" Churchill folded his paws and settled atop *Animal Disturbances*. Joe scanned the audience. There were numerous cats in people's laps. Outside the arched windows a dozen more prowled in the grass.

"Can't you … won't you please leave?" Ranna said.

"I've contacted the cops," Urside said, looking up from punching something into a phone.

Joe drew in another long breath. "Okay, everyone, I think I know what happened. I can't believe it, but I must have *time-traveled*." He met Churchill's icy blue eyes. "That explains how heavy I feel. Because I'm back in Earth gravity. God, you can't believe how fast you get used to one-third G on Mars!"

"No! That's crazy!" Urside shouted.

"No, I was reading about the CTESOPE conference just last

night, and somehow this afternoon must've triggered it. I mean, I've heard that one of the ways is these *huge emotional surges*. I don't know how it happened!" Again he met Ranna's eyes. Once more, that sense of scary mature female command.

"Please get off my stage," she said. "We have a conference to do here."

"When Glasgow came up with that theory last September, I mean, nobody took it seriously, but there've been all these weird *reports*. Man, I can't believe I did it! Glasgow even called it Heuristic Time Transition. He named it after von Goertner's stupid book! Can you believe it? Everyone thought he was nuts!"

"Look, we'll talk to the police," Ranna said. "We'll make sure they don't arrest you."

"Well, let's get one thing straight, lady. Nobody's gonna give *me* any trouble. I could turn a whole army of cops into teeny piles of broken glass with this Martian shattergun."

More gasps from the audience.

"Oh God, when will they *get* here?" someone moaned.

"Oh, don't worry! Look, it was just a silly joke! Trying to break the ice and all! All I'm trying to say was that all this is so trivial that the book I was reading doesn't even mention any weird problems with the CTESOPE conference. I'd never even heard of this conference until I was reading this book."

"He's crazy!"

"No, forget it! I think the book would have mentioned if I'd shattered a bunch of cops at the 2028 CTESOPE conference, don't you? So basically, nothing much happened. *Is* happening, I guess."

"What damn book?" Ranna shouted.

"Ranna--Kikken, have I got that right? Your picture was in the book! You look exactly like her!"

"Dammit, you're wrecking my conference!"

"No, all the book said was that the conference did go on for a few days and was totally inconclusive, like everything else in 2028."

"*What damn book?*"

"Well, it's called *The Reamers,* which is a silly title, but basically it's analyzing all the fears of humanity in the first three decades of the twentieth-first century. Talking about all the events that were *reaming* everybody's mind. 'Course, I shouldn't laugh, it was only eight years ago, but God, it feels like a hundred! Everybody feels that way!"

Atop the lectern, Churchill calmly licked his leg in front of the assembled conference attendees. Why was this cat accepting him? Was it trying to calm him? Because by all rights Joe should be hysterically raving. But here he was chatting about time travel to 2028 as if it were an everyday matter.

"Would it interest you to know," he went on, "that the Committee to End Suffering on Planet Earth actually continued up through 2031, but this first conference was the only one you ever had?"

"Get out!" Ranna snarled. "We'll be having this conference every year until we fix all the *crap* on this planet! And leave my cat alone!"

"I'm not doing anything to your cat!"

"You've hypnotized him or something! C'mon, Churchill, get down from there!"

Joe laughed. The cat regarded him lazily but didn't move. "I think it's time for CTESOPE to hear some stuff. So what if I screw up the timeline?"

"No!" the skinny Urside screamed. "You can't *mean* that!"

"Urside, stay out of this," Ranna commanded.

"No*! I know what he's doing!*"

Joe briefly met Urside's shocked deep-set blue eyes. Okay, he had to get some control here. He'd battled the Central Asians, he'd evacuated the earth, he'd fought Martians and Alpha Centaurians, he damn well could get a grip on Heuristic Time Transition. He leaned toward the mike and flipped a switch.

"This thing on?"

SCREEEEEEEEE

Hundreds of hands jammed over hundreds of ears, but Churchill gazed back lazily, rubbing his neck against the mike as he continued washing himself.

SCRUHHH SCRUHHH SCRUHHH

"Wow, this thing has its own volume control," Joe said, dialing the mike back down from ten to three. "That better? Wow, can't believe there are still *analog dials* hanging around in 2028. Haven't seen one in ages!" He laughed at a new thought. "Hope I didn't come to this conference myself! *That'd be weird!*"

"Ranna, you didn't really hire this man as a clown or something?" said a horse-faced woman in a dark blue executive power suit.

"Absolutely not." Ranna glared at Joe. "We'll just have to wait for the police to drag him off."

"They won't be here for at least half an hour. This place is so isolated!"

"And, meanwhile, this bozo can ruin my conference! Won't anybody just take him away?"

"I tried to, but he's got that gun!" Urside said.

"Whoa, let's not get all out of control," Joe said. "First of all, I *can't* be here. And obviously I have no memory of being here eight years ago, so we're all okay."

"I can't believe it!" Ranna cried. "I spent *six months* organizing this thing!"

"Look, maybe I should introduce myself."

Silence from the audience. A muted *scruhh ... scruhh ... scruhh* from Churchill. "Okay, my name's Joe Commer. And I guess you're wondering why I'm wearing this, uh, I guess you could call it, like, a NASA uniform."

More silence. Then a hoot from the rear: "Forget it! That's no NASA uniform! Try again!"

"Huh. Yeah, you're right. But hell, NASA wasn't much of a space agency anyway. Not until people finally got their act together and founded the USSF. Well, I guess I was trying not to mess the timeline up too much, but since you're on to me, sure, this isn't any stinkin' NASA uniform, this is a United System Space Force uniform, circa September 2035. We went crimson for some reason. Hell, I wore it less than a month before I quit."

"If I don't get some able-bodied, courageous men to get up

there and remove him," Ranna declared, "I'm going up there myself!"

Well, there was a woman with balls. Not many people wanted to think about arguing with a Martian shattergun. Upon closer inspection, Ranna Kikken was a fine-looking female with generous breasts tight in a russet ribbed sweater that almost matched the color of her wild hair. One of those rare brown-eyed, redheaded women. But of course she was just another nonprofit lady running a civic organization.

Row upon row of these unfortunate nonprofit ladies arrayed themselves behind Ranna, outnumbering the men here five to one. Right this second in the backs of their passionate narrow minds these women were organizing library book sales, setting up charitable foundations, and mustering docents for the latest museum opening. They were sincere, frustrated, time-harassed, intelligent, and blocked. Later these smug cows would pose in bulging, low-cut gowns in the Opera Guild Sunday Supplement rotogravure section still being published, on paper, in 2036.

The audience rumbled. Joe whistled through the microphone.

Silence. Churchill cocked an ear at Joe, then settled down and closed his eyes. Joe stroked the cat's soft gray fur. His duties in the USSF had included an occasional speaking engagement. How was this really any different? "Okay, gang, looks like Joe Commer is your first speaker, for better or worse. So listen up. The very fact that I'm here means the timeline isn't going to get messed up. So I guess we're safe for now."

"What's he *talking* about?" a lady whined.

"Heuristic Time Transition," Joe said. "I still can't believe it, but, God, it must be true, or I wouldn't be here, would I? I mean, zapped straight to here from--" Okay, Joe would have to figure out later about *Jackie on the bed*. "Well, we have to deal with actual reality right now, don't we? I mean, even though for Glasgow it's just a physics experiment, everyone says it's been explaining a lot of people's reports since I don't know when. Like I say, any sane person thinks he's nuts, but, hell, maybe he was right all along."

"No, that can't be real!" Urside cried.

"Hold on there. It *is* real. Did I mention I'm from 2036? January 26, 2036, to be exact?"

"Aaah, forget it," said the same heckler who'd taunted him about NASA. "This is a serious conference about human suffering, and you're just providing more of it!"

"No, it's not really about suffering. Unless it's about how afraid you all are." More silence. "Well, I'm more or less quoting *The Reamers,* but any fool can see how the last few years, and this year especially, have shaken you all up pretty bad. I can't say I was immune from it either, but hell, I was just out of the Naval Academy, and somehow I didn't get so worked up about it. Jack had graduated two years before me and he'd already made up his mind to get into space, and when the USSF came along, well, we both were thinking that, hell, if the solar system is gonna break down on us like this, we're gonna be in on the *fix*."

"Get to the point!"

"The point is just this: you have this conference, you think you're doing something to get to the bottom of all the insanity, when in reality you're all damn hysterical about what's gonna happen to your poor little nonprofit asses."

"Dammit!" Ranna Kikken flared. "Where are the cops?" She paced up and down in front of the first row. "For your information, I formed the Committee to End Suffering to *eradicate* all the dishonesty, all the cruelty and delusion on this planet! Of course everyone's concerned about the recent events. But we can only deal with what we can deal with. Which is why I wanted Dr. Norsen to start off with his analysis of the animal disturbances, but nooo, we have to listen to your crazy science fiction *drivel!*"

"Civilization's breaking down," Joe said quietly, petting Churchill. "Deep down, you all sense you aren't gonna make it. Nothing's been working right for some time. You're all afraid you're doomed. Well, let me tell you something just a few years in your future. You're right. You *are* doomed."

More silence. It was spooky, to be in such control of an

audience. Any protest they made was futile and they knew it. Joe would go on speaking until he was ready to stop. Oddly, this sense of confidence seemed to center around Churchill napping on the lectern. Joe had a momentary panic that he'd fall apart if the cat jumped away.

"What's the point of this?" someone shouted. "It's just more suffering!"

"The point is, your confidence was already shaky before this strange year got underway. Before February 6th. And now you *know* you won't recover. There are forces at play now, out-of-control forces."

He felt their rising hysteria. It hadn't touched him so much in '28. He'd been a strong, resilient, space-minded young man, one of four space-minded Commer brothers. He remembered 2028, the year that brought the first disasters but, more importantly, the USSF itself, much differently than these people living it now. "I'm here, really, to talk about the asteroids, I guess."

"Oh, God …" Urside gasped from the front row by Ranna. Everyone sagged.

"Freaks you out, doesn't it? Freaked everyone out much worse than the feeling that our entire civilization was doomed. Because of course now some nameless evil was involved. Maybe because of the dates. Weird coincidence, or deliberate evil? Actually, I can let you in on a secret: the dates *were* a weird coincidence. The, uh, *entities,* I guess you could call them, don't have our concept of time. They'd never think to try to scare humans by playing on our calendar superstitions."

Joe cleared his throat. "So, February 6, 2028. Just three months ago for you all. Minor planet Ceres suddenly drops out of orbit, and accelerates directly into the sun! All within a few hours. Nobody can believe it. The astronomers and physicists are baffled, to say the least. How can Ceres, the largest asteroid in the solar system, come to a *complete halt* in its orbit and start accelerating into the sun? A lot more than just simple gravity's involved. There's no way Ceres would've fallen in on its own in just nine hours. There was *deliberate acceleration*."

"Okay, what's the point?" Ranna snapped. "They haven't figured out about the asteroids yet, but I'm sure they will."

"Do you have the slightest idea how much *energy* it takes to bring a six-hundred-mile-wide planetoid to a dead stop in its orbit? Or to accelerate it down? *The Reamers* quoted one astronomer explaining this as a quantum possibility or some such crap, a one-in-a-googol event. He sure shut up on March 6, 2028, when Vesta, the second-largest asteroid in the solar system, stopped dead, and shot down into the sun as well."

The faces were gray with shock. Joe did recall feeling sick when he'd heard about the second asteroid. Jack's advice had been to treat the whole thing logically, to study his physics and prepare to move out into the solar system to study the phenomenon up close. Somehow Joe succeeded in following Jack's example. He spent weeks grimly keeping a mounting panic at bay about what would happen if the earth itself should come to a dead stop in its orbit.

"Then April 6, 2028. Pallas, the third-largest asteroid in the solar system, shoots straight into the sun!"

The audience was doubled up in mourning for those big balls of rock they'd never given a thought to but which, once lost, represented their own imminent extinction.

"We know, look, we know," Ranna said. "We can only hope …"

"That your precious CTESOPE can do something?" Joe mocked the nonprofit lady, ashamed of his cruelty, unable to resist it.

"Dammit, I didn't know about any asteroids, none of us did, I just wanted a Committee to End Suffering, was that so bad? Who the hell are you anyway, to wreck everything like this?"

"Today's May 5th. Tomorrow's May 6th. Anybody want to tell me the name of the fourth-largest asteroid in the solar system?"

More silence. Finally the polo-shirted Urside said: "Hygiea. They're saying it'll be Hygiea. On the sixth."

"That's correct. On the sixth, Hygiea goes into the sun."

"*Ohhhh …*" came from the audience.

"But that's just superstition!" Ranna protested. "What're they gonna do, drop every asteroid in the solar system into the sun on the sixth of every month?"

Joe smiled. "Interesting. Interesting to see you confirm that by May 2028 there really was a thought that there was a *they* behind it. I was freaked out, I remember, but I don't recall feeling it was *them,* whoever *they* were. I just thought it was a physical breakdown of the solar system. I just couldn't buy the alien intervention theories. I'm not really sure I should say anything about them. Timeline concerns, I guess. Or, hell, I don't know. Maybe I will tell you."

"You're drunk! Messed up on something!" someone shouted. "There are enough two-bit prophets running around these days!"

"Well, tomorrow you should know I was telling the truth," Joe said. "You may be even more convinced on June 6th."

Audience gasp.

"When *nothing* happens. No more asteroids go into the sun. Apparently they'd finished their first experiments with Amplified Thought by that time."

"Get off my stage, leave Churchill alone, take your little shattergun and your stupid red flight suit and get the hell out!" Ranna screamed. "*Where are the cops?*"

CHAPTER TWO
Are You Ready for This, Nonprofit Ladies?

"*Ranna* ..." Urside whispered, daring to pat her russet arm. He couldn't bear to see her upset. He wondered if Mandy had bothered to come here today. Then again, she probably wouldn't want to be in the same room with him after the fight they'd had yesterday.

"Damn him! Damn him!" Ranna sputtered.

But what was a fight with Mandy compared to what this time traveler was doing on stage? Would that man actually unravel everything? Was there any word he could utter that would collapse the universe? And in these doomed final moments, shouldn't Urside put his arms around Ranna Kikken and tell her how much he loved her?

Okay, he was a puppy. A thirty-two-year-old puppy in love with a forty-seven-year-old woman. It was total insanity. Why had he confessed all that to Mandy? Now she hated him. And Ranna had never wanted a thing to do with him anyway.

Everything was disintegrating. Half the world was sure that Hygiea would be the next lottery winner. Every astronomer on the planet had had Hygiea in his or her telescope for the last week, looking for the slightest sign of orbital slowdown. The nearest spacecraft, the unmanned *Emerald 4,* had been diverted to get as close as possible, but wouldn't be within twenty million miles by tomorrow.

"Get off my stage!" Ranna shouted, turning to Urside, brown eyes furious. "Damn it, get up there and drag him out of here!"

"He's got that gun!" Urside protested. "I already went up once! We have to wait for the cops!" But should he charge the stage for real this time? Would the time traveler shoot him? Would that be the breakdown point for the timeline? Or--chilling but somehow welcoming thought--would Urside's death *cure* the timeline?

Because hadn't he probably wrecked it himself?

"Then, Robbert, *you* get up there!" Ranna fumed.

The old bastard to her left shrugged. "Well," Robbert Geswindoll drawled, "it looks as if we have to wait for the police to handle this, my dear, don't you think? He does have that gun. I do think it's best not to rile him."

"Dammit!"

"But we don't need to worry, love, the Celestions will protect us," the geezer went on.

"Oh, great, the *Celestions*. I can't believe this!"

Urside grimaced. Geswindoll was the street person who'd showed up last month. Somehow he'd become Ranna's pet project, though it was painfully obvious he was an alcoholic on a bender. Dammit, this wasn't some commune or spiritual retreat, but Ranna thought the ancient derelict would be an asset to CTESOPE. "Maybe we'll have some readings of his poems," she'd said.

Why did she laugh at his off-color jokes? He was a hairy bearded garbage dump, tottering about like a stick figure in that filthy plaid coat that stank like a wet dog. Why was he always at Ranna's side these past few days?

"Now calm down, Ms. Kikken," the crimson-suited man on stage spoke through the microphone. "Looks like fate's appointed me your first speaker, and then we'll let Dr. Norsen come forward with his theories about the animals. Meanwhile, I've still got some future history to rattle off for you all."

"He can't do this!" Urside protested. "He'll spoil everything!"

"From here in 2028," Joe Commer went on, "major pollution and social insanity grow exponentially despite all you do-gooders. You thought the previous couple decades were bad, but you're really just starting the Nightmare Era now. But one good thing came out of that. When the remnants of NASA turned into the USSF in '28, we started to have some capability of fighting *back*."

"We're fighting back now!" Ranna cried. "With CTESOPE!"

Commer waved this away. "You're *cringing* with CTESOPE. You're hoping this futile little gesture will save you.

But it won't."

"Damn you! You son of a bitch!"

"Ranna, perhaps if you didn't lower yourself to his level," a woman leaned in from the second row. Urside hadn't noticed Hedrona Bhlon behind them. The tiny, tight-faced blonde, hair tied to the back of her skull, cold blue eyes glittering as always with shrewd ambition, incongruously wore a sexy black low-cut cocktail dress, boobs dangling every which way.

"Damn it, Hedrona!" Ranna snarled, barely turning to register her. "Stay out of this! For once, just stay out of this!"

The Operations Manager of the Cat Farm blinked, shrugged innocently, then settled back in her chair. "Just trying to be of help."

"God, my conference is *ruined!*"

Urside bit his lip, unwilling to chance any further Ranna rage. How Hedrona had managed to avoid being fired was a mystery to all. Ranna railed about Hedrona to everyone, but they all knew and appreciated, probably even Ranna herself appreciated, Hedrona's genius for guiding her noxious bomb loads in just under the radar. The Cat Farm had been a financial mess before she'd been hired a year and a half ago. Now it was one of the most successful nonprofit organizations in the country.

"Listen up, people," Commer said. "You luck out for a year. No more asteroids get dumped in the sun. But next year, on June 12th, Pluto is *hurled* from the solar system." Commer swept his arm towards the arched windows where thirty cats had come to gaze in at the ruckus.

"Dammit, he's just trying to scare us," Ranna muttered.

"Just think. Again, can you imagine the *energy* it takes to accelerate a planet to its own escape velocity from the sun? Scientists calculated that Pluto accelerated precisely that amount. Could any rational person have any way to grasp that? No, nobody could. Deep down everyone was completely freaked out."

Urside gasped along with the rest of the audience. The others thought Commer was building on the current disasters to make crackpot prophesies, but Urside knew Commer was a fellow time traveler. What he said had to be true. And if one planet could be destroyed, couldn't any planet? Including the one they were standing on?

"I pretended I wasn't scared, but by now I was, I guess," Commer went on. "I enrolled in some post-graduate physics, all the hard sciences I could. But get this: later in '29, in October, the planet Neptune just blows up! Imagine that! Now we were really freaked. And then a month later Uranus starts dropping into the sun! Accelerating just like those asteroids! A lot of the planet flaked away just like a comet, but we all watch this huge mass shoot right past the earth! Man, everything was disrupted! Our orbit, the moon's orbit, everything. We had incredible environmental disasters! We lost a billion people out of eight and a half billion right there!"

Silence from everyone. "Oh, God," Urside moaned. "It's *true* …"

"So you can imagine the USSF started getting almost every available federal dollar. All four of us Commer brothers were in by that time. Later the USSF changed from United States Space Force to United *System* Space Force, because the world just *had* to unite into the United System."

More silence. "Okay, I'm getting off the subject. But you people have got some more shocks ahead of you. The worst disaster of all comes in July 2031. Saturn and Jupiter blow up simultaneously! Jupiter was in the night sky and was visible. Saturn was almost 180 degrees on the other side of the sun, but our probes discovered it immediately. Both of them gone! Can you believe it? All that's left are some of their largest moons floating in what we now call the Jovian Fragment Field and the Saturnian Fragment Field."

"God …" Urside gasped amid general groans. "*God …*"

"Again, the energy involved to do that just can't be comprehended. By this time we were certain we were faced with some mysterious force we had no defense against.

"Yeah, we'd founded the USSF and believe me, all sorts of scientific research was accelerated. Before long we had the Xon bomb, which could rip half a planet open, and believe it or not, one of the fondest dreams of scientists for the past century came true: in 2030 we invent Star Drive! We can get to Alpha Centauri in fifteen minutes! Can you believe that?"

"Wow!" Urside said.

"So what do we do with that first visit to Alpha Centauri in '32? Well, I'll tell you: Admiral Cromwell busts in there, finds intelligent life, and decides to test-fire our first experimental Xon bombs at it! God knows why! Within an hour we're in a full-scale war with the Centaurians!"

There was no way Urside could drag his lips back together. Even Ranna had stopped fidgeting. Head bowed, she sank into her seat and let the revelations from the future deluge her.

"2033. Even while we're deep in a space war in Alpha Centauri, we can't keep peace at home. The Central Asian Powers are out of control by '31. They've been stockpiling H-bombs in factories under the Himalayas, and all of a sudden they're blackmailing us with 'em, knowing we can't knock 'em out with regular nukes. By now the USSF had developed a Super Xon bomb that was thousands of times more powerful than our first design. And once CAP knew we had it, they had to have it too.

"Now we tested our Super Xon in deep space and just measured the results, but CAP decides to test theirs on the moon! Half the planet watches the moon erupt! Only about three-quarters of it was left. And it finally blew up totally a couple months later, once we were into the Evacuation."

"Can this be true?" Ranna moaned, long sexy fingers in her unruly red hair. Urside stared back at the most sensuous feminine beauty possible. Why couldn't they have made love? At least once?

Ranna had told him no four days ago. He was such a fool. He'd been in love with her for so long, and wasn't he so smugly sure she secretly loved him back, even if they were so far apart in age? But apparently she flirted with him just as she did with every other man she came across. Monday afternoon Urside just couldn't stand it any longer. Was it because all the asteroids were going into the sun, and May 6th was coming up and everyone knew Hygiea was going in as well, and everything was doomed?

Whatever the case, he'd tried to take Ranna into his arms in the server room. He was astonished at how fast she'd wriggled free. He had to admit she'd been pretty gentle about it, but she made it clear there was no hope. That even though she was single, she didn't want a relationship now. And she had to piously point out that he had his girlfriend Mandy to think about. "I'll drop her! I'll drop her!" Urside had yelled to his shame.

He was offered the consolation prize of Ranna's continuing friendship. He wasn't sure he wanted it. But he was too weak to leave the Cat Farm and his webmaster job and he knew it.

For a few days he thought the Ranna insanity might finally be over. But when he got the courage to tell Mandy yesterday that he'd made a pass at his boss, he'd somehow wound up declaring that he still loved Ranna, that he knew he could never have her, but that he just needed to be honest with Mandy in the face of the asteroids and everyone's fears of the coming destruction of the entire solar system.

None of that had gone over too well. Urside had just been babbling whatever twisted nonsense would get him through the next lying minute. At least she'd stomped out before he'd started in on Heuristic Time Transition.

And he would've told her. He would've piled all his fears in Mandy's lap. Because for months Urside had worried, had dreaded, that somehow his own experiments since January had caused the asteroids to fall into the sun. That had to be madness, though, didn't it? But wasn't everything about Urside's life madness now? Because that man on the stage was confirming Urside's guilt.

"So you have to understand where we were by October '33," Commer said. "We'd already been at war for over a year with these insane Centaurians who won't accept our apologies for blundering into their space, and we know we can't afford any disunity on Earth if the Centaurians invade *us*. But meanwhile the Central Asians blast off a chunk of the moon, then they launch a few H-bombs and wipe out New York, Paris, and Berlin, and we're at war on *two* fronts now. We don't want to use our Xon bombs on this planet, but hell, CAP fired off one Xon, maybe they've got another. In fact, they're threatening to wipe out the U.S. with one, so ..."

"*No* ..." Urside groaned. So many scenes down the corridors of all his travels were beginning to make sense. What people in the future felt, what they meant when they referred to *the old Earth.*

"So Jack's flying the *Typhoon I,* and I'm copilot, and we do it! Jack gets the order from General Scott and we drop the Xon. We carve out a crater five hundred miles wide! The Himalayas are totally gone! The mass of mountains absorbing the bomb probably kept the earth itself from being ruptured, but Jack and I blow Central Asia and a big chunk of this planet off into space! We destroy the earth! Are you ready for this, do-gooders? Are you ready for this, nonprofit ladies? *In 2033 we destroy this planet!* You have five years left! Five goddamn years!"

CHAPTER THREE
Planetary Malaise

Ranna Kikken refused to burst into tears as the smooth-faced, dark-haired prophet ranted about the end of the world. A fruitcake in an idiotic Halloween costume had ruined her conference, and the police would never get here. He was just trying to make everyone sick.

Commer was a powerful, well-built young man, and she was appalled to note that, despite his fantastic, cynical words, his steady voice inspired trust. People were falling for what he was saying. How could she repair the damage? In a way he was right. He *was* the first speaker. But as soon as the cops hauled him away, Ranna would be the second. And she'd tell everyone why Commer stood for all the superstitious negativity they had to fight. She'd get the conference back on track.

"In November '33 comes the decision to evacuate the earth," Commer went on. "Ten thousand spaceships of all descriptions. The amazing new tech and the exponential growth of the USSF really paid off, although we also threw in antiques from your day like old near-Earth orbit stuff, up through pleasure cruisers and military vehicles like the *Typhoon I,* which could do one-thirteenth light. Jack and I, and our brothers, flew hundreds of flights towing giant passenger shells. We helped plan the Evacuation with General Scott, but I think, really, we were trying to atone somehow. Nobody was really sure if Mars could be terraformed, nobody was sure if it was wise to move billions of people off the planet, but damn, within one month of the Final War we've got *ten thousand spaceships* in gear."

Why was Ranna allowing this? That voice was so damn *soothing.* And it held so much bitterness and sorrow. Was that why he'd crashed CTESOPE? That he'd seen enough suffering himself, but was so scrambled he couldn't say why, so he made up this fairy tale?

"Nobody knows how many people Jack and I killed with the Xon, but out of seven and a half billion people left after the Uranus disaster, only two billion ever made it to Mars. One estimate is that the Xon killed two and a half billion, then mass pollution and radioactivity killed another two billion, then maybe half a billion were left behind. You know, we just couldn't get to everyone, and some people refused to leave. A lot of the Evacuation was accomplished by force. That's a dirty little secret the USSF doesn't talk about much."

Joe sighed. "And if you're adding all those numbers up in your head, you realize half a billion *more* people died en route to Mars. With ten thousand spaceships doing hundreds of flights, well, there are some accidents. Just about everybody we moved was in a panic the whole time. Wouldn't you be, if you knew one out of five was going to die on the way? I can still see those big passenger shells snapping free on liftoff, and then burning up in the atmosphere."

Silence in the auditorium. Ranna fought the urge to grab Urside's hand. What on earth was wrong with her?

"Into about June '34 we did this. What a damn Dunkirk! We try to terraform Mars, but then we start fighting *Martians*. Can you believe that? Damn if there isn't an ancient Martian culture there after all!"

"This really is getting out of hand," Ranna whispered. She turned from Urside to Robbert at her left in that ugly plaid jacket he refused to have dry-cleaned. Something about a sacred bicycle tour of Australia when he was a teenager, and he'd never wanted to wash the jacket since. She knew she was supposed to take *Robbert's* hand but couldn't bring herself to do so. Mr. Geswindoll was proving a spectacular lack of help today anyway.

"I couldn't even begin to explain all the insanity of that war, but somehow we worked it out, after terrible … loss. Jack and I lost our two younger brothers in that war. Jim, and John, and a bunch of great friends. But we stabilized stuff. We made peace with the Martians, and I even have some good Martian friends now. But after the initial joy of survival, of starting all over on Mars, damn if people aren't saying how homesick they are for good old dead Earth. Not me, though. We screwed up the planet and I'm done with it. I have a new life on Mars now, and, and, man, I don't know …"

The intruder was slowing down. Good. The police would arrest him and maybe later Ranna could question him. She couldn't fathom what Churchill was doing up on the lectern, snoozing beneath Commer's gesturing hands. The blue-eyed cat, the mystical beast, the most affectionate cat of all, the one everyone knew really ran the Cat Farm.

She couldn't possibly manage the place without Churchill. She'd gotten the idea for the Cat Farm from him. When she'd found him here that spring, hanging out by himself, it had all just come to her instantly. They'd hardly ever used the summer estate anyway.

Could she let this madman screw up six months of work? She'd raised twelve million for this conference. She was good at this nonprofit business. She'd made the Cat Farm out of nothing, she'd made CTESOPE out of nothing, she could raise the cash for twenty more nonprofits if she felt like it. She was not going to let this sci-fi nutcase wreck the First Annual Conference.

Commer fingered Churchill's fuzzy gray neck. Everyone could hear the cat purring through the mike. "But the insanity *continues,*" Commer said. "Jack and me, and his new wife, Amav, we take off in the *Typhoon II* for Alpha Centauri. We're gonna negotiate peace with these totally insane Centaurians. But we screw it up. *I* screw it up." He took a sharp breath.

"*I betray Jack!* My own brother! I get brainwashed by the Alpha Centaurians! What do you think of *that?*"

Everyone froze at the cry. Churchill stood up on the lectern and arched his back.

Ranna peered closer at the tormented man at her lectern. Although everyone here seemed convinced that Commer really did know something about the future, in reality it was something with his brother that had unhinged him. This man was Afflicted. He had the Planetary Malaise. God, that was what this conference was all about. *Ending* such suffering.

"Jack and Amav were *tortured* out there while I collaborated with the enemy! They had some way of absorbing you! I would have prevented it if I could, but it was the women that triggered it. They had all these women who were brainwashed. I couldn't resist 'em. Don't know why I'm saying any of this, not what I came to talk about. Who am I kidding, I didn't mean to come here at all!"

Commer reached for Churchill. "Good cat, good kitty." He gulped for air. "We were finally rescued. Jack and Amav too. But I was such a coward! God, I can't get it out of my head! We get a sort of shaky truce with the ACs, and we get home. But nothing's ever gonna be the same!"

"Look, Mr. Commer," Ranna called up. "I don't know who you are, or what your story is, but we can get you some help."

"No! I'm cut off! I'm out of it now! They sure as hell don't want me in the USSF anymore! People tell me I have this new life, this new start! I say crap on that! The damn do-gooders always say that! What if you've screwed up so bad you can never recover? Don't you think that happens?"

"But look, we can make it all right!"

"No, it'll never be all right! Not after people start *time-traveling!*"

"God, *yes!*" Urside cried.

"Heuristic Time Transition! As if we didn't have enough insanity! HTT has to be a real physical phenomenon. Glasgow must be right! Because I've just done it! I HTT'd here! I mean, I guess I have! Look, last fall this Glasgow guy at the University of Mars claimed he had scientific proof, even though it was all limited to quark behavior. Everyone dismisses this guy as a crackpot, but somehow we all know it's true. There've been too many rumors of people actually having done it, and what I think is that since last fall everyone on Mars has been scared some bozo is gonna HTT and blow the timeline to hell!"

"Oh God …" Urside whispered, eyes wide, face like melted rubber.

"Dammit, what's the *matter* with you today?" Ranna snapped.

"I mean, it's been a fad for ages, like astrology, we all know that," Commer continued. "That idiot von Goertner wrote that book on Heuristic Time Transition a few years back. Wow, I guess it's current now! Well, it looks like the idiot's right, all sorts of people have been doing it, there's no control at all! I mean, I never thought *I* could do it, I could never be one of those poets and artists who do it. Anyway, von Goertner's book is making a big comeback on Mars now. About having these incredible *emotional surges* that transition you to *different times*. Glasgow also says something about the high amounts of energy involved. He calls it quark chi, some sort of raw energy. I don't know, I've never had any real emotions, I guess."

"*Wow* ..." Ranna whispered along with Urside.

"Glasgow says HTT depends on connecting the *inner* chi to the *outer* chi and flowing along and finding these *links* to other times. He thinks maybe because of the upheavals so far this century, there are all these big, repressed emotions, this chi crap or something, and they're opening up these time-travel links. I mean, maybe people are trying to get back to Earth, you know, *before* ... or maybe the links are totally scrambled, and people from all times can now go anywhere."

"*Yes!*" Urside screamed. "I knew it all along!"

"You--you do not!" Ranna said. "Just stop this *craziness!* I've got a conference to run here!" She took a deep breath and gazed coolly up at the stage. "Mr. Commer or whoever you are, your time is up. I'll speak now, and then Dr. Norsen."

"Ranna, he's got something important to say!" Urside pleaded.

"Dammit, Urside!"

"So I quit the USSF!" Commer cried. "In October last year, that's 2035 to you, I just quit it! And I've thrown in with someone my brother *hates!* I'm in business with Huey Vespertine, a traitor to humanity! At least that's what Jack says! What do you do-gooders think? Ah, what the hell, you don't know what a jerk Huey is, you haven't lived through all the insanity on Mars yet!"

Ranna sank back in her seat. That was pure Planetary Malaise up there on stage, racking itself to pieces. And she was supposed to be the one to do something about it? Wasn't it time to admit how much it really disgusted her? Why was she fooling with the Malaise? Who was she to think she could deal with it?

Joe Commer was right. Ranna was just another nonprofit lady. Her whole life was *nonprofit*. All of them, she and Hedrona Bhlon and everyone else here, all nonprofit ladies who couldn't even cure their own Malaise. Couldn't even figure out what it was.

Hell, Ranna knew what her Malaise was.

She *wanted* that jerk on the stage. Oh, yes she did. He was gorgeous. That red flight suit on that hard body was stunning. And she believed his stupid story herself because she found him so attractive. She wanted him this instant. She could take him to bed right now.

She flirted with everyone, she led them on, she *destroyed*. Just as she'd destroyed Urside.

At least Ranna hadn't ended her marriage out of unfaithfulness. She'd been such a good girl. She'd taken so much crap. Then came the night Bartlett got drunk and started swinging his golf clubs at her. It sure woke her up. Why had she ever allowed that son of a bitch to eat up seven years of her life?

Then the men. What had she really been looking for? Ten men, twelve men over the last two years. She'd lost count.

But in any case, Urside Charmouth would never be one of them.

Ranna had been delighted when what looked like a dreamy adolescent with long goofy red hair showed up at the Cat Farm looking for a tech job. Three years ago, just a couple months after she'd founded the Farm. It had only taken him a minute to convince her how badly she needed a webmaster for the Cat Farm, and one more minute for the two of them to act like old friends.

She'd been stunned to find that Urside merely looked like a teenager. In reality he was a twenty-nine-year-old who'd been drifting along at menial tech jobs at various universities ever since both parents had been killed in a car wreck in 2016. Apparently he'd split an immense insurance payment with a half-brother, and now, with funds drying up, he was eager for better computer work. But he'd always seemed oddly unaffected by the deaths of his parents, and had no contact with his brother. Was he just repressing some trauma? That was another reason she'd been drawn to him. She wanted to be available for Urside when he finally needed to talk. A friend.

At least she'd thought that was what he wanted. For some time she'd suspected he was mistaking their friendship for something else. She'd hoped that whatever such notions he might have would eventually evaporate. But Monday he'd made a pass at her. Propositioned her in the server room. She'd refused in shock mirroring his own.

They'd had no contact since then. She'd let him sit beside her today just to see if he could be just a friend. Had she really been leading him on? Had she destroyed him? He looked so sad.

Beyond the arched windows, across the fields on the lake, four bamboo houses rose on stilts. The lake was the most beautiful part of the Cat Farm. Cats loved trotting across the piers to gaze down at hundreds of huge Japanese goldfish. She recalled the evening she and Urside had laughed themselves sick to see two cats pawing for the same fish, colliding with each other, and flailing into the lake amid laughing flashes of gold and orange. Urside had waded in and dragged them both out, getting his arms raked in the process.

Wasn't that supposed to be friendship? And what did they have now, after Monday? He'd told her he *loved* her. But his girlfriend Mandy was the most beautiful woman Ranna had ever seen. What did Urside want with a woman pushing fifty? Who was beginning to break down, physically, mentally, every way?

Ranna shook her head. She had to be responsible now, had to pay attention to the crazy man on stage rambling about Heuristic Whatever. But she found herself focusing instead on his handsome mouth. Here was a splintered, suffering man, ruining her conference, but all she wanted was to get up there with him and kiss those lovely lips.

She had to stop this idiocy. She had a responsibility to CTESOPE, to all these people who'd registered for a real conference. Okay, so a lot of them were nonprofit ladies, but they supported her, they supported an end to Planetary Malaise.

Maybe their money distorted them, but they were her allies. She had to focus and be respectable. She couldn't be fantasizing about taking this conference crasher to bed. She had Robbert now. She had the calming influence he'd already brought to her life.

Calming? Who was she kidding? When just this morning he was whining about "needing to get away and write," because his goddamn poem ideas were starting to flow? Right when she needed him for the conference? There was so much hassle on opening day, but did he care?

Was he going away to write, or to drink? She'd had to drag him here by the arm of his smelly old coat, and he'd been snuffling in self-pity all morning. Was he an alcoholic? Was that his Malaise?

Urside was undoubtedly jealous. Ranna was sure he suspected about her and Robbert. Maybe that explained why Urside derided him as "the BS poet." But Urside couldn't know all the details. He was so out of things. For the billionth time Ranna wished for full telepathic understanding between all human beings. Why call it Gaia if they couldn't share complete soul contact? Where everyone knew everything directly, where by definition there could be no secrets?

And up on the stage he refused to relinquish, the lunatic with the erotic lips and intoxicating dark eyes was still spewing his time-travel fantasy.

"*Can* Heuristic Time Transition harm the timeline? Or has it *already* harmed it? Is that what's been causing the total paranoia of the twenty-first century? This unease you all feel?"

"The animal disturbances!" someone shouted.

"Yeah," Commer said, stroking Churchill. "The poor animals, coming unglued, but toughing it out. But don't really worry, people, the animals are okay. All you're seeing here in 2028 is the same sort of craziness that gets into animals before an earthquake. They know the Final War's coming, and the breakdown of the solar system. But they'll be okay. They're just a barometer now. But, meanwhile, the greatest threat *has* to be HTT. Have I screwed things up by showing up here? If I tell you that CTESOPE was a total failure, that it contributed nothing to our survival or our understanding, does that change anything?"

"No!" Ranna protested. "He can't mean that!"

"Just listen!" Urside said, with a hand to her arm.

Confusedly, she patted the hand, then grasped it. "Urside, I … I don't know …"

"It's all right, Ranna, I can take care of this," said Robbert Geswindoll, standing up. "The Celestions are guiding me."

"Robbert, what on earth are you doing?"

"Do we assume that old theoretical physics workaround that we create an entirely new universe every time we HTT?" Commer continued. "I can't buy that. Who would keep track of all those universes? Makes me dizzy to even think about it. No, my theory is that all the time travel is preordained, that it's been going on by definition from the beginning of time, and so our linear concepts of time just aren't true, that we can go wherever we want, say whatever we want to anyone, and it all just doesn't matter."

"I hope he's right!" Urside cried.

"Robbert, get back here!" Ranna snapped.

"And look," Commer said, "I know I failed Jack. I slunk away from the USSF because I just couldn't handle anything anymore. But what I'm thinking now, doing my first HTT here, is maybe if we coordinate things right, we could *reverse* the destruction! What do you think? Maybe I'm wrong about everything being preordained. What if we carefully went back and engineered fixes in just the right places? We could save the asteroids. We could damn sure prevent the moon from exploding! We could damn sure prevent the Final War, or blundering into Alpha Centauri, or *Jim and John dying*."

"Aw right, buddy, I think everyone's heard enough BS," Robbert said as he gained the stage.

"Forget it! We could save the earth! And really *do* it, not just talk about it like you do-gooders!"

"Robbert, what are you *doing* up there?" Ranna cried.

"You need a man to end this fiasco, you just call on me," Robbert said, then turned to Commer. "Young man, it's my duty to inform you that the Celestions have called upon me to end this farce."

Joe blinked. "Later, dude, I've got to talk to the people here."

"Surely, young man, you're aware that time travel is nonsense. You say you read about CTESOPE in some future book. Then why didn't it mention you showing up and disrupting the conference?"

Commer sized his opponent up, and Ranna thought he was going to punch the shaky, emaciated old man out on the spot.

Commer stepped away from the lectern. Ranna gasped at his muscular body in that tight maroon uniform. "Well, the book didn't go into any great detail on CTESOPE, it was so insignificant. It was just one more example of futility from '28. It's weird, but now I remember that *The Reamers* did mention that there was a debate about time travel at this conference."

"Get off this stage," Robbert said, "before I kill you with my bare hands."

CHAPTER FOUR
The Celestions

The maroon fool had the effrontery to laugh. Robbert became aware of how silent an auditorium could be. He took a deep breath and said: "I repeat, sir. Off this stage, immediately."

"Robbert, get back down here!" Ranna called.

"He's got that gun!" came Urside's shout.

Okay, Robbert had forgotten about the gun. Nevertheless, Urside was a frightened child. And Ranna? Inclined to panic. Robbert eyed the advancing Joe with a new wariness. "Don't worry, everyone, I'm certainly not afraid of a Martial Splatter Gun or whatever he calls it. Oh, I admit I was a little upset about this weaponry at first myself. But I finally realized I was the man to come up here and set this entire matter straight. After all, the Celestions wouldn't let me come to any harm."

"Oh, God …" came Ranna's groan.

Robbert shrugged. Mr. Joe Future had stopped inches away, doing his best to glare malevolently. But the power of the Celestions was confirmed, whether Ranna wanted to believe in it or not.

"Let me get this straight," Joe said. "You get up here, an old coot, and you threaten *me* with physical harm? Hoo-boy!"

"If I have to manhandle you, I will. But we all hope you'll see the light of reason and simply depart."

"Robbert, get back down here! You're making a fool of yourself!"

"Aw, forget it, Ranna!" the Urside child said. "Everyone knows he's a wino! I'm sure he's drunk right now!"

"I am certainly *not* drunk!"

"Hey, I can smell the liquor on your breath," Joe said. "C'mon, old man, sit back down and let me finish about HTT."

"I refuse! And the *ageism* at this conference appalls me! I'm only fifty-eight, and everyone treats me like *crap!*" He whirled to the audience. "All right, so I thought the Cat Farm was for recovering alcoholics! Your damn advertisements sure made it look like that! Who wouldn't have been fooled?"

"*I* wrote those advertisements, you ninny!" Ranna screamed back. "They plainly said a retreat for three hundred cats! *Cats!*"

"Well, Ranna, if you knew how often your writing does miss the point," Robbert began with a wry chuckle, then regretted it as Ranna set her lips into battle formation. Her two-day sulk after he'd compared his "direct" style to her "indirect" still left a stench.

He had to focus on what was crucial here. The Celestions demanded *focus*. After all, they monitored his most insignificant thoughts. He had to keep his mind clear, even when Ranna tore her hair out. Silly woman, panicking at the slightest trifle.

"We're getting off subject here," Joe complained, steering Robbert by the elbow. "C'mon, guy, just sit down."

"I will not! Unhand me this instant! I am not some old fart you can manhandle!"

Joe backed off. "*Whew …*"

"Robbert, get back here right now or you can leave the Farm for good!" Ranna snarled.

"*Whew …*" Robbert echoed Joe, with enough comic timing to get a soft laugh from the audience. Yeah, just what was needed to get everyone *focused*.

"Okay, dude, where were we?" Joe said. "I was standing here giving a lecture on Heuristic Time Transition and its relation to the CTESOPE conference of 2028, and you walked up here threatening to kill me. Have I got that right?"

Robbert folded his arms. "This is the Celestion Posture of Confidence." He held it perfectly. Hell, he'd memorized those videos. Yes, let the Celestion Energy rise to the Sufficient Point.

The fool Joe smirked. "That's another chapter in *The Reamers*. All these idiots thinking *Celestions* are here to help 'em!"

"Nevertheless, I live my life according to their dictates. My unfolding thoughts and perceptions are funneled into the Celestion Overview of Existence. The Celestions saved my life, young man, and I can never forsake them."

"Robbert, get down here or you're history!" Ranna hissed.

Robbert turned the Posture of Confidence on the entire

audience. Let Ranna soak up the energy. Let them all soak it up.

"Goddammit, stop preening yourself and get down here!"

"No one can ignore the Posture!" Robbert sputtered. "Not even you, Ranna!"

"I sure as hell can! Get off the stage or leave the Farm immediately!"

"You can't say that to me! Not your Robbert!" He noted in horror that his arms had slackened. The Posture was gone. "Not when I was *inside* you last night!"

The audience moaned. Ranna looked as if she'd taken a .38 slug to the lungs. "Get the hell out! I never want to see you again!"

"No, everyone! It's true! I *had* her last night! For the first time!"

"R-Ranna?" quaked the Urside child.

"The *last* time!" Ranna screamed. "The *last* time, you hear me?"

"Whoa, this is getting interesting," His Militaristic Future Excellency Joe chortled. "You banged the old coot?"

"I am *not* an old coot!" Robbert repeatedly slammed folded arms to his chest. "Obey the Posture! Obey!"

"This is fantastic!" Joe laughed.

Robbert whirled to the audience. "All of you! For your information, Ranna Kikken and I became lovers last night! At midnight, out in the fields! We made it three times! She came all over the place!"

"Damn you!" Ranna cried. "Of all the *ungentlemanly* things to say!"

"You were begging for it! Begging for it!"

"I was not!"

"Ranna!" Urside wailed.

"Get him out, Urside! Someone get him out!"

"Ranna, this is *unbelievable,*" a woman blatted. "Surely you wouldn't associate with--"

"The BS Poet!" Urside screamed.

"Don't you dare denigrate my poetry!" Robbert shouted. "I refuse to listen to that! I am a published poet! You are *nothing!*

I've published four books of poetry! Four! I wrote *The Most Beautiful Poems of the Universe!* I am Robbert Geswindoll!"

Laughter from the entire audience.

Celestions, kill them all!

No result.

"No! God, no! I can't believe it! Robbert Geswindoll! *You!*" Mr. Future Joe gasped.

Robbert whirled. "Have you got a problem with that, you ageist monster?"

"Dammit, I know you from the *future!* I can't believe it's *you!*"

"Of course it's me! Who the hell else would it be?"

"But you're not a wino in *my* time! I mean, you're always incredibly well-dressed, and, man, this is *weird!* It can't be, but it is! Robbert Geswindoll! We all knew you'd written that poetry thing a long time ago, but, wow, I guess I shouldn't mess up the timeline any further than I have!"

"Celestions, convert this man to the Way! He's deranged!"

"I mean, in *my* time, I swear you look ten years younger! I didn't recognize you!"

"Enough of this ageism! I'm only fifty-eight! You oughta respect that, mister! I was born the day NASA first landed men on the moon! I thought you were a goddamn astronaut! Don't you guys stick together?"

"We're supposed to *interview* you tonight! On Vespertine and Commer! I can't believe this! Is that why I HTT'd here? Because *you're* here?"

"I have a fifth volume coming out any day now! Any day! As soon as I finish it and find a publisher!"

"All right! Okay! Timeline be damned! In my time, this man will become the head of the USSF Public Relations Division! A high-ranking Space Force bureaucrat!"

"That's insane! I would *never--*"

"And Huey and I were gonna tear you apart on the program tonight! Because the USSF is nothing but lies and deceit now!" Joe turned to the audience. "Can you imagine that, do-gooders? The jerk who wrote *The Most Beautiful Poems of the Universe* must've cleaned up his act, because he makes it to Mars and starts spreading *lies!* I loved the USSF, and now it's gone straight down the tubes! My brother's the head of it, but this Celestion insanity is everywhere now! The USSF is *going* Celestion!"

"Then that's an excellent thing, whatever you're talking about, because the Celestions are here to save us!"

"What are they talking about?" someone said.

"Hey, Ranna!" Joe called down. "You picked yourself a real loser here! He believes Celestion *insanity!*"

"Where are the cops?" Ranna muttered. "Robbert, I never want to see you again!"

"You can't throw me out! We're *lovers!*"

"Urside, just throw him out!"

The Urside child bounded on stage in that silly green polo shirt. Well, maybe not just a child. He was skinny, but taller than Robbert, with well-muscled forearms. "You … heard her," Urside gasped.

"Celestions protect me," Robbert said, making his right thumb and forefinger into an arrowhead which he thrust repeatedly at Urside.

Urside didn't drop dead, but merely frowned. Well, surely the Celestions had much more grisly plans for his demise.

"Look, kid, anyone can tell you're upset about me and Ranna," Robbert said, "but believe me, even as noble a woman as Ranna Kikken has to come all over the place now and then! Last night, in the fields, she was wild! Wild!"

"Get out …" Urside managed.

"Yeah, get out," Joe said.

Robbert's heart sickened to see Ranna slam down her conference program and stamp up the stairs.

"I mean it, Robbert, out of here! I'm never going to see you again! Last night was an insane mistake! And for your information I was just putting on a show! I didn't come at all! So there!"

"God, Ranna!" Urside whimpered.

"Hell, women always say that when they get pissed off. In

two days you'll be begging for it again!"

"Forget it! Even our party crasher here would be better than you!" Ranna said, jabbing a finger at the crimson Man from the Future.

"Well, hey," Joe said. "Thanks, but--"

"Ranna, this--this is *disgusting!*" Urside said, fleeing down the wooden stairs.

Robbert turned to the rapt audience. The moment was magnificent. He could feel the perfect poem congealing out of all this.

"Are you still here?" Ranna snapped.

"Well, yes, I'm here, I suppose, uh, to make a final report, of sorts, to the Celestions," Robbert stammered. "Because the Celestions command it. They say you cannot rile me!"

He was interrupted by someone else climbing on stage. Now the *piece* was here, in leather pants and electric blue silk blouse, with frizzy dark brown hair and rich sculpted lips, with sharp, haughty blue-green eyes that were paradoxically fuzzy. The whole package was drenched in exquisite turquoise jewelry from New Mexico. "Well, I see the fashion model's arrived," Robbert joked, masking the other urge since he'd met her last week, to pull her down to the floor on the spot.

"I just had to come up!" she said in her lilting Texas accent. "To meet this lovely young man! Isn't it exciting, a man from the future!"

Ranna turned away. "God, no wonder CTESOPE failed!"

Robbert surveyed the young slut's perfect boobs and thighs. What would it be like to grab that ass in those skintight leather pants? Breasts big and round and tight in that blue blouse? Damn, it was unbuttoned to her navel.

He was distracted by Joe Commer, Martian Militarist, fingers outstretched and quivering. "Who's *that?*" he moaned in an unfathomable mixture of horror and lust.

"Oh, that's just my sister," Ranna said. "She's always like this. Drunk and stoned on her ass at my first conference. Don't pay her any mind."

"Jackie! God, it's *you!*" Joe groaned.

CHAPTER FIVE
Jackie in Turquoise Jewels

"Well, yes, it *is* me!" Jackie cooed. It seemed as if the masses of turquoise looping around her neck were all that were keeping those breasts from jiggling right out of her unbuttoned blouse.

Joe's mind shut down. It couldn't be her. *His* Jackie was elegant and regal. There was no way she'd ever dress like a whore. The eyes in front of him were potted, drugged. But the face, the voice, were definitely *hers.* "You must be--twenty-eight? Not thirty-six?"

"Do you know …" Ranna Kikken began.

"Well, that's right, handsome," Jackie said. "I'm twenty-eight, if you must know."

"I can't believe you're *here!* I can't believe I'm meeting you! I mean, *now!* I mean, I can't believe your hair!"

"What about my hair?"

"I mean, it's beautiful! Lovely!" What was he saying? It was a *mess*. Jackie would never wear her hair like that. "I mean, in all the craziness I've ever seen, I mean, even in *battles,* I never expected to see you *here!* In the past!"

"When *did* you expect to see me, honey?"

"In … in the *future!*" Joe stared into that scary opening of that superb tight blouse. Hadn't he just had those babies in his hands a few minutes ago? Or eight years from now? And then came this time transition, and here they were again, on display for any man to drool over?

"Jackie," Ranna sighed, "what the hell are you doing up here?"

"Well, everyone was having a party here, and I figured, hey, lemme see this cutie spaceman! Before I puke all over the place, that is!"

It was the exact same face, the exact same body. It had to be her. But *his* Jackie was sophisticated. Joe had never seen her drunk or obnoxious. And this Ranna woman had to be twice as old as this Jackie. "How can you two be *sisters?*"

35

Ranna sighed. "Two different mothers, if you have to know, mister."

"God, Jackie, if you only *knew!*"

"Mr. Commer--that is your name, correct? I do wish you'd stop leering at my little sister."

"Oh, it's okay!" Jackie giggled. "He likes me, Ranna! I can tell!" Joe gaped at the thick jewels around her neck, turquoise designs harboring what looked like diamonds and rubies. He didn't know anything about gems, but somehow knew those weren't glass. The jewels matched those vacant blue-green eyes.

"She's just drunk and stoned again. I can't believe she even made it up on stage without passing out."

"Hey, I'm co-owner of this damn Cat Farm, and I can get drunk if I wanna! And stoned! And I can do anything else, with anyone I wanna!" she cried, brutally latching onto Joe's eyes.

"God, I still can't *believe* this," Joe moaned. "Your maiden name's *Kikken?*"

"Well, I ain't no maiden, if it's any of your business, and I suspect it is," Jackie giggled, "but Kikken's the only name I got!"

"No wonder the emotion dragged me here! It was *you!* Jackie Vespertine! I know you as Jackie Vespertine!"

Jackie blinked. "Whoa, this guy's more messed up than me, even!"

"It's certainly all disgusting," the old coot Robbert put in.

"Shut up, Robbert," Ranna said. "I'm very pissed at you."

"Watch your language, dear, everyone can hear what you're saying. The Celestions are certainly recording all this."

"Dammit, who gives a good goddamn about your goddamn Celestions?"

"No! This is crazy!" Joe said. "That *Geswindoll* should be here, too! Man, did I come for Jackie, or did I come for *you?*"

"You tell us," Ranna snapped. "You've probably got half a minute before the cops get here. At least I hope so."

"You don't understand. In the future, I fall in love with *Jackie!* She's an entirely different woman!"

"Wow!" Jackie said. "Man, that's weird!"

"You're damn right it's weird!" God, Joe's Jackie had once been a *slut*. Did that explain the incredible hold she had on him in his own time? Sure, the 2036 woman was elegant and poised, but did her devastating sexual power find its roots in this putrid past?

"Hey, like I'm gonna barf or somethin'," Jackie grunted.

"Oh, God, not again," Ranna muttered.

"Jackie, I don't know how to say this, but *I love you!*" Did he? What did that even mean?

"Well, I love you too, cutie, but I'm feelin' *woozy* alluva sudden."

"You never told me you were mixed up in political stuff! This CTESOPE crap!"

"Hey, honey, just came here for a visit, just for the damn summer. Then I'm blowin' it!"

"Why didn't you ever *tell* me about any of this?"

"Ranna, this guy's drunk! Cute, but drunk! Drunker 'n me! Drunker 'n everyone!" Before anyone could react, Jackie Kikken tumbled into a frizzy-haired, silk-and-leather heap, jewels clanking on the glossy stage planks.

"Well, she won't remember any of this," Ranna observed. "She always drinks herself into a stupor. She never remembers what she did, who she slept with, anything."

"There, there, it's all okay," the old coot Robbert said with a pat to her forearm.

"Goddammit, get away from me!" Ranna snarled, whirling to the audience. "Everyone! This man is *cast out!* He is unwelcome at the Cat Farm! This is an official Cat Farm edict!" She turned back to Joe. "Dammit, listen to me! I don't know why, but I believe you! I believe everything you're saying! Do you understand me? Your entire story! About the future! About everything!"

"But--you're a nonprofit lady!" Joe gasped, snagged in her brown eyes. "But you're real! Somehow!" And now he recalled *The Reamers* and the tiny picture of Ranna Kikken. She was an afterthought, an illustration of how CTESOPE never accomplished anything, and Joe had dismissed her fate. After all, so many people had died in the Evacuation.

But now that he knew her, hell, now that he *admired* her, what could he say? What could he make of the parenthesis after her name?

RANNA KIKKEN (1980-2033)

Joe had been part of her death. She was just one more of the billions who didn't make it off the planet in '33. Joe could now add her to the long list of his crimes.

He fought for breath. He couldn't process this. Jackie there was breathing, she was alive, she'd make it through '33. Somehow she'd mature and marry Huey Vespertine. And she'd either seduce Joe or Joe would seduce her, and he'd be totally crazy and time-travel to *here.*

But, deep down, was Jackie Vespertine even one-tenth the soul of Ranna Kikken?

Jackie never mentioned a sister who died!

"Someone call the police?" came the kind of voice Joe had trained with, worked with, respected. The comrade voice. Authority and order. The police. The army. The United System Space Force.

But Joe felt his legs giving way. "He's right--well, he *was* right here, officer," Robbert Geswindoll said, but his words warbled down an infinite echoing well. And Churchill the cat cried his own Animal Disturbance into the acoustic chaos, and Joe was sailing down that cold dark well himself.

"Where'd he go?" Robbert said, his volume fading. "Ranna, where did Mr. Future ..."

CHAPTER SIX
Logon to the Big Shared Nightmare
Saturday, October 15, 2033

"Urside, where are we?" Mandy whispered.

Urside's eyes adjusted to the dimness. Angled rafters above them. Below, two-by-fours nailed into a grid. "Watch out for the spaces between the boards. Looks like we're in an attic. That's just drywall for a ceiling there. I know, I put my foot through a ceiling like that once." Ahead, faint moonlight dropped through a vent.

"An attic? This is crazy! Ow!" Mandy said, bumping her head.

"Crawl slowly, after me." Urside crept across the two-by-fours with Mandy grunting behind him. "Set your weight only on the boards." Too bad they'd jumped into such a difficult spot, but it wasn't the first time he'd done that. You just figured out what your next step should be.

"Great, so somebody will hear us clonking up here and shoot us."

"I told you, nobody's ever hassled me on an HTT jump. They *can't*. They don't ever know we're here." Urside came to the vent and squinted through the slots. "Wow, looks like we hit a whole town of mansions or something. Some incredible grounds down there. I think we're three stories up."

Mandy came up and glanced out. "Huh. So how long do we have to stay?" Moonlight shone on her face, but worry was canceling her usual loveliness.

"Look, it's okay. We just find proof of the date, like from a computer, or else a news printout or something. Then we either go home, or maybe jump somewhere else."

Mandy looked away. "I'm not so sure this was a good idea."

"But it liberates all these wonderful energies! Didn't you say that sounded great?"

"Yeah, but I guess I didn't think we'd really *go* anywhere. I thought it was going to be more like, I don't know, just meditating and having this vision of going to another, like, time zone, whatever you were saying."

"No, you really do go there. I thought I told you that."

"You did, but …"

"That's one reason I like to confirm the date, to prove the jump really happened. Also it seems emotionally necessary somehow. It sort of balances the energies."

Mandy shook her head. God, how he wanted to kiss her breasts in that tight sweater. The energy was flooding him. Why wasn't she feeling the same?

"You don't understand," she said. "One second we're in your room, the next we're here in somebody's old attic."

"That's true. We linked to a different space and I'm sure a different time."

"Can we get back?"

"Oh! Of course we can! *That's* what's worrying you! No problem! We just *feel* the emotional resonances, then just glide along the HTT links. It's just like being on the Internet, following the links wherever you want to go."

"Except you never know exactly where you're going to wind up! God, Urside, this is stupid! What are you *doing* with this HTT stuff?"

"Look, the more you explore, the more you follow the links, the more you learn how to connect your chi to all these *possibilities*." Urside knew he was parroting von Goertner's *Guide to Heuristic Time Transition,* but he had to reassure Mandy that he knew what he was talking about. "We learn as we go along. Get more and more confident. You know why von Goertner uses the word *heuristic?* I had to look it up myself. It means 'encouraging the student to discover for himself.' And that's what we're doing."

"*You* know how to do it. And you dragged me along somehow. But you could go away and leave me here by myself!"

"Shhh! We can't let anyone hear us!"

"You said nobody can know we're here!"

"Well, but just to be on the safe side. I mean, look, it's okay. I would never leave you anywhere. I really do love you."

Mandy turned her beautiful cold moonlit face away.

"I mean, sure, you need my help at first," Urside said, "but after that, you'll know how to flow with the links yourself. But we have to be emotionally *together* now. We can't be arguing and losing contact."

Mandy's brown eyes grew large. "We could separate? Get stranded here?"

"Only if … if we don't keep loving each other." Urside reached for her and she climbed into his arms for a hug. "I know it's scary the first time, but really, you'll feel the energies, I promise. You're probably feeling them right now, it's just that you got scared and they're coming out backward."

"Maybe … maybe that's it."

"Let's try to find a way down from this attic and we'll feel better. I mean, fear is just another HTT link flowing along, and you can choose to jump out of it to … to *pleasure,* let's say."

"Oh … okay. I'll try."

"You'll be fine. Look, here's a little door right here." He opened it. A ladder led down into what appeared to be a closet. "Yeah, this'll be easy." They edged backward down the rungs. "That attic was way too cramped." He opened the closet door and they found themselves in a huge dark room lined with bookshelves. Moonlight shone through a window thirty feet away.

"Wow, the mansion's library," Urside joked.

"And they really don't know we're here?" Mandy said, sticking close as he ran his hands over disordered shelves of paperbacks and hardbacks.

"Really. Well, to be honest, there've been a couple times I've noticed odd reactions in people. I can be in the same room with them and they suddenly shiver and look around. They never see anything, though, so we're safe that way." But that sure didn't explain why everybody could see that Joe Commer guy a week ago. What if he really had transitioned from the future? What did he say, 2036? What if he wasn't just some jerk imposter milking their fears? Sure, he'd been right about Hygiea going into the sun, but half the world thought it would be May 6th anyway.

"Oh! I don't want to see any people! Can't we just find a printout or whatever and leave?"

"Well, okay." Urside found a lamp and turned it on.

"No!"

"Relax, if anyone happened to come in here, they'd just think they'd left it on. Believe me, they definitely wouldn't think two people had HTT'd in from 2028 to turn their lamp on."

"Well ..."

"Besides, I also get to look at you," Urside said, admiring her low-cut purple sweater and her tight white pants, now smudged with attic dirt. "You're so beautiful."

"Well, thanks," Mandy said, moving anxiously towards a large wooden desk cluttered with books and papers. Urside gazed helplessly after her. Why wasn't she feeling the sex energy? Hadn't he told her that the entire experience would be a deep emotional bonding? After all, Von Goertner's *Guide to Heuristic Time Transition* said that intimate lovers could HTT together even if only one knew how. She'd been skeptical last night when he told her about his HTT trips. She said it sounded like a drug that college students would abuse.

But Urside knew he had her when he'd told her that Heuristic Time Transition was about deep connecting emotions. That to have her in his HTT life would be his ultimate fulfillment. That his HTT trips had always seemed like plugging himself into the fate of the world, and that she had to be there with him.

"Look, here's a news feed!" Mandy said, pointing to a tablet glowing on the desk.

"Wow, what's the date?"

"*October 15, 2033!* God, Urside, can this be real?"

Urside read the headlines: *Effects of Xon Bomb Debated. Scientists Study CAP Crater, Radiation Levels. Jack Commer and Crew Awarded USSF Medal of Honor. Earthquakes Raise Questions of Global Structural Integrity.*

"Oh, *wow*." What had that Joe guy said last week? And wasn't Jack Commer his father or brother or something?

"Urside, that guy who crashed CTESOPE was named

Commer, too!"

"Well, from my experience, all the future zones you get into are just possible alternatives, not the real ones," Urside said, hoping he wasn't lying.

"But this one sounds an awful lot like what that Commer guy was saying!"

"Well, maybe it's just a possibility, not the real thing."

"You've time-traveled to other futures where this *didn't* happen?"

"Well, I've never seen anything like this before. I've only been past the 2020s a few times. Mostly I've seemed to stick around the late twenties. And I've done a few backward jumps, like 2018 or so."

"Huh," Mandy said, looking over the news screen.

She was so beautiful. Those deep brown eyes, those perfect breasts. "Look, Mandy, the HTT linking is for *feeling*. We came here to *feel*."

"I'm really not feeling anything except hyper. I really just want to leave. So we have our proof. Do we take this thing with us?"

"No, that wouldn't work. It probably wouldn't make it back with us, and if it did, anyone could say it was just a fake," Urside said, confused that his arm around Mandy wasn't warming her up. "We haven't *felt* yet. I mean, you being hyper is just raw energy going nowhere. If we could focus it …"

"How would you focus it?"

"Like this," Urside said, turning her face and kissing her hard. After a moment's surprise she accepted it, gave a little back, then broke.

"What was that for?"

"That was the energy coming out of me."

Mandy smiled faintly. "No, that was you stealing a kiss."

"No, it's the raw energy. That's because the jump is always emotional, there's always this connection to incredible *power,* and, well, for me, it always comes out in being really, really *horny*." He touched the cleavage of her sweater.

"Well, I don't think …"

"But--" Urside said, running his hands over her breasts.

"But what?" She let him fondle her. So wonderful. God, he'd missed her. She had to have missed it too over the past week.

"We should make love ..."

"Why ... would we want to do that?"

"To align our energy," Urside said, rubbing, squeezing. "To make sure we stay aligned, and together. I'm so horny for you."

"You mean here? In this house?" Mandy's eyes widened. "You mean, we might get lost if we don't align our energy?"

"No, I don't really think that would happen," Urside said, kissing her neck. "We just want to make sure nothing, you know, bad happens, and we need to express all this *energy*." He moved his lips to her mouth, and then, at last, she was responding. He pulled up her sweater. She wore that transparent bra he loved.

"Oh, Urside, are you sure?"

"Yes, I'm sure. I'm so horny for you. Let's sit down here." Urside pulled her back to a couch along the wall.

"I mean, are you sure now ... about your feelings? I mean, about Ranna?"

"Of course, of course," Urside said, ears heating. "You know it was just a stupid crush. Nothing ever happened. But Mandy, for you and me ... it's been so long ..."

They landed on the couch and Urside finished pulling her sweater over her head and undoing the front bra clasp. "God, you're *unbelievable*."

He'd been a fool to confess anything about Ranna. He and Mandy hadn't talked for a week, though much of that was Urside's terror about CTESOPE and Intruder Joe. Was he really from the future? Worse, had Urside's experiments with Heuristic Time Transition *caused* Joe to appear? Had he in fact screwed up the timeline?

But he couldn't help it. The vast energy of HTT, the life-affirming eros of time travel, was so *necessary*. Wouldn't such joy *heal* the timeline and repair any breaks anyone else might have done out of power lust and ego trip?

Last night Mandy had reluctantly accepted his abject

apology about Ranna. In fact, Urside got them both laughing about the absurdity of having a fantasy crush on such an older woman. He reiterated his deep commitment to Mandy and she seemed happy with that. They talked about everything, including their fears about Commer's prophecies. And Urside told her about his HTT adventures over the past five months.

And now they were naked on the couch. "Oh … oh, yes, Urside …" she moaned. Yeah, it was all working perfectly. She'd just needed to warm up and get into the energy flow. "Oh, yes, I *want* it!"

"See? Don't I have good ideas now and then?"

*

Urside was abruptly aware of where they were. Woozily he knew he should fight for clarity so he could evaluate their position. But he was unable to do anything but close his eyes and drift.

"Okay, Mr. HTT Space Cadet," Mandy said, poking his stomach. "Now that we're done with the main course, how do we get out of here?"

"Well, let's see, we got the date, we know we jumped to at least a *possible* 2033. And we did express our energy. So all we need to do is get dressed, and …"

"And? I thought you knew everything there was to know about this, sir." At least she wasn't still panicking. Making love had been the right idea.

"Well, usually you have to wait until you find the right emotional resonance, then you feel you can let go and jump. It's easy once you have the right resonance."

Now Mandy did stiffen. "Wait a sec. We have to wait for some resonance thing to get straightened out before we can go back?"

"Well, it means we're about ready to go, we just have to, you know, slow down, mellow out, be ready to sense the next link."

"The next link *home,* I hope you mean."

"Sure. Of course. We're heading right back home. To 2028, I promise you. I always get back to more or less the same time of departure."

"Hmm." Mandy climbed off him and surveyed the pile of their clothes. "I don't suppose this library has a bathroom. It'd be nice to clean up before we go back."

"See, that's a good idea. You're getting the hang of it. Clean up, sort of mentally freshen yourself, get dressed, then we'll see that we're all ready to go. Just like getting ready to go on vacation. You lock the house, walk out to the car, and drive off."

"Huh," Mandy smiled warily. "I guess you do know, if you've come and gone--how many times?"

Urside shrugged. "I tried to estimate that a couple weeks ago. I figured I've HTT'd about eighty times since January."

"*Eighty times?* God, Urside, that can't be good for you! How much time have you spent tripping into all these other places?"

"Well, it's funny, but the time differential is weird. It's possible to do *hours* of HTT trips and only lose a few minutes from your home time. Some of mine have lasted whole days. One was four days, can you believe it? And I only lost five minutes of real time. In fact, one reason I got interested in logging my hours was that I wanted to see how much extra experience I'd gotten since January. I figured I might've gotten something like four hundred hours of extra time."

"Urside, no! That's crazy! How can you possibly have the energy to add an extra four hundred hours to your life since January? I mean, wouldn't you have to expend, I don't know, food energy, sleep time, just to make it through four hundred hours? What's that? Two weeks? Two and a half weeks?"

Urside took in her magnificent nudity, her hands on her hips, her sharp rising energy in shocking contrast to his own lethargy. "Well, I actually think the sex energy you feel during HTT is what fuels the linking process. I've never felt it get depleted."

Until now, he thought with a shiver of horror.

"Dammit, Urside, you mean to tell me you get horny on

eighty HTT trips? Do you find women to screw on them? I can't believe it! You just wanted me along for entertainment!"

"No! I've never had sex with anyone on an HTT trip! I always feel the energy, but I don't act on it with anyone! I did want to share the sex energy with you, but--"

But dammit, I never considered that depleting it might strand us here.

"Okay, okay! But after what you said about Ranna, what can I believe anymore?"

Urside inspected the library's Persian carpet. It would probably be a big mistake to tell her the real reason he'd pursued his HTT experiments: that he was searching for Ranna Kikken in other times. Would they have gotten together in the coming years? What if he went far enough back to find a Ranna his own age? What if he found Ranna at sixty-five? Did any of that matter? No, because it was *love*. Surely all these Rannas would be aware of the time traveler and love him back, wouldn't they?

Yet he'd never seen her. Not on eighty HTT trips. He'd obsessively tramped across the Cat Farm in 2026, observing Dr. Norsen, Donna and Carl Franklin, Arnold Templeton, everyone who lived here, but not Ranna. He'd hunted in her bedroom, her bathroom, in all times. There was something blocking her from him. It was the core sadness of his life. Urside was a sinner who would never be redeemed. He was wrecking the entirety of human destiny so he could unite with Ranna Kikken beyond time, but in the real world, she scorned him. She'd spurned him for that mealy-mouthed Geswindoll.

"Look, I admit I'm confused," he finally said. "I don't understand why we're not just linking back right now. We got what we came for, we should be heading home."

"Okay. Okay. We can sort all this out when we get back. Meanwhile, I guess I'll follow your advice and clean up. Now where would a bathroom be here?" She crossed to what appeared to be the main door of the library and reached for the doorknob.

The door opened. A little man stood there in a shiny golden robe.

CHAPTER SEVEN
Dar

"Oh my God!" Mandy cried.

"Don't worry! He doesn't know we're here! We're not in his zone!"

"It's--oh my God! Oh my God!"

Urside stood up dizzily. "For God's sake, Mandy, don't panic! He can't see us!"

"HELLO HELLO HELLO WARE AMM I?" croaked from the--

"*Oh my God!*" Urside screamed.

"HELLO FRENNLEE HUUMANNS! WARE AMM I? HOWW DIDD I GETT HEERE? WHAZZ GOING ONNN?"

Urside fell back on the carpet. "God, Mandy! I'm sorry! I'm sorry! We must've opened up some interdimensional *hole!* Oh my God!"

A creature five feet high, like a giant fish. Huge unlidded eyes. A pink fin protruding from a golden robe.

"Oh my God!" Mandy gasped, backing towards a bookcase. "We have to get out of here!"

"No, wait! We need our clothes!"

"Just grab them! He doesn't know we're here!"

The being scampered into the room. It was sickening to watch its little feet slap on the wooden floor and then scuff into the loose carpet. Then it stood right on their pile of clothes. "HELLO, HELLO, HOWW DID I GETT HERE? WHOO ARE YOOO GUYZZ?"

"He *does* know we're here!" Mandy screamed. "His voice is in my *mind!*"

"DOO NOTT PANIKKK, MY FRENNS! DOO YOOO NOTT KNOWW TOO REED PROPPURRLEE THE THOTS OF A MARRSHUN?"

"No! God, no!" Urside met those unlidded eyes and his mind burst into hyperventilating madness.

"THE GRAVITTEE HEERE ISS SOOO HIGHH. THISS CANNOTT BEE FURST HOMME, I THINKK."

"I'm crazy! *Crazy!*"

"No, Urside, wait!" Mandy cried. "I don't know how, but I'm *aligning* with his thoughts! They're making sense! They come together if you just relax!"

"God, Mandy, I'm so sorry! I'm so sorry!"

You are Urside? came the voice in his mind. Then, uncannily, something did relax and the voice in Urside's brain now exuded nothing but calmness as the creature continued to speak: "You are Urside, and she is Mandy? And we must be on Planet Marble because of the gravity? And yet the air is not polluted nor are we dying of radiation poisoning? So by definition we are in the Alaskan Earth Terraforming Project Zone? And you have never seen a Martian before? Have I got that all correct?"

"Planet--planet--" Urside gasped. "You--"

"Yes, Planet Marble is Earth!" Mandy said. "Yes, that's right, we're on Earth! And you're Dar, Emperor of the Martians! How the hell can I *know* that?"

"I have *radiated* that, friend Mandy. You have never seen a Martian, nor ever received the outradiance? How is that possible? Unless--"

"God, are you from the *future?*" Urside cried. "Because that Joe guy talked about Martians!"

"Time travel is not possible! I do not accept this Professor Glasgow's theories!"

"We're from 2028!" Mandy shouted.

"This nonsense you humans call Heuristic Time Transition--"

"It's true! I've done it eighty times!" Urside said. "Believe us! We're from 2028!" He had no idea how he could be standing here naked, shouting at this fish creature, and still be in some possession of his sanity. He had to admit there was something damned comforting coming out of this little thing. Could it really be a Martian? Urside strained to recall this concept of "Martians" showing up now and then in some of his post-2030 HTT trips.

"We are in 2028? Do you believe that? On Planet Marble?"

Dar said. "We are not in Alaska on--what is your time reference--January 26, 2036?"

"No! At least I don't think this is Alaska!" Urside said. "And what is it, Mandy? 2033?"

"Yes. We found this news feed. It has the date," Mandy said. "Here, on the desk. Look for yourself."

The pink creature skittered over to the desk. Urside saw that its robe was really thousands of tiny colored golden discs wired together. Somehow he was certain those discs were solid gold.

"Hmm," Dar said, pulling the tablet to his face. "This device could of course be providing nonsense. It proves nothing."

"Oh, my ..." Mandy blurted.

"What?" Urside said, then felt his mind relax even further. He was flooded with perceptions, images, and history he could hardly make sense of. Human cities on Mars, some great Evacuation off this ruined planet. A war with Martians. Another war in Alpha Centauri. And he knew his naked girlfriend was also relaxing, taking in the same outradiance from this being. "No, this is all a *dream*," he gasped. "Just one *possibility*."

"Have I really time-traveled?" Dar mused. "Amazing if it is true! For I am instantly transitioned to high gravity. I was on First Home, now I'm apparently on Planet Marble, or else in some clever gravity chamber built to deceive me, yet I have been transported here instantly, the air is rich with your human nutrients, and there are two humans who apparently have never heard of a Martian before."

"It's true!" Mandy said. "We're all time travelers! Urside and I came here from 2028! You came here from--did you say 2036?"

"Yes. The year is 2036 in your reckoning. You know, there *is* a call in the Amplified Thought Program to a theoretical quantum time disruption."

Urside almost threw up at the wave of calculus and programming logic pouring through his mind. "God! Stop! We get the picture!"

"This is really quite marvelous. It would solve some incredible problems in AT if we could just consider time as--"

Urside backed away. "Please, not again!"

"Then again, I must remain skeptical. I certainly can't accept that I've time-traveled on the basis of some theoretical computer code and the testimony of two young humans."

Mandy sighed and pointed out the window. "Maybe taking a look at the moon would help."

*

Have I flipped out? Urside wondered. How could he be causally walking over to this window, naked, with naked Mandy and a fish thing pumping dream images out of its mind?

The Dar creature looked out the window, turned back to Mandy, and nodded. "Yes, friends. That is proof. I do accept that today is October 15, 2033. And that time travel most definitely is possible. I am really quite astonished."

Could this thing read the position of the moon against stars and somehow calculate an exact date? Urside went to the window and looked up.

"*No* …" he gasped, grabbing for the windowsill as his legs failed him.

He felt Mandy's arm around him. "It's okay," she whispered. "It all makes sense now."

"No, it *can't* be!"

"I noticed it when we were first looking out the attic. I kind of canceled it out, but all along I knew it was true. Everything Joe said is going to happen."

"*No* …" The moon *wasn't right*. In last quarter, the bright left side was a smooth circle around the bottom and side, but at the top, most of the moon was … *gone*. Red infection seethed in the depths of a vast jagged hole, fueling glowing scars all across the remaining surface. Tiny white fragments floated nearby. Scraps and powder of *Luna*.

Joe Commer was right. Someone in Central Asia had really blasted the moon with some superbomb. And the moon was supposed to completely explode later.

Urside whirled. "Okay, Mr. Emperor--" But the fish

creature was gone.

"He--he just *went!*" Mandy said.

"He can't! We need him! I mean, hell, I don't know what I mean! Why the hell did we come here? To this stupid mansion?"

"Well, I'm sure it was to meet the emperor."

"That's insane! Then why did *he* come *here?*"

"Well, to meet *us!*"

"That's crazy!"

"To prove to us that this is all real! That in 2033 they're gonna drop some sort of superbomb, and it'll wreck the earth, just like Joe Commer said! He was right about Hygiea, he's gonna be right about all the other disasters! And all that stuff from Dar's head, about our new life on Mars!"

"No! That can't be! This is just a suggestion of what *could* happen." Urside spied his underwear on the floor and jerked it on. "C'mon! Get your clothes on! We have to stop hallucinating all this insanity and get back to 2028."

"But you've admitted you don't know *how* to get back, haven't you?"

"We can get out! I know we can!" Urside fought to calm his racing heart. If only Ranna were here. With Ranna, he'd be feeling the *sex energy* that would save them. How could that gorgeous woman have refused him? How could she have stranded him here with Mandy Frederick? "Look, Mandy, someone has to be in *charge* of the HTT energy!"

"But it's me now. *I* have the HTT energy."

"Forget it! You don't know the first thing about it!"

"Shhh," Mandy said, effortlessly opening an HTT tunnel.

CHAPTER EIGHT
Vespertine and Commer
As aired on the Vespertine and Commer Hour on AresNet,
Saturday, January 26, 2036

Jack Commer, Supreme Commander, United System Space Force: Listen, how can you have this *jerk* on the program? I actually called in to *fire* him!

Joe Commer: *Oh my God, where are we?*

Huey Vespertine: Damn, Joe, where the hell have you *been?* I thought I was gonna hafta do the damn interview myself!

Robbert Geswindoll: You can't fire me! The Personnel Rules clearly state that a newly-hired Grade 44 has six months to--

Jack: Forget it! I'll change those rules myself!

Geswindoll: The United System Council decides--

Joe: *Where the hell are we?* I'm dreaming! This has to be a dream!

Huey: That's right, jerk! Have you snapped? Only showin' your damn ass now!

Joe: I am insane! *Insane!*

Churchill: Riaowl!

Joe: Oh my God, *Churchill's* here! He must have been sucked along with me! But that's crazy! I couldn't have been in 2028! But if this cat came along--

Huey: Where'd that damn cat come from? You know I'm allergic to cats!

Joe: We're on *Mars?*

Jack: What's going on there? Did you just get in, Joe? Huey said you didn't show up!

Joe: I'm insane! I time-traveled! I actually time-traveled!

Huey: C'mon, dude, you scared the bejeezus outa me, sneaking into the studio like that!

Geswindoll: I swear that seat was empty just a second ago!

Huey: And that damn cat!

Joe: Ow! C'mon, kitty, don't rake me with your--

Jack: What's going on there, Joe?

Joe: Jack, is that *you?*

Jack: Yes, yes, it's me, calling into your stupid program to fire Geswindoll!

Geswindoll: Our glorious Supreme Commander! But his hands are tied and he knows it!

Joe: How can you be calling? Huey! We're in the studio! With Geswindoll! *How'd we get here?*

Huey: Are you crazy, man? I had to start the interview without you, you wouldn't pick up your comm!

Joe: We're on the air? *Now?*

Huey: Yes, for God's sake!

Joe: It's--January 26th?

Huey: Yes!

Joe: *2036?*

Huey: Yes! Are you nuts?

Joe: We're in Marsport? It's really January 26th again? But later? Because this afternoon--oh, God! Jackie!

Churchill: Riaowl!

Joe: I was at the CTESOPE conference! Eight years ago! And *Jackie* was there! A twenty-eight-year-old Jackie!

Churchill: Riaowl!

Huey: *Why'd you bring a goddamn cat here?*

Joe: And *Geswindoll* was there! In 2028! But he looked older then than he does now!

Geswindoll: Well, I dare say the Celestions keep my body young for whatever nefarious purposes they may have in store for me.

Jack: You're fired, Geswindoll! And if Easterling gives me any trouble, I'll fire him too!

Geswindoll: Bob has full authority to hire anyone he wants!

Jack: He *waits* until Amav and I are out of town, and then hires someone outside the USSF, with no public relations experience!

Geswindoll: He knew the USSF needed a *poet!* I remind you, sir, that I have twenty published books of poetry under my belt!

Jack: Sheesh!

Joe: Wait, this is the Geswindoll interview?

Huey: Of course it is! What the hell are you *on* tonight, mister?

Joe: Is Jackie here?

Huey: No! Why should she be here?

Joe: I don't know! I mean, this afternoon she was bringing over your questions for the interview, and somehow I *time-traveled!* I saw her in 2028! And *this* guy!

Geswindoll: Of course I've kept my mouth ever since you Commer dudes got so famous back during the Evacuation. I knew nobody would believe I'd seen the great Joe Commer back in '28! But I finally knew that Heuristic Time Transition was *true.*

Joe: Yes, it's true! Oh my God!

Geswindoll: So you're saying you just got back right now from the CTESOPE conference?

Joe: Yes, but I'm sure back in civilian clothes if it's true!

Jack: I can't believe you'd be a party to putting this jerk on the show, Joe!

Joe: *Churchill's* proof! Churchill came with me! From 2028! This is Ranna Kikken's cat!

Huey: Who?

Jack: Huey I can understand. He'd do anything to embarrass the USSF. Putting a Celestion worshipper on the show! Someone illegally hired by that idiot Easterling!

Geswindoll: I was hired perfectly legally according to United System Council rules!

Jack: Aw, forget your rules!

Joe: I can't believe it's *you* again!

Geswindoll: Yes, it's me, and all this proves that time travel does exist!

Jack: Glasgow's a charlatan! Everyone knows that he's just trying to find in physics what that idiot von Goertner used to prattle about before the Evacuation!

Geswindoll: Obviously the Celestions have given us time travel in order to fully understand ourselves!

Huey: Great! I knew we'd get into the good stuff real fast!

Jack: People just want to believe in time travel so they can go back to save the old Earth!

Joe: Yes! Yes, that's it!

Jack: But it's not gonna happen! What happened, happened!

We've got to move on!

Joe: You're calling into Vespertine and Commer? Jack? That's really you?

Jack: Of course it's me! I can't stand that stupid name of your program! Vespertine and Commer! Who listens to stupid talk radio shows anyway?

Huey: C'mon, dude, it's definitely enjoying a renaissance here on Mars.

Jack: Huey, I really had to swallow my distaste to even call in and talk to you, after all the treasonable crap you've pulled over the past few years.

Huey: Free speech isn't treasonable!

Jack: Aiding and abetting Sam Hergs in the war, for God's sake!

Huey: I was *not* aiding and abetting!

Jack: Advocating that we all just die on Earth instead of evacuating, instead of reaching out to build a new life!

Huey: It's a crappy new life if you ask me!

Joe: You don't understand, Jack, I *needed* this job, I've had to work things out, and this program is a way that people can talk things out!

Jack: So you start a radio program with this traitor!

Geswindoll: Well, this is certainly all interesting. I thought *I* was the one being interviewed tonight.

Jack: Look, Joe, I know it's been hard on you, I know you needed to get away from the USSF, but really, this program! Huey Vespertine! Someone who betrayed our family!

Joe: What the hell do you care if the family gets betrayed, anyway? *You* broke away from it all right!

Jack: Look, dammit, I'm sorry, that's not what I mean!

Joe: Are you back in Marsport? I thought you and Amav were off to the Jovian Fragment Field until next month!

Jack: I'm calling in from the JFF by superspace radio! I just couldn't bear to know the two of you were interviewing this *illegal hire.*

Geswindoll: Not illegal! Not illegal!

Jack: This public relations expert for Celestionism! I know I'm not supposed to get involved in politics or talk radio, but dammit, this goes too far! This Geswindoll character! I'm firing both him *and* Easterling!

Geswindoll: Let me clear up the confusion here, listeners of Mars. The fact that I remember Joe Commer from 2028 means that we have at last proven that Heuristic Time Transition does truly exist! Praise the Celestions!

Joe: But you were a *derelict* then! You looked like you were about to drop dead!

Geswindoll: That's the power of the Celestions, my boy! They understand *life force!*

Jack: God, Joe, Huey's brainwashed you! How can you be on this program and listen to this crap?

Joe: I am not brainwashed! I am not brainwashed! Take that back! Take that back!

Jack: C'mon, Joe, take it easy.

Joe: No! You bring that up all the time! How I got brainwashed by the Alpha Centaurians last year! You're saying I'm susceptible to brainwashing!

Jack: Look, Joe, anyone could have gotten brainwashed by the ACs. I understand that. The whole crew got brainwashed! Even Dar did. They would've gotten me too, Amav and I just held out a little longer than everyone else, God knows why.

Joe: I put the *Typhoon* in danger! Me! The copilot! I abdicated all responsibility so I could go screw with the women! *That's* what I'll never forgive!

Geswindoll: Wow, this is amazing! Listen, Joe, the Celestions can help!

Huey: Lay off the poor bastard, dude.

Joe: I am not a poor bastard! Oh, dammit, man, who cares?

Jack: Joe, it's not what you think. Everyone knows you've needed time to recover.

Joe: Who cares? Who the hell cares?

Geswindoll: The Celestions care! They have a hundred-fifty-five-step plan for you!

Jack: God, how could anyone hire this man for *anything?* What was Easterling thinking?

Geswindoll: Easterling knew we needed a *poet* to helm the PR office in this time of crisis! Face it, Commer, the USSF has a very, very poor public image right now! Everyone's just waiting for the next AC attack and the USSF is doing nothing!

Jack: That's nonsense! We've had a truce since last year, and that's given us and the Martians time to build up the Amplified Thought Early Warning System.

Geswindoll: The EWS won't help if the Centaurians warp in a million battle cruisers!

Jack: I can't believe it! The USSF PR Head is openly *defeatist?*

Geswindoll: So you admit I'm the USSF Public Relations Director!

Jack: Forget it! You're fired!

Joe: Huey, I swear to God I don't know what we're doing here! I just transitioned in!

Huey: Wow! I didn't know you did drugs!

Joe: I'm not on drugs, dammit!

Churchill: Riaoowwwll!

Jack: I've said it from the beginning, this stupid Vespertine and Commer thing won't last three months!

Huey: Wow, this is *great!* Joe, your goody-two-shoes brother is having an epileptic *fit!*

Joe: You shut up! Just shut up!

Huey: We've been going for a month and a half now, for everyone's information!

Geswindoll: Hey, does anyone have any questions for me, the USSF Public Relations Director, as certified by none other than Jack Commer, Supreme Commander?

Jack: I'm telling you, you're not employed by the USSF! We'll pay you from Wednesday to today, but that's it!

Joe: I'm a disgrace to the family! I'm sure Dad and Mom are listening to this right now!

Geswindoll: Wait a second, your parents are *here,* on Mars?

Joe: Of course! They're over in Clalcaj, trying to live down the shame of Joe Commer!

Jack: Look, Joe, you don't have to get so hysterical about everything!

Joe: *Don't you understand that all I've wanted the past year is* *to tell you I can't handle Jim and John and I want to die myself?*

Jack: God, Joe, really, I mean, on the *air* and all!

Joe: Do you think we could ever sit down and have a little talk and work things out? No way!

Jack: Look, Joe, of course we can talk sometime.

Joe: We haven't talked since I don't know when!

Jack: You haven't *wanted* to talk!

Joe: That's why I *quit* the USSF! Because no one can come out openly and *talk* about how they feel! About Jim and John dying, for God's sake, about the whole *Typhoon* crew dying! That's why I joined this stupid talk show! At least people *talk!*

Huey: Hey, pardner, I thought you were *committed* to this concept!

Jack: C'mon, everybody calm down and let's discuss this rationally.

Joe: Nooo, Jack never loses control! *He* knows what he's doing with his life! *He's* Supreme Commander, *he* protects the solar system!

Geswindoll: Not very well, if I may add!

Joe: When I just mess everything up! Everyone knows that! I betray everyone! Me, Joe Commer! Formerly of the goddamn United System Space Force!

Churchill: Riaoowwwll!

Huey: Great, now you've riled the goddamn cat up! What're we supposed to do, just sit around and wait for it to scratch our goddamn eyes out?

Joe: Man, you really don't like cats, do you?

Geswindoll: I thought everybody was supposed to be interviewing *me!*

Joe: Churchill wouldn't hurt anyone!

Huey: Aaaaa-choo! Aaaaa-choo! There! Is everyone satisfied?

Churchill: Riaowl!

Joe: Let's get back to the point! I *time-traveled!* I did Heuristic Time Transition! Back to 2028! Von Goertner's right! Glasgow's right! I met Geswindoll there!

Jack: Oh, calm down, Joe, of course that's nonsense!

Joe: Dammit, Jack, that's exactly the attitude I'm trying to talk about!

Geswindoll: But I can confirm it. Joe did appear at a conference held in Texas in 2028. It was the Committee to End Suffering on Planet Earth. Joe gave us all a warning of the horrible coming events of '28 on, and if anyone cares to look at the video of his speech, it's on AresNet, just use search term CTESOPE. I reviewed it myself last night in preparation for this interview. That is, if anyone would care to ask me, the USSF Public Relations Director, a single question!

Jack: God, I can't believe this insanity! How did Easterling ever hire this guy?

Huey: C'mon, don't you know the upper echelons of the USSF have been converting to Celestionism over the past year? That Easterling's a committed Celestionite?

Joe: You're saying the Deputy Director of the USSF is a *Celestion worshipper?*

Huey: Yes, of course! That's why he hired Geswindoll!

Geswindoll: Because he knows we need the Celestions to defend this solar system! After all, they do stand guard over the entire universe!

Jack: No! Absolutely no!

Huey: Oh, this is priceless! Priceless!

Geswindoll: You may not laugh at the Celestions!

Joe: I always knew Easterling was a little flaky, but to hire *Geswindoll?* Dammit, why the hell *were* you at that conference? Why did I HTT there? Why am I back here now?

Geswindoll: Obviously so that both of you may convert to the Love of the Celestion. In fact, so that anyone within the sound of my voice may convert!

Joe: Stop using the word *convert!* I hate that word! That's what the Alpha Centaurians did to us! They *converted* us! Brainwashed us!

Geswindoll: You're ready to convert right now! I can tell!

Joe: Why was Jackie at the conference? *That's* what I don't understand!

Jack: That's it, Geswindoll! You're fired! Using the USSF to proselytize your private religious beliefs! That's it! You're out!

Easterling's out too!

Huey: Man, this is good!

Jack: Dammit, we need the USSF to be sane and rational! We have to be alert to the Alpha Centaurian *threat!* Especially right now! Do I need to remind everyone that they told us, a year ago, they had plans to attack us in *one year?* They emphasized that, *one year.* They even translated that into our time figures. So even though we have this weird kind of truce with them--

Geswindoll: Forget it! The Celestions won't allow any such warfare!

Jack: Great, you go on believing that.

Joe: Look, if all this talk of Celestionism taking hold in the USSF is true, then--

Huey: Then your precious USSF is doomed, is that what you're saying?

Jack: I will not sit here and listen to you malign the USSF, Vespertine!

Geswindoll: Of course the interests of the USSF and the Celestions coincide!

Joe: Shut up! Shut up! I can't stand it!

Huey: For all we know the Celestions are renting a couple floors of the United System Building!

Geswindoll: Do not mock my religion, sir!

Huey: I'm not mocking it! I confess I'm *fascinated* by your Celestions! That anybody could believe that crap about Disembodied Beings of Interdimensional Love!

Geswindoll: Those of us with faith understand that the Celestions guide our destiny! Some of us have special contact with them. I'm not ashamed of my spirituality! It's taken me sixty-six years to develop it!

Jack: Let me get this straight, then. You're saying Bob Easterling has bought into this crap? And other USSF officials?

Geswindoll: Sir, a man is free to believe as he chooses in our society!

Jack: USSF officials are openly espousing *crap* about goddamn Celestions?

Geswindoll: You profane them at your risk, sir!

Jack: You're fired! Fired! Get off the air!

Geswindoll: You're not even on the planet, Monsieur Commer! Your superspace radio may enable you to speak instantly with us here, but you shall not still my voice!

Jack: Damn you! I can be there in an hour or two!

Huey: Forget it, Jack, you can't shut this program down! Let's just listen to this guy's insanity and have a good laugh! Aaaaa-choo! Aaaaa-choo! Damn cat!

Churchill: Riaowl! Riaowl!

Geswindoll: I may as well go ahead and tell Lord Commer that the real powers in the USSF have been running things without his interference for some time!

Jack: That's insane! The USSF is a highly motivated military organization!

Geswindoll: Aw, c'mon, man! You've just been a figurehead ever since you got back from Alpha Centauri last year. You think you're running things, but you're not!

Jack: You son of a bitch!

Huey: Whoa, I've never heard the great Jack Commer call anyone a son of a bitch before!

Jack: Why are you doing this, Huey? All this anti-USSF propaganda?

Huey: Lovely! The great Jack Commer finally deigns to talk to Huey Vespertine!

Jack: Dammit to hell! Why do I bother?

Geswindoll: Listen, everyone, I actually bought presents for Huey and Joe. This lovely fifty-pound leather-bound Celestion Bible! I have a Celestion Bible for each of you! And I'll even send one to Jack on his precious vacation out there in the JFF!

Jack: It's not a vacation, it's a fact-finding mission! Damn you!

Joe: Back up a second! You say you saw a video of CTESOPE? From 2028?

Geswindoll: Well, yes, it's been on the Internet, and now AresNet, for a few years, but nobody was ever curious about it.

Joe: There's a video of me speaking at the CTESOPE conference?

Huey: I heard about that one myself. It's a fake. They just morphed in a Joe Commer character, dressed him in the '35 USSF uniform, and had him spew out all his predictions. It had to be made in the last couple months or so.

Geswindoll: Nonsense! I saw that video myself in '32.

Joe: But Jackie was there! Jackie would be in that video!

Huey: Huh? How could Jackie be there?

Joe: She was there! In Texas! In 2028! Didn't she ever tell you that?

Huey: Well, not really. We've sorta made a pact never to talk about the past. Like most people on Mars these days, you know.

Joe: She probably wouldn't even remember it herself. I mean, she passed out and all.

Geswindoll: But what a *piece* she was then! That's what you're thinking, right?

Joe: No, of course not!

Geswindoll: Man, I lusted after that bitch for years! Man, oh, man! She exuded nothing but *raw sexual intercourse!* Even the Celestions wanted a piece of her!

Joe: This is Huey's *wife,* you know! Jackie Vespertine!

Huey: My wife exudes *raw sexual intercourse?* Well, of course she does! I knew that!

Geswindoll: Well, as you can verify from your own Celestion Bible there, and may I quote *Fluttering Disunions,* Chapter Four, Verse Six, "They shall lay their wives at the feet of the Elders of the Phallus of the Celestions." See, look, on page 556 there's even a picture of a young lady kneeling in front of--

Joe: Damn, you are stone crazy!

Geswindoll: I'm revealing sacred principles of the Celestions to you dimwits! I *am* an Elder of the Phallus, you know!

Jack: I'm going to *clean out* the top command of the USSF!

Geswindoll: Your blasphemy is hereby noted, Mr. Supreme Commander. But even your own wife, the lovely Amav, shall kneel before the Phallus!

Jack: You bastard! I'm coming back right now to beat the crap out of you!

Huey: Wow! This is unbelievable!

Churchill: Riaoowwwll?

Joe: I know it's insane, little guy, I know! Do you have any idea that you've been blasted eight years into the future? Is that weird or what?

Churchill: Rowl!

Jack: Why am I *listening* to any of this?

Huey: This is what I love about AresNet talk radio!

Jack: Shut up, you traitor to the USSF!

Joe: Listen, everyone, this is Ranna Kikken's cat!

Huey: Who the hell is Ranna Kikken?

Joe: Think, Huey! Jackie's maiden name! Kikken!

Huey: Huh?

Geswindoll: Oh, this is wonderful! Joe's conversion to Celestionism is proceeding smoothly! His mind's so fragile he's about to Celestionize himself all on his own!

Jack: Hey, that's my *brother* you're insulting there, jackass!

Geswindoll: The Celestions know every detail of Joe's twisted cesspool existence! They know your sole goal in life is to bang Huey Vespertine's wife!

Joe: No! Forget it!

Huey: Here we go again! *Everyone* wants to bang my wife!

Joe: Huey, I swear--

Geswindoll: The Celestion Archives tell the truth! That is, in the form of the USSF surveillance video of Joe Commer's very interesting afternoon today at his apartment. Too bad this really is just talk radio. Our listeners will have to miss the video I'm playing on this monitor here.

Joe: No! This--this is a violation of the rights of a Marsport citizen!

Geswindoll: Correction. According to USSF Personnel Directive 3440-GR, all current and former USSF personnel are to be continuously monitored!

Joe: There's no such directive!

Geswindoll: It was passed yesterday, Mr. Commer. In the face of the magnitude of the threat that possible Alpha Centaurian operatives might pose to USSF personnel and to the secrets they maintain in their brains, Bob and I thought it best to act fast.

Jack: That directive is canceled! Canceled, do you hear me?

Geswindoll: Observe Jackie Vespertine arriving at Joe Commer's door wearing, for reasons one can only guess at, a luscious, low-plunging, tight mini-dress! Her neck and wrists covered in diamonds! And a diamond ankle bracelet! All this to give Joe a copy of the interview questions for this evening!

Joe: Well, well … I mean …

Geswindoll: Joe answers the door and look at his eyes pop out!

Huey: Huh? Jackie?

Geswindoll: Yes, your own wife! Bringing the interview questions to Joe's apartment in the middle of the afternoon! God knows she could've emailed the entire batch!

Joe: Look, Huey--buddy--I'm *sorry!*

Geswindoll: Observe the instant embrace!

Huey: Damnfire!

Joe: I think it just blew up in our faces!

Geswindoll: Observe the mad dash to the bed!

Huey: Wow! Every man wants her is all I can say!

Joe: *Every man wants her* is all you can say?

Huey: Well, hell, Joe, Jackie's one hell of a sexy woman! Who *wouldn't* want her?

Geswindoll: Observe!

Joe: God, I can't watch this!

Huey: Yep, she's a stunner, all right. Why'd she take up with a flabby lard bucket like me is beyond comprehension!

Geswindoll: Everyone's wondered that!

Huey: Oooh, good move there, Joe, rip the shoulder strap. Do you have any idea how much a slinky black dress costs? I *pay* for those dresses, you know!

Joe: Why did she come to my apartment wearing a slinky black dress?

Geswindoll: Observe Joe Commer and Jackie Vespertine completely naked on the bed!

Joe: No!

Huey: Whoa!

Joe: I'm so sorry, Huey, man, we've been flirting for months, and, really, it just blew up!

Geswindoll: And now observe Joe Commer *wink out of*

existence!
Huey: Wow!
Joe: God!
Geswindoll: And Jackie Vespertine's reaction of total disbelief. It takes her fifteen minutes to calm down! You can practically see her trying to put her mind back together. Have I flipped out completely? she wonders. You can almost see the moment when she settles on: The bastard just up and ran away! I won't get laid after all! And if you watch all the way to the end, you can see her put her little dress back on and let herself out of the apartment.
Joe: This is all so wrong! So intrusive!
Huey: Man, she *was* upset when I saw her right before I came over here. Huh, Joe, I never woulda guessed it. Or hell, maybe I would have. Who cares?
Joe: Are you crazy? This is your own wife! I must be out of my mind!
Jack: What in hell's going on there, Joe? Now you're having an affair with Huey's *wife?* For God's sake!
Joe: You stay out of this!
Jack: I swear you waste your life energy traipsing after every woman in the solar system!
Joe: Damn you! You think you know everything now that you have this so-called great marriage with Amav!
Jack: I won't be talked to like that! I absolutely won't!
Joe: I won't be talked to like that either!
Jack: Well, then, have it your way! I never should've called into your stupid Vespertine show! What a zoo! You're all obviously *brainwashed!*
Sound: CLICK!
Joe: Dammit! Jack? Jack?
Huey: He hung up! Man! Before we could take any calls from our listeners!
Joe: I'm outa here, too!
Huey: No, you're not! Sit back down, boy!
Churchill: Riaowl!
Joe: Crap! Goddammit!

Geswindoll: We don't need Lord Commer anyway! And look, you're both missing the most important thing about the video! Joe winks out of existence! He *time-travels* to 2028! Observe the sense of blurred shrinking as I rerun the video in slow motion. Believe me, if you run the end of the CTESOPE video you'll see Joe Commer in 2028 doing the exact same thing! Transitioning to back *here*.

Joe: I don't care about time travel! I care about being an honest, normal human being! I've betrayed everyone! Everything! I allow myself to be brainwashed by everyone!

Geswindoll: The intense emotions you experienced caused you to perform two Heuristic Time Transitions in a row. Believe me, the Celestions are interested in *that*.

Huey: Oh yes, the Celestions! They're interested!

Joe: You're driving him insane somehow, Geswindoll! Driving us both insane, showing us that video! Huey's always been unhinged, but now you're making it worse!

Geswindoll: Convert! Both of you! Now!

Joe: Jackie never told me about a sister who died!

Huey: A sister?

Joe: Ranna! Ranna Kikken! She founded CTESOPE! But she died in the Evacuation!

Geswindoll: Oh, yes, did you know Ranna was actually my wife? We got hitched a year after CTESOPE, about the time Pluto went flying out of the solar system. But she got in the way of the Celestions, so they offed her!

Joe: Your wife? She *married* you?

Geswindoll: You wanted to bang *both* sisters! I can see it in your eyes!

Joe: Of course not! I was just sorry that she died! God, we killed so many people in the Evacuation!

Geswindoll: Oh, don't get so riled up about lusting after some big-boobed bitch! It's the typical mistake you youngsters make! Confusing the desire to hump a woman with some sort of mystic vision of love!

Joe: Look, I'm not talking about any of that!

Geswindoll: Oh, just sit down! Now you're in love with this

Jackie woman, or you think you are, and it's gotten you all riled! Don't worry about it! The Celestions love you!

Joe: God, you are crazy!

Huey: Don't you just love talk radio! This man comes in and shows me a video of my buddy getting naked with my wife!

Joe: Look, I don't know! About anything! I'm so damned confused!

Geswindoll: It's just *raw sex!* I know, I used to be as obsessed as you are. But the Celestions fixed me. By the time I got to Mars, I'd grown far beyond all that.

Joe: Well, of course, you're just an old fart!

Geswindoll: Age has nothing to do with it! I still go down to Donbottor Street and score some pussy with the whores when I need it. The Celestions don't care as long as I don't get hung up on it.

Joe: God, those are the teenage girls who--

Churchill: Riaowl!

Geswindoll: What of it? They made their choice!

Huey: Hey, dude, those are the orphan girls who fell through the cracks!

Geswindoll: Hey, one time I banged a *Martian* woman! I didn't think that was possible! It was weird! Well, maybe I shouldn't say that on the air. Maybe I should *retract* that statement! There! I retract it!

Joe: There are *laws* against interspecies--

Geswindoll: I know, I know! I retract it utterly! It never happened!

Joe: Damn, Huey, why are we sitting here talking to a corrupt old fart?

Geswindoll: It's the idea you can merge your soul with anything but a Celestion that's at the root of human misery! I went through that myself. It was obvious to the Celestions, and finally to myself, that Ranna was just draining my energy, so I dumped her, even though she made it look like she was dumping *me!* We married in '29, called it quits in '31. Worst couple years of my life. Bitch!

Joe: I don't know. I guess I really admired her. And I was so sorry …

Geswindoll: That she bought the farm in the Evacuation? Hell, the Celestions told me she had to be dispensed with. She was doing something that was interfering with their plans, so she pulled the short straw in the great Evacuation lottery!

Joe: God, I can't believe you're so *callous!*

Geswindoll: Listen, young man, I don't need any sanctimonious crap about how callous I sound. The Celestions want me to be callous, so I'm callous! Ranna bought the farm and to the Celestions that works out fine for the universe.

Joe: That's evil! From what I saw of her, Ranna Kikken was a noble, forceful--

Geswindoll: Fantastic sexy bitch with killer boobs, huh? I can see how a young man like yourself, lost in orgasmic fantasies of this Jackie bimbo, would have a hard time tearing your eyes away from Ranna's sensational body. Have to admit, it did wrench me a bit when the Celestions told me she'd bought it on the *Pegasus.*

Joe: *What?*

Geswindoll: Passenger Shell *Pegasus.* They gave 'em all names, you know. Keep up morale during the Evacuation and all.

Joe: Idiot, I *know* that! I *ferried* those shells! The *Typhoon I--* no, I can't believe it!

Geswindoll: And I was wrenched, no matter that the Celestions told me I shouldn't be, that getting rid of her was all to the good.

Joe: She couldn't have been on the *Pegasus!*

Geswindoll: The Celestions made me write this poem about it, called "Bitch Bought the Stupid Goddamn Farm."

Joe: No, look, I've got to *think.* Got to process this. Ranna died on the *Pegasus?*

Geswindoll: *bitch bought the goddamn farm / on this goddamn stupid attempt / to escape the goddamn destruction / the goddamn USSF got us into*--something like that--

Huey: C'mon, Joe baby, pull yourself together! You USSF'ers lost a lot of passenger shells, after all!

Joe: I know, I goddamn *know!*

Geswindoll: *I am a clone, cleaning out your toilets / waiting for some bitch to harvest my goddamn guts*--something like that--

Huey: Man, those shells would just crack right off whatever ship they were attached to! I had to be totally sedated to get on *my* shell!

Joe: Of course I remember our six shells! A thousand people on each of 'em! And our record was a hell of a lot better than most. We did over five hundred transports ourselves, and only lost six shells. Six goddamn shells!

Geswindoll: I've wondered whether I should maybe go back to poetry full-time.

Joe: At the time, you couldn't feel much. After all, we'd just Xon'd CAP. That was two billion people dead there. You were just *numb* with all the death.

Geswindoll: But what I've really been thinking about recently, and our conversation is really spurring this on, is putting all this amazing sweep of a life into an autobiography!

Huey: Wow, man, make it a book-length poem and all!

Geswindoll: My poetry career, the Celestions, my stupid marriage to Ranna, the Evacuation as seen by an Elder of the Phallus, then getting this fantastic PR Director job and knowing I'm in the right place to really convert this sorry planet!

Joe: I remember all our shells! *Neptune,* and *Aurora.* And *Nebula IV* and *Endymion* and *Chalice.*

Geswindoll: What a slice of human history is contained in this one amazing life!

Joe: And *Pegasus.* That was one of the times we launched from New Mexico. I can still hear the ripping sound, and the groan that went up throughout the ship. Because we knew it'd happened *again.* There was nothing to do but watch it crash. They cobbled those passenger shells out of old airliners, oil storage tanks, whatever they could find.

Geswindoll: Yep, there's still a million liability lawsuits tangled up in the courts about those awful shells!

Joe: I killed Ranna Kikken! I can't believe it!

Huey: Dude, this is talk radio at its best!

Geswindoll: Now you're really ready to convert!

Churchill: Riaowl! Riaowl!
Joe: *I killed Ranna Kikken!*

CHAPTER NINE

Found in the Wreckage of Passenger Shell *Pegasus*
Ranna Kikken's diary, Thursday, June 14, 2029, 10:30 PM

Of course we're all edgy. Robbert simply came apart this morning. Completely drunk. He can't take Pluto. But can any of us?

Five days ago. Just Saturday. Some people are saying Pluto's not such a big loss. After all, it got downgraded from "planet" to "minor planet" a long time ago, who cares, who needs it, it's just a ball of rock, and so on. But what everyone doesn't seem to want to acknowledge is the total insanity of an entire planet, minor or not, taking off on its own out of the solar system. There's so much we don't know. Each report further smashes our dimming confidence in an orderly physical universe. I can't remember any of the figures for speed or distance. I don't want to know.

And for the past two days I've been wrestling with whether I should go ahead and publish our video of Joe's speech last year. Arnold at least had the wits to record the last three-fourths of it. It clearly shows Joe predicting Pluto.

Up to now I haven't considered posting his talk to the Internet. I knew it would further weaken CTESOPE. I admit I've never recovered from him crashing the conference last year. But all the while I've been torn. He moved me. All along I've believed he was telling the truth, even though I consciously thought he was mentally ill.

Last year we got enough explanations of "oscillating quantum gravitational cycles between the outer planets" to make us feel there's at least some reason why asteroids would suddenly accelerate into the sun. A billion people have written their crackpot opinions anyway, so what good would publishing Joe's speech do except further discredit CTESOPE? Why should I publish his prediction about Pluto, and all the stuff about Jupiter and Saturn and Uranus? So many people are nattering about "end times" anyway. Why add to it?

But I see another reason I haven't wanted to publish the

speech, and this is spooky to admit: my fear of damaging what Urside calls the timeline. Deep down I can't shake the feeling that Joe Commer really is from the future. If asteroids can shoot into the sun, if Pluto can be hurled from the solar system, why can't there be time travel?

Urside flatly says there has to be time travel. He talks about the timeline, and alternate universes, and time travel paradoxes, with an unnerving authority. Maybe it comes from his science fiction reading.

But that doesn't help me decide to post the video. I have this dread I'm about to wreck something. And this is hard to admit: what might publishing the recording do to a certain spaceship pilot named Joe Commer?

I definitely have the diary on UltraSecure Mode, not only with RetinalScan but also with a password that would take a supercomputer six hundred thousand years to crack. Or I would not reveal the following to my diary:

A few days after Joe's speech, I did a search on "Joe Commer." I netted thousands and thousands of Joe Commers, and I almost gave up in dismay, but then I thought: Fool! He gave you the names of three brothers! It was absurdly easy to add in the concepts of Jack, Jim, and John Commer.

So there was the result: Jonathan Commer, U.S. Air Force, retired, with four sons, Jack (25), Joe (24), Jim (22), and John (20), the eldest three having graduated from the U.S. Naval Academy, all having majored in aerospace. They'd all transferred to the new United States Space Force and were assigned to the new *Typhoon E* project with its breakthrough high-tech nuclear drive. The youngest, John, started the Academy himself in 2027. Not only did I find photos of all four brothers, I got a crisp video of Joe Commer playing soccer. There were even their Deerfield, Illinois high school yearbooks. Fifteen-year-old Joe Commer's interests included physics, geology, chess, and, amazingly, theater. He played Macbeth in a high school play, and got good reviews.

I downloaded it all. Those files are on UltraSecure as well.

The verdict? Yes, that is my Joe Commer, the man I confess

I--what the hell--fell in love with last year.

Yes, I write it down! So sue me! Does it matter anymore? Isn't it sinking in all over the world that we have to be faced with malevolent alien contact? Isn't that the only possible explanation at this point? That beings of frightening technological prowess are demonstrating that they have us at their mercy?

Joe talked about a war with *Alpha Centaurians*.

Everyone's going crazy, but nobody's talking much, everyone's cowed. We don't know what we're fighting. We have no idea what's next. Could publishing Joe's prophecies somehow prepare us for the next stuff? Neptune blowing up this fall, Uranus flying past us a month later, Jupiter and Saturn and some Final War? We can only hope they're just Joe's torment. We have to believe his final prophecies are distorted, delirious.

But above all, there's the fact that I still haven't dealt with my romantic feelings for that troubled man. Joe Commer. I guess now's the time, two days before my marriage.

I know Robbert and I have to marry now. Because time may be short. It may be our last chance to be rational in this world. We need this marriage. We will surmount all obstacles.

Like my feelings about this house. Why did I wake up at three AM last night, looking over at Robbert and panicking? What does it mean when I keep thinking I really don't want him here, in the soul house I built for myself off to the west, away from the rest of the Cat Farm, the house I built for soul meditation?

I really only had this house for a month. Planned it for two years, started building it last March. Moved in on October 19th. But within a month, Robbert was also here. I still don't understand how it happened. After all, didn't I tell him he could have the old house to himself, that we should take it slow?

All right, I admit it, the sex is incredible. People look at Robbert and I can tell they think he's a flake because, hell, he *looks* like a flake. But do they know how perfectly sexually compatible we are? Nobody has ever given me this much satisfaction.

I know this marriage will work. It has to work. We're too

much alike. And I'll go over to Robbert and tell him so as soon as I finish this entry. If he's still in the house, if he's not going out after some coffee.

Coffee? Who am I kidding?

Is he really an alcoholic, deep down? I agree, even Robbert agrees, that he came damn close, but we can both see a closure to that. Getting married, making the commitment, is part of the healing. I don't have to listen to everyone's stupid opinions.

Sure they all wish Robbert would go away. I know Urside hates him.

As for Urside, something major changed in him after CTESOPE last year. There's a new distance. It's strange that he's backed off. I really thought I was going to have to fire him. But after he did that crazy confession of "love" for me, he changed. And he's seemed so eerily calm and accepting of everything since then.

I don't know why. Maybe it also had to do with his girlfriend Mandy leaving him around that same time, leaving the area for good. Apparently they'd had some major fight and, as he told me, "She just got in her car and drove off." I wondered guiltily whether Urside had told her about his feelings for me. But I also know Mandy was hot-tempered under that sunny exterior. After all, she'd gotten estranged from her family and left them. Maybe she got estranged from Urside the same way. Like Urside, she looked much younger than her thirty years, and I'd always suspected she'd never really matured.

After Mandy left, I really expected Urside to be looking at me again, but it never happened. I guess we've all assumed he's found a new woman somewhere, but we've never seen her. He sure doesn't confide in me the way he once did.

Although once we talked all day about Churchill, and somehow he calmed my grief at losing the best cat of them all. Churchill who must've shot out of the room along with Joe at the CTESOPE conference. And never returned. I was heartbroken for months. At first I was totally irritated at Urside for glibly talking about "Churchill having transitioned to a better place," and that Churchill is somehow "waiting for me," but somehow Urside healed me, and our friendship has resumed, though it's more distant than before.

But all this stays under UltraSecure Mode. Nobody will ever see this. But I have to get this down, get it out of me. I won't censor anything.

Robbert and I have changed each other. That's what people don't understand. He's steadied me at a time when I was flying apart. I have stability now. I'll be a married woman again. That was comfortable. I won't have to fend all these men off every two seconds. Or succumb to half of them.

I'm rambling and so what? Why am I still thinking about Joe?

I admit it! I've been fantasizing it's *Joe* I'm marrying Saturday! Don't you understand that sexual compatibility with Robbert isn't really anything? But what does any of this matter? This marriage is going forward no matter how insane it is!

He's going to El Slobbero to get drunk! I know it! He's racing my car at a hundred miles an hour on those back roads to get stinking drunk! When he comes home he'll babble for hours about the goddamn Celestions! It's like he's some old, crippled, incestuous *father!* I hate the way he operates!

But Joe knows what's going to happen. He predicted Pluto, so all of his story must be true! And so there must be some future for me with Joe! And I've thought, okay, go ahead with the marriage, fate has ordained it, but someday you'll meet Joe again! You need him!

Can you believe it, dear diary on UltraSecure Mode? Believe it, because I'm going to destroy this entry. It's gone way too far off base. But I suppose I need to run off some steam for a while. Release all the tension.

Joe needs me! Wasn't that obvious from the start? Just as I need him?

CTESOPE *failed.* I still can't get that review out of my mind. In fact, I'll paste it in here as a monument to my failure:

"Her striking, off-balance beauty was the only highlight of Ranna Kikken's failed attempt to eradicate All Human Sorrow with a misguided Committee to End Suffering on Planet Earth, a conference that opened pitifully with a clown masquerading as a Wise Man from the Future predicting various environmental disasters, and then dragged on for four days of utter cliché and boredom."

No wonder I want to marry Robbert. *Everything* in my life has failed. He's drunk at El Slobbero, right now! I can't believe I wanted to think of him as swarthy, as earthy, as sexy! In harmony with the guts of the earth like some primitive tribal god! He's a *mess!*

All the nonprofit ladies snicker that he's an alcoholic and I'm doomed!

Destroy this entry, now! It's obscene and wrongheaded. It's nothing like the poems I wrote in college, things I wouldn't show even to a boyfriend, just my best friend Donna. Could I write a poem now?

Who am I kidding? What does it matter if I write a poem? If I marry Robbert or not?

Who can bear to consider Joe's final prediction, the one we never mention?

In 2033 Joe drops that bomb and destroys the earth! Every one of his predictions is his agonized memory of what *did* take place for him and what *will* take place for us! We have four years left before obliteration! Four years to continue pouring ourselves down the sewer!

So why shouldn't I marry an old coot alcoholic? Why shouldn't I be CTESOPE's perfect nonprofit lady? Why should I waste my time on poetry?

Dammit to hell! It's forty-five minutes of hell later! This stupid DiaryWriTA program! I can't delete this goddamn entry! RetinalScan still responds to lock it but somehow the program won't let me delete the entry!

In fact, this file is really screwed up because I can't even delete individual words.

Can't even backspace over this crap I'm writing! Just like life, huh? Can't take anything back!

I can't go backward in time and correct all this, Joe! So I just have to STOP! STOP EVERYTHING FOREVER!

CHAPTER TEN
Home
Friday, January 26, 2036

Bumping, sliding to the right, through several lanes. Mandy fought her nausea.

"Mandy! Wake up! Please!" someone moaned next to her. Urside?

"Sorry, guys," said a man in front of them, big hairy hands on a steering wheel. "They haven't fixed this part of the Interference yet. The potholes are pretty bad. Kinda gets to ya at three hundred miles an hour."

Mandy blinked. Night sky, and skyscrapers that seemed made of wires and lights. A freeway pouring past. "My God, we're in a *taxi!*"

The driver cocked his head. Urside squeezed her hand. "*It's all right,*" he whispered, as she noted with relief that she and Urside had their clothes back on. Well, not their real clothes, but something like thick black tunics and pants.

"Yeah, okay," Mandy whispered back. "But where are we?"

"I thought you said *you* had the HTT energy. Don't you know? You've been practically unconscious all this time. I was starting to get worried."

"Let me think. I felt this energy, and I wanted to come *home*. But what's all *this?*" Those buildings were so tall and spindly. The name on the dashboard of the taxi said *PhoboStar 880*. Its speedometer appeared to register 380 miles per hour. Mandy felt too light. They were cresting the hills of an elevated freeway way too fast.

They hurtled past complexes of white domes, billions of multicolored lights on spires and spheres that reminded her of oil refineries. BALAMMA OXYGEN PROCESSING, read a sign.

Other vehicles passed, sharks with bubble tops, flashing by in an instant and then gone. "Can you imagine?" the driver went on. "They built this freeway only a year ago, but already it's got potholes! If the City Council had its damn priorities straight!

Wants to break us with some stupid Friendship with Venus Pavilion, but won't repair the freeways! Hell, there's only a couple thousand idiots on Venus in the first place! Nobody can live there! Now half of Marsport's probably gonna vote for that Gooney dude! Can you believe it? A Martian? We're gonna have a *Martian* Mayor?"

"Did--did you say M-Mars?" Mandy gasped.

A sign said MARSPORT--NEXT 21 EXITS and then flashed over the roof of the taxi. "*Damn*," Urside whispered. "I can't believe this! Is that why I've been feeling so light?"

"How'd we get here?"

"We were in a building. I can't remember much. I'm still pretty dizzy myself. We were on a bench. Dressed in these black clothes. First thing I saw was a bunch of kids on exercise machines or something. Someone was playing basketball. I remember freaking because the ball took forever to go into the basket."

"What are you talking about? How'd we get in this car?"

"I don't know! I didn't know where we were, I tried walking you around, you were mumbling all this stuff about *Norcaj,* I think you were saying."

"That's right, the Norcaj Rec Center," the driver put in.

"Shhh! He can hear us!" Mandy whispered.

"The taxi was waiting in this garage in this building. I got you into it, I don't know why. I knew you needed help."

"*How can he hear us?* I thought you said people couldn't know we were here!"

"I don't know! I don't know!"

"Hey, you kids okay?" the driver said.

"Yes, yes, we're fine. Mandy is just--just--"

"Upset. Homesick. Yeah, I guess we all are."

"*Home* ..." Mandy whispered. A boxy, glassy skyline grew on the horizon. It reminded her of her hometown Houston, but the structures were impossibly high, with calligraphic flourishes of slender skyways looping around the buildings. Ahead came the flashing, changing words on a giant electronic billboard:

MARSPORT HOTEL

NEW LOW RATES
CORNER CANAL AND GANYMEDE
11:20:42 PM

"So where you want me to let you kids off?" the driver said.

"Oh my God, Urside," Mandy whispered. "What are we gonna do?"

"I don't know! You made the HTT link, not me!"

"Help me, Urside! I'm really--really--" She caught the driver's eye in the rearview mirror. "Really *homesick,* I guess."

"Uh, we'd like to go to the, uh, the Marsport Hotel. I mean, we're supposed to meet Mandy's parents there, aren't we?"

"Uh, right. The Marsport Hotel," Mandy added, impressed with Urside's quick thinking. The driver nodded, drifted across eight lanes, and shot the taxi into what looked like a four-foot-wide tunnel at three hundred miles an hour.

Blurs of light and darkness, then more glass buildings and the street slowed sickeningly to twenty miles per hour, crowded with other cars. People bounced along the sidewalks in shiny iridescent clothing. Another billboard was framed against the night sky, flashing GREENEY GOONEY FOR MAYOR.

Then a picture of a fish-man.

"A *Martian!*" Mandy cried. "Oh, God, Urside, it's true! It wasn't a dream!"

Urside leaned over to look out the window. "Man, just like what we saw! I mean, did we really see that--that *thing?*"

"We read its mind! It looked just like that!" The sinister fish creature brandished a tiny pistol spurting what looked like broken pieces of glass that congealed to spell: VOTE FOR ME! Then the image faded, replaced by: *Paid for by Greeney Gooney for Mayor Campaign '36, Phil Sperry, Treasurer.*

"A *Martian* running for mayor!" the cabbie said. "Nobody can believe it! Of course they're citizens of the System, same as us, but, sheesh, Gooney's a terrorist! He set up the Douglas assassination two years ago!"

"My God, Urside, what have I done? Where have I brought us?" Mandy moaned.

The driver leaned back. "Listen, kid, are you really okay?

Are you both okay? Because you guys seem, like, really out of it, y'know."

"We … we're fine. Just that I haven't seen my parents in a while, and I'm sorta nervous. We're both sorta nervous and all, I guess."

"Huh." The cabbie steered the PhoboStar to a halt in front of a plaza filled with geometric sculptures. "Well, here's the Marsport, guys. Hope it goes okay and all." Mandy leaned against the window, focusing on a black tetrahedron stretching into the thin pink sky, and felt for the door latch.

A warning buzzer came on. The latch vibrated painfully and Mandy let go. "Not so fast, young lady!" the driver said. "Gotta get rid of the air in here or it'll blow you guys right out on the sidewalk." He pressed a button on the dashboard and air rushed around them. "Knew this guy Ernie who blew this old lady fifty feet outa the taxi. He had his seat belt on so he didn't go nowhere, but they fired him quick!"

"Uh--guh--" Urside gasped. Mandy also felt air sucked from her lungs.

The driver sized them up. Somehow Mandy knew he'd seen this look on people's faces before, that everyone who lived here was probably extremely alert to this sort of look. "Dammit! You kids don't have your EnviroFields!" He pressed the button again and cool air rushed from vents all around Mandy's head. "Wow, I woulda gunked ya both! Man, what're ya doing without EnviroFields?"

"Wow …" Urside said. "We just, uh, forgot 'em! Thanks so much for catching it!"

"Hey, lemme pull you guys into the hotel airlock." The driver roared down an alley into a tube. In a few seconds, they were sealed in a small chamber where air buffeted the vehicle. Then a door slid back and the car moved into a glittering garage four stories tall where scores of other taxis discharged passengers from ten lanes.

"Man, are you kids really okay? When I picked you guys up at the Rec Center I had no idea you didn't have your EnviroFields! Man, we came close, dudes! But I shoulda thought! Next time I pick up any kids from the Norcaj airlock I'll know! Damn, I'll know!"

Mandy met his bright blue eyes. He was huge and bald and friendly. How could he be aware of their presence? But Urside had said that sometimes people knew you were there, and wasn't that after all what had happened with that *creature?* Dar, the Martian?

"Well, we're sorry," Mandy said, "but just don't have the-- the EnviroFields." She was about to say *And what's an EnviroField?* when Urside squeezed her hand.

"What do you mean, you don't have 'em?" the cabbie said. "Don't tell me you bought those Cramston EFs that've been screwing people up!"

"Uh, yeah, we just threw 'em in the trash, they were so bad," Urside said. "We knew we'd get new ones in town. We just totally forgot to tell you to put us in at the airlock. It was stupid."

"Well, I'm sure glad we caught it! Believe me, I don't wanna be gunking my passengers! Shouldna thrown away the Cramstons, I guess. Waste of resources according to the Recovery Council. But I guess I don't blame ya. The Cramstons are almost like going suicide skinny-gunking in the desert! Anyway, get yourselves a coupla Patterson 950s. Best thing short of a full Mars suit."

"Oh, okay," Mandy said, wondering how they were going to pay for such devices, then worrying how they were going to pay the taxi driver. She noticed a purse at her side, and, dazedly figuring it might somehow have been given to her, she hunted through it until she found a bright purple card that said "AresCredit." To her astonishment it also read "Mandielle Frederick." She nervously handed it over to the driver.

"Thanks, young lady," the driver said, holding the card to the dashboard. "I'm only charging you guys for the cost of hydrogen over here. I ain't doing full price on account of I nearly killed you guys. But I gotta live, ya know. The cost of H is killing me, ya know?"

"Well, I guess that's … all fair enough."

"Good luck, guys! Hey, there should be a Patterson store

right in the lobby!"

*

Mandy and Urside found themselves outside the gleaming red PhoboStar with its TAXIMARS sign. Now Mandy could focus on how light she felt. She wasn't quite floating, but felt she was skipping through the air. As the PhoboStar slid away it began to sink in that she was in the taxi garage of a major hotel on a different planet, alone with a strange young man with whom she was ending a one-year relationship.

"C'mon," Urside said, pointing to a wall of glass beyond which lay a vast lobby of couches, potted plants, and shops. Bouncing out of speakers was bizarre conversation that sounded like some badly-acted stage play:

"--to the Alpha Centaurian *threat!* Especially right now! Do I need to remind everyone that they told us, a year ago, they had plans to attack us in *one year?* They emphasized that, *one year.* They even translated that into our time figures. So even though we have this weird kind of truce with them--"

"Forget it! The Celestions won't allow any such warfare!"

"Great, you go on believing that."

Mandy tuned it out. Damn, it was true. It was all over between her and Urside. She'd only gone on this date to give him a chance to make up after the crap he'd said about Ranna last week. She'd been apprehensive about what he was saying about HTT, but thought she owed it to him to see what he was talking about. But she certainly hadn't expected to actually *land* in that mansion. And the way he'd assumed she'd want to have sex the second they got there. Was he obsessed or what? She'd done it to get it over with.

There was no way she could forget the Ranna thing. Mandy wasn't a fool. Urside hadn't been honest with her all during their relationship. All along he'd had this crush on Ranna Kikken. It didn't even matter if nothing had ever happened between them. His whole confession about Ranna now struck Mandy as being equally dishonest. Did she really have any idea who Urside

Charmouth was? And did she care?

Despite his cleverness in adapting to this bizarre environment, Urside wasn't scoring any points with her. She felt as if she were being dragged through a shopping center by her fifteen-year-old nephew.

"Look, here we are," Urside said, pointing to the gold PATTERSON ENVIRONMENTAL NECESSITIES sign above a shop door. EVERYTHING FOR THE MARTIAN ENVIRONMENT: ABOUT TOWN, CASUAL, FULL EXPOSURE, DEEP DESERT. "We can buy the EnviroFields and walk around a bit, get a feel for the place, or, if you're ready to HTT back, we can head back now."

"Well, let's get a couple EnviroFields and look around. We need to get the date, after all." She knew Urside's unspoken words: *I can't get back myself, I don't have the energy, I need you to do it.*

"Oh, okay. But you have to watch what you say here. Let everybody else take the lead in conversations. Flow along with whatever they say."

"I can handle myself, Urside."

"Hey, you're not mad, are you? I mean, because I know we can get out of this. I mean, if all else fails, we can probably just fall asleep and wake up back home. I've had to do that a couple times."

"No, I'm not mad. We'll get back home. I'm sure we just have to wait for the *right emotional thing* to happen."

Urside turned away, obviously unable to face the *right emotional thing.* Did he know his lies had caught up with him? Did Urside Charmouth, with his meaningless Abstract Art Comics and his HTT trips, his glib explanations and his inability to directly face anything, have the slightest clue what was about to happen to his relationship with Mandy Frederick?

"Hey, this might be a news terminal." Urside stopped at a kiosk where a hologram six feet wide, four deep and four high showed changing tableaus of citizens at meetings, people walking on the street, soldiers in carriers crawling across red rock, desert landscapes, and spaceships in orbit. A narrator spoke: "Today the United System Council approved a five trillion-dollar overhaul of the East Balamma Oxygen Recycling Station in the Kilpatrick Desert. This move, coupled with …"

"Look at the date cycling on the printed part down there," Urside said, pointing to flowing crimson three-dimensional letters:

Friday, January 26, 2036. 11:34 PM. Marsport, Mars Edition of AresNetNews.

"Urside, this is another of Joe's predictions! Didn't he say the whole planet had to evacuate to Mars? Didn't he say he came from 2036? Isn't this his time, then?"

"Well, maybe …"

"C'mon, why don't you just admit his predictions are true? Why don't you just admit that the earth was destroyed and everybody had to come to Mars?"

"Shhh!" Urside said, gesturing towards a man within earshot. "You can't let people hear you!"

But when Mandy turned to face the man, he nodded sympathetically. This puzzled her, but only momentarily.

"Sorry," she said. "I guess it's still pretty hard for everyone to admit."

"Yeah, you got that right," the man said, scanning the AresNet tableau. Mandy felt she could reconstruct from his tone how many people that one man had lost in the catastrophe. Something about the set of his shoulders said *wife and children*.

"Some of us still just can't believe it, I guess."

The man didn't turn. "Yeah."

"C'mon, we've gotta keep moving," Urside grunted, steering Mandy across the lobby to the Patterson store. "Man, I can't believe how easily we're interacting with everyone here. I've really only had interaction in a handful of cases, but it was all weird and hazy."

"Maybe it's the same thing as when that Joe guy came to CTESOPE. Everyone saw him, he saw everyone." Mandy had missed the meeting, but had seen the partial video of Joe Commer's speech. "Looks like we're just going to have to interact with these people here until that *certain emotional thing* gets accomplished."

Urside grimaced. "Look, let's just get a couple of these EnviroFields and get outside and explore a bit."

Mandy let Urside do the negotiating in the Patterson store. The salesclerk wasn't surprised they didn't have EnviroFields. Apparently so many visitors came in without them, from the two Martian moons, Venus, and what the salesclerk called the Jovian Fragment Field, that the Patterson store did a good business right from this hotel. The Patterson 950 was, as the cabbie had told them, the top-of-the-line model, and quite expensive. She wasn't sure what sort of line of credit she had here in the future, but the salesclerk's machine accepted the amount of AresCredit 32,786 and soon Urside and Mandy walked out of the store with two smooth black boxes on belts around their waists.

They waited in the main airlock with others as the lock cycled hotel air to equal the one percent Martian atmosphere. When the main doors opened and they moved out onto the plaza, Mandy felt the electric buzz of the EnviroField kicking in around her. Again she was struck by the giddy lightness of her steps in the Martian night. "The gravity is so much less!"

"Something like one-third Earth gravity. I've been reading up on Mars the past week, ever since, you know, the Commer guy and all."

"Oh, so I weigh forty pounds now!" Mandy laughed, bounding across the plaza to the bright light of a giant electronic slab. It was another information terminal, but unlike the lobby interface, this one was two-dimensional, twenty feet high by ten wide. People clustered about it gathering information. She found that reassuring. People apparently hadn't changed much in the last eight years, even after this awful Evacuation.

She was puzzled that so much of the two-dimensional display was in what appeared to be Chinese symbols, side by side with English text. Then, noticing that many of the people here were Asian, she understood that the evacuation of Earth must have remixed all the races, and she was seeing the two dominant languages of Earth represented here in Marsport.

She moved back to take in the electronic god face everyone

worshipped. Information was survival here. People needed to absorb all this data just to live another second on this planet. Not only no air and no pressure, but wasn't it true that the ultraviolet light alone would kill you? She definitely hoped the Pattersons were filtering that out as well. And what about those sandstorms that could cover the whole of Mars in a couple days? What other disasters had these people run into here? "This is amazing!" she said. "And it's only been a couple years after this Evacuation thing?"

"If--if it really happened," Urside whispered.

"No, I mean, look what they've built in such a short time."

"No, damn you, *override!*" came a cry. "You stupid piece of crap!"

Something banged hard right next to them.

"I'm staying *anonymous,* you hear me? You damn thing! *Override!*"

CHAPTER ELEVEN
Alycia of the USSF

Mandy turned to a blond woman in an outrageously skimpy outfit pounding a keyboard at the base of the info slab.

"Dammit! *Override!*" the woman snarled. A few more jabs, then: "Okay! About time! You stupid piece of junk!"

Mandy's first impression was that nobody should be so unprotected out here, but then realized that anybody's street clothes, including hers and Urside's, were wholly inadequate without EnviroFields. All you really needed out here was the EnviroField belt around your waist. You could be entirely nude otherwise.

This blond woman came close to that. Her halter top consisted of two fabrics, one a solid green diagonally across her left breast, the other an outrageously transparent light blue gauze that crossed her right breast and tucked inside the green. The right nipple was clearly displayed for any man's attention, although he'd also have the advantage of seeing about seventy percent of both breasts outside the crisscross.

The blue gauze was echoed below in her low-slung wrap. Mercifully this wasn't transparent, but both well-defined hipbones were exposed and much of her ass showed in the rear, with the black belt of her EnviroField draped casually around all this tantalizing sculpture. There was so much long slender exposed torso, and so much long slender exposed thigh, that Mandy had a hard time believing this woman's figure was real. It all seemed like a computer simulation.

Urside's mouth was open big enough to swallow this female whole. His eyes locked on that right nipple as the woman turned to the interruption of her keyboarding.

"C'mon, Urside, it's just the way the natives dress here," Mandy said, although nobody else was dressed like that.

"Uh, I know. I mean, I wasn't looking."

Mandy laughed. "You were *goggling!* Haven't you seen wilder things on all your eighty trips?"

"Well, actually, it's just that I probably need to regulate my oxygen flow." Urside fiddled with a dial on his belt marked O2. "Yeah, I couldn't focus properly because my oxygen--"

Instantly he turned blue and staggered.

"Urside!" Mandy cried, catching at him, flailing at the unfamiliar Patterson dials and buttons.

"God, what an idiot!" said the blond woman, moving over to stab a button twice on Urside's box.

Urside gasped and collapsed, but once on all fours he shook his head, took a deep breath, and shakily stood. He rubbed his forehead with a tiny buzz of what Mandy guessed was force field meshing into force field. "Wow ..."

"Hey, guy, what's gotten into you?" the woman said, as Mandy distanced herself from this ultra-sexy computer simulation creature. "You just shut down all your oxygen and all your pressure! Don't ever touch the O2 dial on a Patterson! That's for emergencies only, like if you have a system malfunction. Everything on a Patterson's automatic. You shouldn't ever have to worry about that."

"Uh, well, this is my first time using a Patterson."

"Yeah, I could tell." The woman adjusted the Patterson's ride on Urside's hips, then finally deigned to take in Mandy Frederick. "How about you?"

"Old hat for me," Mandy said without knowing why. Somehow it was true. She felt fine on this planet. The low gravity and the thin atmosphere spoke to her soul. She was *home*. The Patterson was nothing more than a shirt or a set of car keys. She used it because she needed it, without stopping to drool over how it worked.

"Uh, we're just in from the, uh, Jovian Fragment Field," Urside babbled.

Mandy saw that part of being home was realizing that she was outside the merely human society transplanted to this planet. She stood back watching Urside drool over this sex beast who'd inexplicably fastened onto him.

"Huh," said the blonde. "Believe me, we must have twenty people who gunk themselves every day in Marsport. A few people forget their EnviroFields, can you believe that? They usually just die in the airlocks as soon as it hits Mars pressure. But I saw this one guy get out of a car in front of Bfulli's Bookstore and he must've staggered a hundred feet before he finally bought it. It was like he was doing some weird ballet. Disgusting! Of course, after we first got here we had hundreds of people kill themselves by ignoring pressure rules, and we didn't have EnviroFields the first few months. But you'd think people would know by now."

"Well, you saved my life!" Urside said, reveling in all the flesh on display for him.

"No prob. My name's Alycia. And you guys?"

"Uh ... Urside Charmouth. And this is--" Urside gestured.

"Billy Sue Jones," Mandy said, straining to transmit directly into Urside's addled brain: *Idiot! Don't reveal checkable personal information to the natives!* Of course, Mandy had already inserted an AresNet credit card into the Martian economy, and possibly revealed even more than Urside had. But this Alycia woman was a different case.

"Huh," Alycia said. "Look, I'm just making some comments here." As she pointed to the keyboard, a lamppost spotlighted her transparent right boob, which in turn lit up Urside's intoxicated face. "If I can just send off this one diatribe, I could show you guys around Marsport."

Mandy was stunned. What a *carnivorous* woman. What *gall*. Surely Urside had the sense to refuse such a brazen ploy.

"Hey, that would be great," Urside said. "So you can just use the terminal here to write?"

Mandy sighed. Urside was *besotted*. Public terminals for personal writing had been around longer than even the Internet, hell, they went back to the 1970's. That Marsport had this common feature was nothing.

Alycia flashed a cute little smile. "Sure, silly."

But now Mandy noticed how tight and hard Alycia's blue eyes were. The woman turned back to her keyboard. "Gotta stay anonymous with the keyboard. Else I'd have to patch my EF mike into the Net and they'd know it was me and I don't need that hassle right now."

"Huh," Mandy said, realizing that all communication had to be coming over radio between their EnviroFields. It sounded like normal speech to Mandy. The sound, including Alycia's punching at the keyboard, was evidently transmitted throughout the shell of air around the EF wearer, probably arranged via algorithms to appear as if it were coming directly from the person standing opposite.

Urside had to move in for a closer look, of course. Glancing briefly at the keyboard and then lingering over Alycia's breasts, he said: "So why do you have to be anonymous?"

"Because I just don't want anyone to know who I am. The voice rec software will pull up my ID in a second. So I'm just signing on anonymously and saying my say. It's my right. I can't let you guys see this, either, so just back off."

But by this time Mandy had also arrived at the keyboard and saw words forming within a red rectangle above the keyboard:

SO I SEE WE HAVE A CALLER. WAIT, NO, THIS IS SOMEONE KEYBOARDING ANONYMOUSLY FROM A PUBLIC INFO BOARD.

"Urside! Look at the heading there!" Mandy said. "It says *Vespertine and Commer!*"

"*Man,*" Urside said. "You're right! This Commer guy again!"

"Yeah, Commer caused a real scandal when he signed on with Vespertine," Alycia said. "All he does is freak out on the air every night. The guy's a *mess*."

WELL, I DON'T THINK WHOEVER IT IS NEEDS TO BE ANONYMOUS WITH US. EVERYONE'S FREE TO SPEAK THEIR MIND HERE. C'MON, PATCH YOUR MIKE IN SO WE CAN REALLY TALK!

"Screw that," Alycia muttered, pummeling the keyboard, oblivious to Mandy standing right behind her and reading everything:

As a former USSF Technical Sergeant who quit the service IN DISGUST last August I am APPALLED at the growth of this idiotic religion of Celestionism in all levels of our society, but especially the USSF!

ANOTHER NONBELIEVER! COME ON, HAVE THE
COURAGE TO USE YOUR OWN VOICE.

YEAH, WE HATE LISTENING TO THE SYNTH-
VERSION OF YOUR TYPING.

LIKE WHICH ONE WE GOT GOING, JOE? ROCK
CUTTERBUTT? CAN'T WE DO BOUNCY BERTHA OR
SEXY SATANIA?

NO, I THINK THE PROGRAM DEFAULTS TO
GARAGE FLOOR GEORGE.

RIGHT, THE DRUNK BASTARD! OKAY, LISTENER,
YOU OKAY WITH BEING GARAGE FLOOR GEORGE?

"*Hell,*" Alycia muttered. "Well, maybe it's all for the best.
Hey, guys, back off, let me type my say in peace here, will ya?"

*Yeah, I'm sure you'd find some ways to take reprisals
against me! Cowards! Brainwashed USSF Celestion toadies!*

I'M NOT BRAINWASHED! DAMN YOU! I QUIT THE
USSF LAST FALL, REMEMBER?

*Yeah, yeah, yeah, to start this talk show trip with
Vespertine. So what? If you'd had the guts to stay with the USSF,
maybe it wouldn't have gotten taken over by Celestion creeps
like Easterling and Geswindoll!*

HOW COME YOU KNOW SO MUCH ABOUT THE
GODDAMN USSF, THEN?

*I told you, I was IN the goddamn USSF, I went in after my
brother joined up, I thought I was gonna do some good, I was
training to be a goddamn spacecopter pilot!*

"C'mon, you two, get back, stop staring at what I'm
writing!"

Mark DIED! You KILLED him, Joe Commer!

YOUR BROTHER DIED?

*In the Kilpatrick Desert! When you were at the damn
Martian ruins, and they attacked! And Mark--*

GOD, WAS HE THE ONE--

*I saw him die on television! The whole thing was being
televised! The Martians shattered him!*

HE WAS THE ONE WHO SAVED OUR BUTTS! THE
BLOND GUY! THE EOS GUNNER! YOU'RE HIS

BROTHER?

I'm his sister!

WHOA, GUYS, LET'S SWITCH TO SEXY SATANIA!

HUEY, SCREW THE HELL OFF, DAMN YOU!

HOLD ON, I'M CONSULTING THE USSF PERSONNEL FILES. KILPATRICK DESERT BATTLE CASUALTIES. KLAVE, MARK. SO YOU WOULD BE ALYCIA KLAVE? INPUTTING ANONYMOUSLY FROM MARSPORT HOTEL PLAZA INFORMATION KIOSK? JOINED USSF JANUARY 2034, DISCHARGED FOR PSYCHIATRIC REASONS AUGUST 2034?

GESWINDOLL, YOU IDIOT, SHE WANTED TO REMAIN ANONYMOUS!

"Damn these jerks! Dammit!" Alycia cried. She pressed a button on her EnviroField and yelled to the sky: "That's right! I admit it! A psycho discharge was the only way out! Mark *died!* I couldn't handle it! But at least I thought the USSF would stay goddamn *noble* somehow! Instead Joe Commer slinks away, all the good men slink away and get replaced by these Celestion sons of bitches!"

I SAY PROSECUTE THIS WOMAN FOR TREASON! TREASON TO THE USSF!

HELLO, LISTENERS, WE BREAK INTO THIS PROGRAM TO ANNOUNCE THAT IT'S MIDNIGHT, AND WE WILL NOW ENTER THE THIRTY-NINE-MINUTE TIME SKIP.

"The what?" Mandy said. But she saw, on an adjacent green rectangle labeled "Time Skip Daily Synchronization," a flashing red "12:00 AM," underneath which blue numbers ticked off seconds, and added: *It will remain 12:00 AM for the next 39 minutes, 35 seconds.*

"The goddamn *time skip*," Alycia said. "Don't you people know *anything?* Coordinates us with the Martian day and all. But of course the damn talk show stays on."

OF COURSE VESPERTINE AND COMMER STAYS ON!

ANY OTHER COMMENTS, MS. KLAVE, BEFORE WE

CUT YOU OFF IN MID-WHINE?

"Yeah, just this!" Alycia shouted. "The USSF is being taken over by Celestion worshippers and, meanwhile, you're ignoring the *threat* from the Alpha Centaurians!"

LITTLE LADY, THE USSF IS ENTIRELY PREPARED TO ONCE AND FOR ALL NEGOTIATE A LASTING PEACE WITH THE ALPHA CENTAURIANS. IT'S MILITARISTS LIKE JACK COMMER WHO'VE STOOD IN THE WAY OF PEACE, WITH ALL THEIR XON BOMBS AND THREATS!

HEY, DAMMIT, THAT'S MY *BROTHER* YOU'RE TALKING ABOUT!

*

"Aw, damn your Celestionite asses!" Alycia snarled, jamming at the keyboard, then whirling to Urside. "I can't believe the USSF is flaking out on us like this! Everybody knows the truce with the Alpha Centaurians won't hold!"

Words still formed within the Vespertine and Commer rectangle: THAT'S RIGHT, HANG UP, COWARD! JUST LIKE THAT BASTARD JACK COMMER WHO DIDN'T HAVE THE GUTS TO TALK TO MY FACE!

YOU TAKE THAT BACK ABOUT JACK OR I'LL *PUNCH* YOU IN THAT GODDAMN FACE!

"The truce?" Urside said. "With--with--"

"Don't play stupid! The whole Alpha Centaurian war!"

"The what? Centaurian *what?*"

"The goddamn war with the goddamn Alpha Centaurians! We had a truce just last year! But it can't hold! Don't you know *anything?*"

"Look, I can accept we've landed in 2036 but there can't be *star travel.*"

"But Urside," Mandy said, "don't you remember Joe talking about an Alpha Centaurian war? It's on the CTESOPE video, something about Star Drive."

"No!" Urside moaned. "This can't be real!"

"Ever since '32!" Alycia cried. "Even before we left Earth!

My brother and I signed up to fight both the Martians *and* the ACs! Then Joe Commer gets Mark killed!"

"I know Joe Commer too! I met him at the CTESOPE conference! In 2028!"

"*Urside!*" Mandy hissed.

Alycia spun to her. "You're not Alpha Centaurian spies, are you? Damn, I should have known! You're new here, you don't know how to use your EFs, then you make up this story about being from the JFF!" She turned helplessly in all directions. "Joe! Jack! Somebody *sane!*"

"Hey, take it easy," Urside said, patting her bare arm. Mandy stiffened but said nothing. "We're not these … these people. We're not spies."

Alycia stared back. Mandy didn't like the new intensity in her blue laser eyes as they locked onto Urside's. This woman was too cute, too sexy, too *suffering* for Urside to resist.

"Prove it!" Alycia shouted, mouth trembling, tears rimming her eyes. "Goddammit, prove it! I'm so sick of all this! All this time I've pretended it's okay, that we were fated to come to Mars, and those that didn't make it--that didn't--" She furiously wiped her eyes in a buzz of EF static.

"*Wow,*" Mandy said, wondering about the deep wounds that had to exist throughout this Martian colonial society. Meanwhile, Alycia bravely pulled her shoulders back to take a deep breath that rode her chest high and got Urside gawking again. Damn, flirtation wafted off this woman like knockout gas. Any man around her instantly went under.

"Look, we'll level with you," Urside said. "We're *time travelers*. Mandy and I came here from 2028. We don't know anything about your wars, or an evacuation."

"You can't tell her that!" Mandy cried.

"No, it's true!" Again Urside patted Alycia's arm. "We're really from 2028. From Earth!"

"Oh God," Alycia whimpered, "I knew you were crazy! All that crap about Heuristic whatever it is that people have been mouthing these days, right alongside this Celestion worship! All of a sudden the USSF itself has gone Celestion! What the hell does it mean? And you have the gall to tell me you come from a time *before!* Damn you!"

"*Wow ...*"

"We're all *insane* here! We just don't ever want to admit it! We stole this planet from the Martians, who're so peace-loving they just let us, after our stupid little war with them, that is. Oh, God!"

"Really, you have to believe us, we're *time travelers!* Heuristic Time Transition is real! Mandy and I are from 2028!"

"Dammit, Urside!" Mandy said.

Alycia straightened up. "Okay, everybody knows HTT's this unexplained thing. Last year some scientist said he had proof of it. Big deal. Maybe you're right about it. Maybe it's possible. I think you're crazy, but maybe it's possible that it's happened to some people. But to stand there and talk about *2028!* About a time *before!* I remember all those asteroids dropping into the sun, and everyone got really scared and nothing was ever the same again!"

"God, so it's all *true,*" Urside whispered.

"Nobody wants to admit it, but it all happened! And now we're fighting Alpha Centaurians, and we wrecked the earth-- and--and did I mention Mom and Dad were killed in a passenger shell crash? *Did I mention my brother was killed in the Martian War?*"

"Well, yes, you did."

"We're ... so sorry," Mandy said.

"Killed by a Martian shattergun in the Kilpatrick Desert! For no reason! I'm the only one left! That's why I quit the USSF! I just couldn't stand the *death* anymore!"

"*Man ...*" Urside said with another arm pat. Alycia accepted this as well.

"Look, I'm sorry," Mandy said. "But what about these Martians you keep talking about? Who are they? You were at war with them, now it sounds like that's over with." She was surprised by her fresh curiosity. Despite the fact that Alycia's brother had died in the Kilpatrick Desert, Mandy wanted to head out there now.

Alycia reluctantly took her eyes off her latest conquest and more or less acknowledged that Mandy existed. "The whole stupid thing was an insane misunderstanding. Everyone knows that. The Martians got brainwashed by Sam Hergs and before we knew it, we were at war. Back when the Commers were *sane*. They saved us from that. Didn't save Mark, though."

"We're so sorry," Urside said, again patting her arm when what he wanted to pat was her boobs.

Alycia took another sorrowful, sexy deep breath. "The Emperor Dar came to each family that had a loss and personally apologized. He really is wonderful. I mean, even now I can't hate the Martians."

"Dar," Urside repeated numbly. "Not that *creature* we saw!"

"Yes, the same one," Mandy said. "The emperor. We could read his *mind*." The word "Dar" reverberated deeply. Deserts, caverns, craters, ancient Martian cities. Small people with heads like fish and huge pink fins down their backs, but with human torsos, hands, and feet. Gleaming golden robes worn only by Martian Elders. Ancient rituals of Martian love enacted by emperor and consort. Mandy seemed to be remembering things she'd known about for eons. "Urside, we need to talk to this Dar again."

"Forget it," Alycia said. "There's no way you could get an audience."

"He'll remember us. We met him in 2033, as a matter of fact. On this same HTT."

"We can't spread the story of time travel here!" Urside cried.

"You just did! You spilled the beans because you were flirting with this bimbo here!"

"I was not!"

"Well, excuse me," Alycia said. "He was. I can't help it if he finds me attractive. I think we all just need to accept that and move on." She caressed Urside's arm. "What did you say your name was?"

"Uh … uh …"

"Sheesh," Mandy said, pointing at the Marsport Hotel looming over them. "Look, you two can just get to know each other in there while I go find this Dar."

"N-no!" Urside said. "Mandy, this has gotten all out of hand!"

"So where do I find our Martian emperor?" Mandy knew that beautiful Martians would telepathically understand everything she felt. An image coalesced of a vast white palace at the heart of this city, not an ancient palace, in fact a thoroughly modern structure built by humans and Martians to commemorate the end of the war and to honor Dar's emperorship.

"Mandy, don't be silly! We have to go back home!"

"No! I'm staying here, in *this* time. *This* is my home." The palace was the most beautiful architecture she could imagine, solid clean human slabs mixing effortlessly with soaring Martian spires.

"You're nuts! Everyone has to return to their own time zone!"

"Not if this is my real home! I'm a *Martian*. I've always been a Martian, until somehow, in this last lifetime, I was born into this *human* body."

Alycia and Urside stared. Finally Urside said slowly, as if talking to a child: "No, everyone who does HTT has to retreat to their home time zone, or else there really will be a break in the timeline. From everything I've seen, that's how it works."

"There's got to be allowance for permanent shifts. I've got to stay here. This is my *fate*."

"That's crazy! You're coming home with me, now!" Urside declared, grabbing her arm, closing his eyes, and straining ineffectually to HTT.

"You can't! You don't have the energy!" Mandy laughed, dancing back. "You're just going to have to sleep it off! You're going to have to leave me here!"

"I wonder if her Patterson's set up right," Alycia put in. "Could be hypoxia."

"Mandy, knock it off!" Urside snapped. "I've done enough damage to the timeline myself without you screwing it up further! I'm sorry you came along!"

"Look," Alycia said, "maybe you guys should work this out by yourselves."

"No, don't be silly, Urside needs you!" Mandy said. "There's only one way he can get back. Only one way he can satisfy the *certain emotional need* and HTT back. See, he's way too tense to sleep now, so the only thing that'll knock him out is *sex.*"

"*What are you saying?*" Urside cried.

"Yeah, what?" Alycia demanded, jamming hands to her hips, unfortunately gluing Urside's eyes again to the sight of delightful jiggling boobs.

"Okay, let's spell it out. Urside and I are through, that's obvious."

"It is not--" Urside began, then guiltily scrutinized the cement beneath him.

"We had a year together, but after what you told me last week …" Mandy couldn't bring herself to mention Ranna. If Urside was to have any sort of relationship with Alycia, it was best not to confuse the issue with his puppy crush on Ranna Kikken.

Urside nodded miserably. "I told you I was sorry." But it clicked in even his innocent head that he didn't have an apology that could cover the damage.

"And I'm staying here anyway. I'm staying here to explore Mars. You two will find a room at the hotel."

"What?" Alycia gasped. "What makes you think that I want to do that?"

"Oh, you do. And Urside does. I'm signing him over to you as of right now." She took out her AresCredit card and handed it to Urside. "I won't need this anymore, and we at least know this one works." She reached for each of their hands and stuck them together. As she expected, when she relaxed her grip, Urside and Alycia's hands remained joined.

"This can't be happening!" Urside and Alycia burst out together.

Mandy laughed. "Consider Urside's position: he's done

eighty HTT trips and he's gotten to a place where he's not sure he can get back. He's scared. And his girlfriend just told him it's over, which it is. And Alycia here has had some really bad experiences since 2028, and she's scared too. You two need each other. So you're going to go into the hotel and have a very nice time. And then Urside will be able to fall asleep afterwards and he'll wake up home in 2028."

"Gee, that sounds great," Alycia said sarcastically, but still holding Urside's hand.

"Don't worry, Urside will come visit you via HTT every day."

"This is crazy!" Urside said. "You can't just disappear into 2036! That'll screw up the 2028 timeline! There'll be a missing person report, all that legal stuff."

"Make up any story you want. The timeline will heal itself. Some sort of explanation will gloss it all over. Just tell everyone I moved to Florida or something. Who cares? And if that doesn't work, there've been missing person reports since the beginning of time. How many just HTT'd over to a new life somewhere else?"

"Nobody can do a permanent HTT!"

"I can! I have the energy! It's *fated* I stay here. I don't want to just wait passively for all the crap from 2028 on to happen. My energy is needed now, in 2036. Somehow that makes sense to me. The Martians need my help."

"What about me?" Alycia demanded. "You think I believe this stupid time-travel crap? I think you're both nuts!"

Mandy sized her up in distaste. "You'll believe me when you watch Urside flash back to 2028 in a little while." She felt new knowledge enter from the planet beneath her feet. "After that, you'll have work to do here with us. There are all sorts of problems to work on. Rebuilding the earth, for one thing. Something about animals. And something about the timeline. Dar will know how to proceed."

"You just can't walk in on him!"

"Oh, I'm sure you'll be glad to show me the way to the Emperor's Palace!"

"Look, it's this new place they built in the middle of Marsport, after the war. You just take Douglas Boulevard--"

"I know where it is. You can take me there after you and Urside are through. I'll just wait out here on this bench and soak up some Martian night air."

"But--" Urside began.

"C'mon, let's do as she says, for God's sake," Alycia said, tugging him towards the Marsport Hotel. Hand in hand, they cycled through the airlock.

Mandy grinned. So Urside had always thought of his HTT trips as some sort of dream. Just a dream where he could act like a jerk and still think himself a brave explorer. But it was all too real. It was crucial to human consciousness. And to Martian consciousness. It wasn't a game. But it *was* fun.

She unstrapped her Patterson EnviroField and let it waft to the Martian concrete in one-third G. Eagerly taking in the thin Martian air, she scanned the human-revised but still gloriously Martian capital of her real home as she calmly awaited Alycia's return.

CHAPTER TWELVE
Society is an Awesome Phenomenon, Not to be Lightly Dismissed
As aired on the Vespertine and Commer Hour on AresNet, Saturday, January 26, 2036

Program Computer: Hello, listeners, we break into this program to announce that it's midnight, and we will now enter the thirty-nine-minute time skip.

Caller Alycia Klave: The goddamn *time skip*. Don't you people know *anything?* Coordinates us with the Martian day and all. But of course the damn talk show stays on.

Huey Vespertine: Of course Vespertine and Commer stays on!

Geswindoll: Any other comments, Ms. Klave, before we cut you off in mid-whine?

Klave: Yeah, just this! The USSF is being taken over by Celestion worshippers and, meanwhile, you're ignoring the *threat* from the Alpha Centaurians!

Geswindoll: Little lady, the USSF is entirely prepared to once and for all negotiate a lasting peace with the Alpha Centaurians. It's militarists like Jack Commer who've stood in the way of peace, with all their Xon bombs and threats!

Joe Commer: Hey, dammit, that's my *brother* you're talking about!

Klave: Aw, damn your Celestionite asses!

Geswindoll: That's right, hang up, coward! Just like that bastard Jack Commer who didn't have the guts to talk to my face!

Joe: You take that back about Jack or I'll *punch* you in that goddamn face!

Churchill: *Hsst!*

Geswindoll: Get that damn thing away from me or I'll shatter it!

Joe: Put that gun away! You'd shatter a *cat?* What kind of monster are you?

Huey: You'd shoot a rare and endangered creature? C'mon, dude, there's probably only a hundred cats or dogs on the whole of Mars!

Joe: We had to leave 'em behind! Almost all the animals! What idiots we were!

Geswindoll: Don't tell me you're getting softheaded about the stupid animals! You know there was no way we were gonna ferry all fifty gazillion goddamn animals to Mars, so just forget it! If there's one less goddamn cat to bother us, why then--

Churchill: *Hssssstt!*

Joe: Holster the weapon! Or I'll declare a crime in progress and get the Autopolice!

Geswindoll: Aw, sheesh. I never thought Joe Commer would be a *wimp*. Didn't you say you racked up two billion people yourself when you dropped the Xon?

Joe: Damn you!

Geswindoll: You're the killer, not me!

Joe: Dammit, it was just pure karma that it fell to me, and Jack. And to Jim and John, and the rest of the *Typhoon* crew! The other guys were lucky in a way, when the ship was destroyed at Mercury. They're dead now, they don't have to carry that load. Jack and I have to carry it! *We're* the ones! And now *Ranna!* Oh God, Ranna!

Geswindoll: Watch what you're saying, young man! You sound as if you still have the hots for her! That's my ex-wife you're talking about!

Joe: *Why am I on this show?*

Huey: Hey, Joe, I tried to distract you from all this pathetic grief by taking some callers, but nooo, you've got to wallow in it like you always do!

Joe: But the Xon, and all the people who died! Those *passenger shells,* and now *Ranna!*

Geswindoll: So now you're in love with my dead wife! I thought you were in love with Huey's goddamn wife!

Joe: I need to talk to Jack! Jack, call back, please!

Geswindoll: You're hysterical! But the Celestions tell me that you need to get laid! Right now! You're a typical young man who needs to get laid!

Joe: Screw that! I love Jackie Vespertine, and I'll never betray her!

Huey: Joe loves my wife! Well, why the hell shouldn't he? I admit she's a piece! Everyone knows it! *She* sure does!

Joe: Dammit, Huey, I'm sorry, but face the facts, I love her!

Geswindoll: Forget it, my horny young friend! The Celestions tell me you love *Ranna Kikken,* even though she was blown to atoms two years ago!

Joe: Ranna died! On the *Pegasus* shell! How can you just sit there and *laugh?*

Geswindoll: You'll never get inside her! Or her little sis Jackie for that matter!

Joe: You're a son of a bitch, you know that? Jackie is everything to me!

Huey: Hey, man, you having a goddamn nervous breakdown or something? Just chill out, will ya? It's no big deal about Jackie.

Joe: *No big deal?* Dammit, you're *crazy! I'm* crazy to be here listening to this!

Geswindoll: And their insanity shall convert them to the Way of the Celestion, and Universal Peace, to quote the Celestion Bible.

Joe: I will *not* convert! Don't you dare use that word to me!

Geswindoll: Convert now! Both of you!

Joe: Don't use that *word!* Damn you, I remember what it *felt like* to convert to the goddamn Alpha Centaurian Grid!

Geswindoll: Oh, right, like I'm supposed to change my language habits just because you're having these silly flashbacks! I'm not talking about your stupid fears of their Grid, dude. We defeated the ACs last year. Between the Martian Solar System Defense and our capability of destroying the AC agricultural worlds, that threat's over. See, I can actually agree with your idiot brother there. I was just jerking his chain earlier.

Joe: That's crazy! They'll never keep that truce! We've got to *prepare!*

Geswindoll: And the Celestions are nothing like what you went through last year. They're a new religion, a new way of life.

Joe: No, it's the same damn thing! It's brainwashing! What if I'm still brainwashed? What if I was given a post-hypnotic command last year to sabotage the United System, right now?

What if this whole HTT thing is the beginning of *total insanity?*

Geswindoll: "And they that puke heresy shall be arraigned before the Annihilating Justice." That's *Prettified Doom,* Chapter 13, Verse--

Huey: Lay off my damn partner, dude! He's got a lot on his mind these days! Xon bombing the earth and offing a couple billion people, getting brainwashed by the ACs last year, and time-traveling! And now getting into my wife's pants!

Joe: Dammit, Huey! I swear my intentions are honorable!

Huey: Aw, you think I really give a damn? You think Jackie gives a damn about me?

Geswindoll: This is incredible! I hereby order both of you to convert to the Way of the Celestion, right this instant!

Huey: Man, alluva sudden I feel *sick.* Man, I can't *take* this!

Joe: Wow, man! What's wrong? You look really *sick,* man! Did this jerk make you sick?

Huey: Jeez, just dizzy or something, listening to this idiot here.

Joe: Dammit, Huey! Don't convert! This Celestions crap is just insanity!

Geswindoll: Watch what you say about the Celestions! They hear everything!

Huey: Oh, man … so dizzy … throat hurts … can't breathe …

Joe: *I* did this! Because I screwed around with your wife! I made you sick! I'm sorry!

Huey: Yeah … or maybe like with your time traveling, man.

Joe: *What?*

Geswindoll: You guys are so messed up! How does this program stay on the air?

Huey: I mean, something about the timeline, and Celestions. All screwed up. Wish I could remember. Feel so *weird.*

Joe: I'm so sorry about Jackie! We fell in love! I think! I mean, I couldn't help it!

Huey: Don't care. Jackie's a fine girl. Doesn't care about me. I don't have a real life … I don't exist, really …

Geswindoll: Incredible! The Celestions are taking his mind apart as we speak! In preparation for a most glorious Conversion! Listen, everyone! Praise the Celestions!

Joe: Back off! He's having a fit or something!

Geswindoll: He's seeing the Light! Praise the Celestions!

Joe: Screw that! Look, we've always known something's *wrong* with Huey. This guy really hasn't been able to function as a human being since he dropped out of the Academy!

Geswindoll: Oh, that's right, I'd forgotten the sentimental story of how he was in the Academy with you and Jack. But now he's converting to the One True Way, and you can't do a damn thing about it. And you're next!

Joe: I'll never convert! Dammit, what the hell's going *on* in the USSF?

Huey: I'll tell you what's going on! The Alpha Centaurian invasion has *begun!* We've *already* been infiltrated!

Geswindoll: Oh, listen to this! Finish your goddamn Conversion and get in line with the Celestions! We're tired of this nonsense!

Huey: I know, because I'm really an *alien!* I'm a goddamned *alien!* I'm a Jujl from Zorex!

Joe: Oh my God! He's snapped! Geswindoll, you hypnotized him or something!

Churchill: Riaowl! Riaowl!

Geswindoll: Dammit, I'm *trying* to convert him! Something's interfering!

Huey: The Zoraxians are here! And they've got HTT! It's really a *weapon!* We've got to warn everyone!

Geswindoll: Dear Celestions, perhaps your Conversion is a little too intense for our subject, who as we can all see is absolutely frothing at the mouth. Please finish Your Process quickly so that he may dwell in the Light of the Celestion forever. Amen!

Huey: They'll tear apart the entire universe! They're so crazy! They don't give a damn!

Joe: You drove him insane! You drove my friend insane!

Geswindoll: Hey, you're the one who was about to bang his wife!

Joe: But fate time-traveled me *out* of there! Fate was trying to *protect* us all!

Huey: Time travel! That's the key! That's how they'll destroy us!

Joe: C'mon, Huey, take it easy, man, you're shaking all over!

Churchill: Riaowl … roo … roo …

Huey: It was me! Me! *I* wrote the goddamn Chronowarp Subroutine!

Geswindoll: Hmm. I think it's time for me to go. This Conversion has been useless. Nice talking to you guys.

Joe: Get your ass back here! *You* caused this! You hypnotized him or something!

Huey: The Zoraxians stole the Chronowarp! They screwed up the timeline!

Geswindoll: I'm out of here! The Celestions don't want me seeing this sort of garbage.

Joe: No! Help me get him on the floor! He's delirious!

Huey: We've got to stop the Zoraxians! Once and for all!

Joe: C'mon, Huey! Please! You'll be all right! Of course we'll stop them if they try to attack us! You don't need to worry!

Huey: No! They've *infiltrated!* They're already here!

Joe: That can't be true! The Martians have their Amplified Thought defense!

Huey: But the Martians never saw a *time attack* coming! The Zoraxians are here! I can feel them! I'm a Zorexian! I should know!

Joe: You can't be a Zoraxian!

Huey: Dammit, Joe, I said *Zorexian!* I'm *Zorexian!* Don't confuse Zorexian with *Zoraxian!* We're two goddamn separate species! Zoraxians are--what is your term?--*monsters!*

Geswindoll: What the hell's this stupid twit saying now?

Joe: Somehow he's talking about the Zoraxians!

Geswindoll: The what?

Joe: You're supposed to be a USSF honcho and you don't know that? The Zoraxians! They call themselves the Zarj! The most militarist species of the ACs!

Geswindoll: So Vespertine's saying he's a spy for the Alpha Centaurians?

Huey: No! I'm *Polot!* I'm Ship's Archivist on *GnlSaljPraraq!*

Geswindoll: This is insane!

Joe: He's sick! Hey, who're you calling? An ambulance?

Geswindoll: Yes, something like that.

Huey: I'm *Polot!* Huey was the only body I could find! He's *soulless!* Been this way for years! So it's okay for me to take him over! But what a weird body!

Churchill: Riaowl! Riaowl! Riaowl!

USSF Airman Carl Posttner: Yes, sir! You called?

Geswindoll: Posttner, these two men are under arrest.

Joe: What? Are you *crazy?* Get an ambulance!

Huey: Polot of Zorex will resist alien torture!

Joe: You there! Point that rifle away!

Geswindoll: Formidable weapon, eh? Shatter-enhanced Electron Oblivion Sequencer, just developed over the last couple months. Our top engineer says the idea for it came to him in a dream. A dream inspired by the Celestions! Praise the Celestions!

Posttner: Do I really have to point my EOS away, sir?

Geswindoll: Hell, no, Airman. Make sure these Alpha Centaurian spies know they'll *cease to exist* if they try anything funny!

Joe: What are you talking about? Huey needs an ambulance!

Geswindoll: Shut up, traitor! Vespertine says he's a Centaurian spy! And you yourself said a minute ago that you were given a post-hypnotic suggestion by the Centaurians!

Joe: Forget it! You hypnotized Huey yourself! Then he went insane!

Geswindoll: Now I see why the Celestions couldn't convert either of you. They found out you're both *traitors!* They unearthed your AC brainwashing!

Joe: Jack! Jack! Help! Are you listening? Stop this insanity!

Geswindoll: Oh, Jack would agree with me here! He'd do anything to make sure the solar system is safe from AC spies! Including locking up his brainwashed little brother!

Joe: You son of a bitch!

Huey: Man, what're all these papers blowing all over?

Joe: God! Our EnviroFields kicked in! We've lost pressure!

Posttner: Sorry, dude, I was in a hurry, didn't have time to cycle the airlock.

Geswindoll: Hey, I had my bodyguard right outside! Can't be too careful, you know.

Joe: That's not the point! Churchill! Where's the cat? *Where's the cat?*

Geswindoll: Who cares about a stupid cat?

Joe: We've lost pressure! We killed Ranna's cat!

Geswindoll: Aw, jeez, if that's your only concern, traitor! Posttner, I've called for a couple jeeps. Just cover these guys until they get here.

Posttner: Goddamn AC vermin, sir, according to the Celestions. We oughta shatter the mothers now and be done with it.

Joe: Hey! Churchill's up on that file cabinet!

Posttner: Back off, or I'll--damn!

Geswindoll: Where'd *that* come from?

Joe: That--that *thought?*

Posttner: Sir! A thought just came! Like a *Martian* thought! Someone called me *dark human!* Told me to lower my weapon! Sir, do we have Martians in this building?

Joe: Are you hearing what I'm hearing? Like picking up a Martian's thoughts?

Geswindoll: I've never felt any Martian thoughts like *that!*

Joe: Oh, the poor cat's dying, and somehow we're getting its thoughts!

Posttner: No, the damn thing's alive! Look at it up there, laughing at us!

Joe: I'm reading Churchill's mind! I'm seeing the whole CTESOPE talk through his memory!

Huey: Hey, man, the cat's *Martian,* dudes, isn't it obvious?

Posttner: Shut up, Centaurian spy! And get that cat out of my mind!

Joe: Churchill's *alive!* How can that be? There's just Martian atmosphere in here!

Posttner: All these cat thoughts, sir! It's disgusting! The damn thing's *enjoying* the low G and the low pressure! And it won't let me shoot these bastards!

Geswindoll: Well, I concur with the goddamn cat there, Posttner. We'll just take these traitors to USSF headquarters and take their minds apart to see what's going on!

Posttner: Sir, somehow the damn cat's playing with my hands! With its mind! My hands aren't steady, sir!

Geswindoll: Easy there, soldier. Just relax. Don't let these spies rattle you.

Posttner: I--I won't, sir. Thank you, sir! Uh, sir, I'm getting word the jeeps are here.

Geswindoll: Okay, then, let's get going. Vespertine, can you walk?

Huey: I don't know! I'm Polot of Zorex! I've never walked in a human body before!

Geswindoll: Aw, crap! Posttner, set your EOS to stun and we'll drag him out.

Posttner: Done, sir. The Celestions report that it was a pleasure to blast him, sir.

Geswindoll: Commer, put that damn cat down!

Joe: No! Ranna's cat has to come! Can you see how much he needs to come?

Geswindoll: What a circus! Okay, bring the stupid thing. Maybe we can sell it on the black market.

Joe: Churchill, stay! No! Ow! Get back here!

Geswindoll: Well, looks like the stupid thing has other ideas.

Joe: He's out in the street! How can he still be alive out there? I've lost Ranna's cat!

Geswindoll: I knew you were still in love with her! How touching! Now how do I shut this goddamn radio show off? This switch here?

CHAPTER THIRTEEN
World Mystery Karma
Saturday, November 12, 2033

Hedrona Bhlon unlocked the Artemis Museum in the chilly darkness and moved across the fractured concrete floor. Outside the smashed windows came a hint of dawn beyond the pines. Not that there'd be much light today with all the clouds and soot from the other side of the planet.

She drifted through the vast interior space, the smell of oil and acrylic paint mixing with stagnant water. She placed a plastic stool beneath a seven-by-nine-foot painting on the wall.

She could barely make out the mushy orange letters MOON MOON MOON across the sloppy purple wash. Climbing onto the stool, she pulled the canvas back from the wall and dug herself under it. She braced the crossbars against her back and reached high for the wire passing through the hooks on the wall. She might be only five-four and 108 pounds, but she knew how to manhandle large paintings.

Up out of the groove--one hook--two--and the painting was free. She backed off the stool, lowered the heavy canvas to the floor, and leaned it against the wall. One down, eighty-four other pieces of crap to go. At least that was the biggest item. Some of the others were just sheets of paper tacked to the walls.

She'd sworn she'd never come back to her museum. Why did she think she needed to take this junk off the walls? Why drag it to the storage rooms? The artists themselves had abandoned it all, and for good reason. It was all putrid. Why did Hedrona think the Artemis needed to be put back in order, here at the end?

She hadn't been here since the Moon Relief Opening. October 8th. Literally the end of the world. In the meantime, the earthquakes had continued to wreck the museum. Somehow she hadn't expected it to be quite this bad. All that glass across the puddles on the floor. Twigs and grass and mud, probably from those thunderstorms last week.

Even the solid Texas Hill Country was experiencing

magnitude five quakes these days. The sickening shift of the ground might last ten minutes. The first few had scared her, then she'd gotten used to it. Everybody had.

She flipped a light switch. Of course no electricity. She hadn't really expected it.

Any reason to look in the office? Anything she'd want to take? No, she was leaving it all. In two weeks she'd be gone. Soon they'd all be gone. She just wanted this trashy art off her walls. Let the Artemis be cleansed at the end. If people ever came back and found the ruins of this place, at least the walls would be bare.

The Final War had ended the Artemis Museum, everything she'd worked for since '27. The culmination of all her life energies. It had come to this abandoned wreck. Yeah, she'd won some prize for the Artemis design back in '31, but now she couldn't even remember the name of it.

Why had she polluted the Artemis with Moon Relief?

Answer: because that bastard Bowe had talked her into it. Well, they were through now. She should never have let him sleep with her. Even more pollution.

Even after the party, Bowe had been on her to get implants. Why hadn't he gone after Ranna Kikken with *her* big boobs, then? He'd been slavering after her at the party, after all. Hedrona had to admit Ranna looked good. She hadn't seen her for a while. It was weird that she'd worked for Ranna for three years and they never were friends. Always enemies. She guessed they still were.

Hedrona picked up a cardboard box filled with gravel and hurled it through a broken window, shattering more of it as the whole mess burst apart on the ground outside. That had been Ricki Foster's "Cardboard Box of Moon," which she'd asked eighty thousand dollars for. Hedrona pulled an unframed drawing off the wall, a listlessly-rendered naked blue woman jamming a flaming orange moon the size of a softball up her crotch. Andy Parkler's "Making it with the Moon," sale price thirty-two thousand dollars, was soon crumpled into a ball suitable for crotch jamming and it followed "Cardboard Box" out the window.

Ranna had apparently lucked out with a reservation for the
Typhoon I on the 26th, piloted by none other than the Commer
brothers. It would make the trip to Mars in a little over a couple
hours. Maybe more like five or six with getting the passenger
shell detached and in orbit around Mars. Hedrona was on the
25th, stuck with a seven-day trip, but it could've been worse.
Some trips were taking two solid weeks.

Hedrona yanked another painting off the wall and stacked it
against the giant "MOON MOON MOON." She'd sling all these
things outside later. Why pollute her storage room, which had
some good art in it?

A new city, Marsport, being built by robots. Other cities
rising from the Martian dust. And they were supposed to
colonize Venus and Mercury too. Maybe human beings might
turn out to be good stewards of what was left of this solar system.
Wasn't that why the United Nations had changed its name to
United System two years ago, right after Jupiter and Saturn
blew?

But what was dear Hedrona Bhlon contributing to this brave
new United System? Answer: *nothing*. All she could do was
come here and grieve over the museum she hadn't wanted to
think about for over a month. A museum where no artist had
shown up to claim a single work; the handful that had been sold
hadn't been taken either.

Hedrona was dizzy. She was flooded with a radio rainbow
of intense colors, thoughts, and moods. Images of red deserts
and red mountains. The thin cold air of Mars, her new home.
How could this ever have come to pass?

*Arrive 3:15 PM 11/25/33 at StarSeed Transfer Center,
Houston, fly to Cape Kennedy, depart for Mars 8:15 PM,
11/25/33.* Sure, some of the passenger shells had fallen off their
host ships and crashed. Sure, some people had died, but Hedrona
was going to take that chance. Was it possible she'd help found
something new and beautiful on Mars?

She pulled up a folded chair and sat down. This wash of
feelings was probably the first real emotion she'd had since the

Moon Relief Party. It was finally sinking in that this was the end of planet Earth. Everyone was leaving for Mars.

How could the moon just *blow up?* Hedrona had been unable to force herself to look at the spreading lunar fragments. She probably wouldn't have been able to see them anyway due to the clouds and smoke covering the earth. The goddamn Central Asian Powers' Xon bomb had blasted that awful chunk out of the moon, but it had taken another month for tensions to build up and for the whole thing to explode.

In the meantime, the *Typhoon I* had paid CAP back with one Xon that wiped the central Asians and the Himalayas out forever.

But the moon was gone. Earth would eventually have a complete ring as Saturn once had. By this time last month scientists knew that the Xon, along with fallout and radioactivity from fifty H-bombs, was too much for the planet to sustain. And that the Uranus flyby in '29 had apparently weakened the structure of both the earth and the moon in ways no one suspected at the time.

This whole damn world could theoretically blow at any moment.

Hedrona tried to stand but she was still too dizzy. Too many images hit her all at once: Mars, new cities, expansion into the universe. The images mocked their listless cousins on these ruined walls. Yet the nasty artworks had their own dark weight. Hedrona realized she could spend hours disposing of all these paintings and drawings and sculptures. It was like fighting an overgrown garden, yanking up an impossible network of stubborn roots.

People spoke about coming back in a few centuries and reclaiming the earth, even repairing serious structural faults. But the moon was gone forever. Deep down, didn't everyone know the earth couldn't survive without its moon? Wasn't that why they all knew it was time to go?

That had to be why the cats left several days before the moon exploded. Any animal on this planet knew the moon had been crippled forever on September 25th. There'd been massive die-offs, absurd migrations to inhospitable places, or that craziness with those hundreds of cougars running into the center of San Antonio last week.

So Hedrona wasn't deeply surprised to hear that every single cat had disappeared from the Cat Farm last week. A hundred eighty cats, *gone*. Hedrona had heard that Ranna had finally lost it and accused some of her people of drowning them all in the reservoir. But Hedrona knew the cats had to be taking a walk straight into the Gulf of Mexico to die honorable deaths. Yeah, they were still her cats. From the time she'd been the manager of the Cat Farm, she'd always loved them. It was too bad she'd never been able to go back, not even for a visit.

She's always wanted to start her own museum, but she might've stayed longer at the Cat Farm if Ranna hadn't been such a controlling bitch. And if Urside Charmouth hadn't turned her down. She'd been a fool to throw herself at him. Saint Urside who'd apparently given up sex after his girlfriend ran away from him.

Yeah, the beautiful, angry one who'd disappeared right after that stupid CTESOPE conference. So long ago, five years. Hedrona had forgotten her name.

Mandy.

"God!" Hedrona gasped. "Who said that?"

Silence through the dark museum, except for the faint rumbling of yet another earthquake.

"Who's there?"

That was right. Mandy *had* been her name. *Mandy Frederick.* As the realization clicked, more images blasted her. Beings. Fishlike people with huge fins. A mix of humans and fish people walking through some alien city.

"What going on? What's this *city?*"

Marsport. Of course, we won't be sending you there.

"Who's there? We can't have squatters! This is private property!" Desert sands, desert in all directions--

Hellas Basin. Where we do most of the work.

A figure emerged from the dank storeroom. With a dog trotting along?

"Hey, really, look, I know the place has been closed, but this is a museum, and we can't have people just living in the storeroom."

We're not living here.

"Oh my God ..." Hedrona could see it was a young woman, and worries of rape and mutilation faded. "Listen, I'm sorry, you scared me, and, I mean, this *is* private property." She gestured at the trash art on the walls. "Well, who cares? It's over with. We're abandoning everything, why not this?"

Commendable, came from--where? From that dog at her side?

Hedrona fought the dizziness. How embarrassing to faint right in your own art museum in front of some stranger and her dog. Only it wasn't a dog. Distinct cat images poured out of it: pouncing and leaping in low gravity, adjusting to higher gravity, memories of wrestling cats in the higher gravity, breathing thin low-pressure air, then rich high-pressure air.

"Riaooowwwll!" said a big dark cat.

God, had she been drugged? She couldn't think straight. Why would anyone drug her?

The figure stepped forward. Hedrona stared. "Mandy! God, it's *you!* I was just thinking about you! What are you doing here?" Urside's last girlfriend stood on the cracked concrete, and Hedrona had the nauseating sensation that billions of thoughts and moods and images were gushing right out of that young woman's head.

"Hey, Hedrona," came the soft voice. "Can we talk?"

"Mandy! How can you be *here?*"

Answers poured from that head. A man-fish creature. The red desert. The alien city. Then cat thoughts mixed in. Hedrona let them all course through her, ashamed how little she'd ever understood cats. Now a focused jumble of sensations, moods, and desires radiated right out of that cat.

"God, that can't be *Churchill,* can it?" she moaned. "Not Churchill from the Cat Farm! That's not possible! He ran away right after the CTESOPE conference!"

Five years ago. What a fiasco it had been, when that insane

guy had crashed the opening meeting and left everybody wondering about his predictions. And dammit, they'd all come true.

"Riaowl!" cried the cat.

"You can't be Churchill!" Hedrona stammered into the blue eyes of a strong young gray cat.

I am Churchill! blossomed in Hedrona's mind.

"Oh my God … uh, hello there, Mandy. I guess I'm confused. I feel so dizzy …"

"No, I can understand. This will all take some explaining. This is Churchill here."

Hedrona came forward into a fuller blaze of Mandy's thoughts. "You haven't changed a bit!"

Mandy's shrug included a spectrum of pulsating colors and images relating to some weird concept of *no time*. "And I see you've really stayed in shape yourself."

"Well, thanks." Hedrona realized she'd been forty the last time Mandy had seen her. "I seem to be picking up what you're *thinking*. Is that right?"

Mandy shrugged. "That's true. I radiate now, like all Martians. So does Churchill."

The cat scratched his chin on Hedrona's shoes, its mind effortlessly unfolding into hers. "Churchill, baby …" she moaned, scratching his furry gray forehead. Then she looked back up at Mandy. "Are you reading *my* mind?"

"No, it's just one-way. I can't read you. But Martians have always radiated outwards."

The fish-men. Fish-women. A forty-thousand-year-old culture on the red planet. And that was Martian years, something like twice the length of Earth years.

"So where have you been for the last five years? You and Churchill?"

"Well, you have to understand this whole concept of Heuristic Time Transition."

"Oh, c'mon, don't expect me to believe *that*." But then Hedrona processed far too much data to do anything but believe. An episode unreeled of Mandy and Urside on an HTT date, a dreamlike sequence about visiting a stranger's mansion, then winding up on Mars amid the bizarre fish people. Yes, this was all *real*. Just as Heuristic Time Transition was *real*.

"Riaowl!" Churchill added to confirm it all.

"My Martian name is Fra'lith. Churchill doesn't have a Martian name, at least not yet. Dar thinks he's a reincarnation of some ancient Martian volcano, but he's not sure. His past is really buried. So we stick with Churchill for now."

"Wow ..." Hedrona said. Massive karma came out of Churchill. The Russian Blue had been struggling for eons, yet he bore it all with happy curiosity. As if he knew that now, as a cat, he was finally grasping the essence of the whole game. Hedrona found she could pull back from the stream of cat thoughts if she wished. She could focus on Mandy's conversation instead of her thoughts. "So you haven't aged at all since you left?"

"Well, a few days," Mandy replied, apparently aware that Hedrona needed talk and not telepathy. "Hey, you like the robe?" She wore a golden robe of thousands of metal circles, embroidered with a deep red collar and cuffs.

"It's lovely. Where on earth did you get it?"

"Not on Earth!" Mandy laughed. "The robe's pure gold except for the trim, which is a kind of ruby filament. I knew it'd get you. See, I can still read you a bit, with good old-fashioned human intuition. Apparently my fate in this lifetime is to be a bridge between humans and Martians."

Hedrona nodded, dazed. Somehow it made perfect sense to be standing in this chilly wrecked museum chatting with a human Martian who'd just time-traveled in. "So you came from--2028?"

"Yeah, via 2036, of course. Anyway, when Urside and I accidentally got to Mars a few days ago, I knew I was home and that I had to stay there."

"So *that's* why you disappeared." Hedrona wondered how she could accept it so easily, but she knew she was getting undeniable proof from Mandy's radiance. And after the Final War, and after a long bungling war with aliens from Alpha

Centauri, for God's sake, anything was possible. Even Martians, when they'd been reassured for years that there was no life whatsoever on Mars. "Urside just said you'd broken up with him. You didn't come around the Cat Farm anymore, and someone said you'd quit your job and left the area."

"Well!" Mandy said in mock anger. "Looks like nobody ever even bothered to file a missing person report!"

"Well, actually I heard that your brother did contact the Cat Farm a few years ago, but I was out of the loop by that time. Apparently nobody had your forwarding address."

Mandy shrugged. "Believe me, we had some serious issues in my family. Of course, now I know why, because all along I've been Martian! No wonder I couldn't fit into their idea of what a normal life would be. But that's not the real issue here. Haven't you bothered to wonder why Churchill and I came to see you, today, November 12th, 2033?"

Hedrona didn't have to ask. The answer welled up from both her visitors. "Well, I'm not sure I'm ready for that," she whispered, knowing it would happen anyway.

"I want to introduce you to Dar, Emperor of the Martians," Mandy said, pointing to a figure looming from the darkness. The creature wore a Cat Farm T-shirt. It was torn, Hedrona saw, to accommodate the huge pink fin protruding from its back.

CHAPTER FOURTEEN
Meanwhile, the *Animals* …

Amplified Thought Document No.: X3344-55667-999.11
Created: January 30, 2036 (Human Time)
Indexed Subjects: Heuristic Time Transition; Amplified Thought HTT Modification; Bhlon, Hedrona; Earth Animal Rescue Program
HTT Contact Dates: Saturday, November 12, 2033; Tuesday, November 22, 2033 (Human time)
Location: Earth
Prosaic Report Title: Emperor Dar's Report on Heuristic Time Transition Contact with Subject Hedrona Bhlon
Poetic Report Description: Somehow the Animal Has Found Refuge within These Structures

By way of background, 3.5 days ago I met two striking individuals whom I've recruited as time agents for the Earth Animal Rescue program: a young Earth woman named Mandy, and an Earth cat named Churchill. Both have proven themselves to be full Martians by their ability to exist in the open Martian environment.

Astonishingly, Mandy is a reincarnation of the Empress Fra'lith who died 13,000 Martian years ago. I didn't want to tell her that myself; I simply gave her the name Fra'lith and decided to let her remember the past on her own. For quite some time there have been rumors among the Martian populace of a reincarnation of Empress Fra'lith, and I figured Mandy would make the connection at the appropriate time.

Churchill, a cat from 2028 Earth, sucked along on Joe Commer's return HTT to the present time, has a more complicated lineage, which I haven't fully traced. But fate has obviously brought him here to assist in the Earth Animal Rescue Program. When Joe was arrested along with Huey Vespertine early Sunday, Churchill managed to escape and make his way to the Palace. He and Mandy in fact came to me at the same time.

When Mandy and Churchill arrived, each surprised to find

the other here, I was deep in meditation concerning HTT. To be more precise, I confess I was recovering from my dismay at having time-traveled myself just an hour and a half before.

Previously I'd scoffed at the ludicrous human concept of Heuristic Time Transition and the human Glasgow's HTT particle physics experiments several months ago. (How convenient these short-term human time measurements can be! I confess I've become quite enamored of them.) But when I returned, I couldn't help but start playing with Glasgow's theoretical framework, which in the light of my own experience pointed to a possible integration of time travel into Martian Amplified Thought. I was dizzy with the prospects. If we can avoid disturbing the timeline, what marvelous changes might we be able to effect!

To my bewilderment, I was now confronted with the same young woman I'd just encountered on my HTT to October 2033. Neither she nor this Earth cat at her side wore an EnviroField to protect themselves from the Martian environment as maintained in the Central Complex. And while I confess I'd failed to fully recognize Mandy when I'd first met her, now the entire history of Fra'lith's last 13,000 years in the *Rar'gasf Triunun'lh* unreeled from Mandy's mind, not that she realized it, of course. Even though she quickly picked up my own telepathic outradiance as I eagerly sorted through Fra'lith's various reincarnations and afterlife recyclings over the past millennia, it must have seemed to her like a jumble of fascinating images, not a history of her life as Empress and Ghost Empress since then.

Then I was brought up short by Churchill's news that the USSF had just arrested Joe Commer and Huey Vespertine in the middle of their talk radio program, on charges of spying for the Alpha Centaurians. It became apparent that Joe Commer had also, in his wild emotional disequilibrium, stumbled upon Heuristic Time Transition. Thus he traveled back to the earth of 2028, to the same time and place where Mandy lived, to deliver a speech which we must now regard as a poisoning of the timeline.

While Churchill is convinced of Joe's innocence on these

espionage charges, I find myself worried that he may in fact be suffering from a relapse into the Alpha Centaurian brainwashing he suffered last year. How awful if this is true! But I certainly have no confidence in USSF officials being able to arrive at the truth of the matter.

Joe's plight surely merits my scrutiny, yet I've avoided him, as I have for months now. Even without being able to read the darkened human mind, I've known that he's suffered such serious problems following his brainwashing that any contact with me would painfully remind him of our disastrous sojourn in Alpha Centauri last year. But I confess that edginess at my own brainwashing of that time may also be part of my reluctance to speak with him. I note that none of the survivors of the *Typhoon II* mission has had much contact with the others over the last year. We all seem to prefer to deal exclusively with Jack and Amav, who managed to avoid the Centaurian Conversion process.

However, two days ago Joe made an appeal to me via AresNetMail in my capacity as emperor. Though I couldn't legally respond, as the Martian emperor cannot interfere in the human justice system, I was able to send one of my staff to inquire about his health, and thus Nluaha'dkldr was able to radiate to Joe my concern for his well-being and to let him know that Churchill was safe with me.

So far I simply cannot understand the ramifications of Joe traveling back to a time and place containing both Mandy and Churchill. Or how Mandy and Churchill can be Martians who have chosen to permanently deposit themselves here in 2036.

And while I'm happy that Fra'lith has reappeared to assist me in this work, I'm reminded on a daily basis of our ancient empress's exceedingly severe nature. After all, she was the cruel warrior goddess who unified the Southern Reaches in 26,866. Within a few minutes of her arrival Mandy was proving adept at sorting through my telepathic outradiance, and, just as viciously as the Empress Fra'lith would have, she seized on my painful knowledge that almost no animals were saved from planet Earth during the hasty human evacuation of 2033-34.

At this point she demanded that we put into action an Earth Animal Rescue Program, which I confess was one of my first dizzy musings when I realized that Amplified Thought and Heuristic Time Transition could be combined.

Well, perhaps *demanded* is not an accurate term. Fra'lith Mandy Frederick, still not suspecting her true reincarnation, instantly took my hazy theories and formulated a comprehensive strategic plan for evacuating almost all Earth animals to Mars 2036. She included justification (the benefit to both humans and Martians from planetwide animal energy); schedule (starting in 2032 for some animals psychically upset by the beginning of the Alpha Centaurian war, and moving straight through the official end of the Evacuation in June 2034); and means (the exceedingly raw draft AT/HTT code I'd been toying with, where, to my dismay, she worked through several muddy subroutines and corrected numerous illogical lines of code).

Like me, Churchill knew exactly who Mandy was, and he drew the entire mass of planet Mars into his concurring purr. So Mandy, Churchill, and I began revamping Amplified Thought HTT, despite my often-voiced fears about initiating such a potentially dangerous program with only four days of planning.

Today we did start the process which will ultimately HTT millions of Earth animals here to First Home. While many will be deposited with miniaturized EnviroFields in human cities and Martian settlements in order to provide animal consciousness amid those structures, most will be sent to one of Empress Fra'lith's favorite hideouts, the Kilpatrick Desert in the Hellas Basin, to await the time when they can be fully integrated into the Martian world. Martian AT engineers are now planning the requisite Earth forests, oceans, and jungles needed, all to be constructed underground at this point, of course. Mandy proposes a full terraforming of the planet Venus for many of the animals.

However, it also pains me to state that, for many of the same reasons I've been hesitant to speak with Joe, so far I've also been unable to bring myself to tell his brother, my friend Jack Commer, head of the USSF, of this project. No human in fact knows. Certainly humans can pick images of what we're doing out of our minds, but so far they appear to consider these images as plans or hopes, not as current activity.

We Martians are incapable of the kind of falsehood and dishonesty which we're still amazed to find in our fellow intelligent bipeds from Earth, yet of course we can still refuse to state the blunt truths behind the images and word patterns coming out of our minds, and so, I must say to our shame, we are in fact capable, for political reasons, of misleading the human authorities in this matter.

I confess that this entire plan for less than honest communication with our human friends emanated from Empress Mandy/Fra'lith, and to tell the truth, I suppose I wonder why I've gone along with this project. Empress Mandy has absolutely taken over its direction and its ungodly timetable. It also pains me to relate that at times I have had to--what is the human word--*fight* with Empress Fra'lith and rein in some of her stronger impulses. I have repeatedly had to remind her who is emperor of the Martians and who is not.

I think it's for Churchill's sake that I've acquiesced in Mandy's hyper-accelerated EAR. Churchill seems to embody why any spirit would choose to be alive in this physical realm. There is something so deep and ancient in him that I must fall down in worship of it. For I also resonate with this primeval spirit that somehow chose to animate itself in this sterile universe. Churchill is closer to it, but we both share it.

Now, coming to the main point of my report, I confess that it was yet another *fight* between Mandy Fra'lith and me that produced the current mission I describe here.

I'd assumed that this undertaking would target only the cats of the Cat Farm, but Mandy had other plans having to do with one Hedrona Bhlon, formerly an administrator at the Cat Farm and, at the point in time we were aiming for, a director of what humans call an "art museum." Such "museums" are full of cult artifacts, crude human attempts to radiate telepathic depth by capturing, in two and three-dimensional displays of form and color, some of the meaning of existence and personal karma. I have patiently endured long tours through several of these nondescript human institutions in Marsport.

Mandy had known the 2028 Hedrona as the Operations Manager of the Cat Farm, and had been incensed at the way the supposedly sensitive, open-minded folk of the Cat Farm ostracized Ms. Bhlon as a cold and ambitious administratrix. Mandy had felt something special buried in Hedrona and was disgusted at her friends' behavior. Couldn't they see her love for the cats? Couldn't they see her grief at the loss of Churchill in '28? Mandy claimed, from studying the Amplified Thought HTT program itself, if this can be believed, that Hedrona had been deeply unhappy with her new art career and should in fact have been something on the order of a veterinarian.

I informed Mandy that all this speculation was very nice, but that we could by no means afford to risk damage to the timeline just to make some Earth woman happy.

This did not go over well with the Empress Fra'lith. She simply coded the coordinates she wished into the Amplified Thought program and told me that the paradigm of Hedrona Bhlon was essential to the unfolding of human and Martian destiny. That Hedrona was the perfect and necessary choice to assist with the resettlement of human animals on First Home.

Before I could open my mouth to protest further, the empress handed me a Cat Farm T-shirt, which I have no idea how she obtained. "Put this on over your robe," she commanded. "It'll insulate her from being shocked at your appearance."

"My--appearance?" I sputtered.

"Oh, come on. You're an alien being to her. She'll freak when she sees you. The T-shirt's there to lighten the mood, that's all."

"So she'll see the Emperor Dar as some jocular, safe monster? What about the dignity conveyed by my Martian emperor's robe?"

"Aw, can it," said Empress Mandy Fra'lith, and, blithely cutting through every Command Override I could muster, ran this mission's program.

And so I found myself stumbling in the darkness and high

gravity of Planet Marble. I quickly adjusted myself. Fortunately my Martian leg muscles were up to the task of negotiating three times normal gravity. No one knows why Martian leg muscles are so strong, but it's been theorized that the original Martians were natives of the weak-gravity moon Phobos, and eventually were able to leap off the moon and somehow float down to the Martian surface unharmed. However, all this speculation is built upon hazy ancestral memories that have nothing to do with the solid Telepathic Archives of the last 40,000 years of Unified Martian Culture.

In any event, hope was soon dashed that Hedrona Bhlon would be spared uncomfortable moments at the sight of me. As I came up to where she stood with Mandy and Churchill, noting in dismay that Mandy was now inexplicably wearing my golden emperor's robe, the Earth woman collapsed on the floor.

"She's had enough," Mandy said, bending over Hedrona and patting her cheeks. "The Final War, the destruction of Earth, and interstellar war with the Alpha Centaurians. I bet she thinks you're a Centaurian yourself!"

"How did you get my robe?" I protested. All I had was the torn T-shirt and human blue jeans, cut off at the knee.

Mandy shrugged. "Check line 3,804,309."

"Dammit! We can't be adding all these complications to the timeline!"

"Hell, the timeline doesn't care what anybody's wearing."

I pointed to the prone figure. "Well, I suppose what's done is done." While I did feel a certain empathy for any being undergoing first contact with an alien species, at the same time my feeling for this Earth woman was not pity. I could tell that Hedrona, even unconscious on the floor, was a strong woman with reserves of immense power.

Certainly we Martians can't obtain telepathic information from humans, but over the years I believe I've begun to develop my powers of intuition regarding these folk. In any event, I could see why Mandy would want to rescue Hedrona Bhlon.

Nevertheless, I went on, I confess somewhat petulantly: "But look, here we've exposed her to me, an obvious alien being, and for what? After all, it's not as if she wasn't evacuated to Mars as planned. I didn't tell you, but I got curious about her, and I found she was evacuated on a passenger shell on November 25, 2033."

"Dammit, what's the goddamn point of being telepathic if you can't understand a goddamn thing?" Empress Fra'lith Mandy snapped. "Pick it out of my mind if it's so damn difficult! And you call yourself a Martian emperor!"

"Well, I ..." To my shame I saw that all along I'd been thrown off by Mandy's human appearance. I'd assumed she wouldn't fully understand the thoughts in my mind. I'd been treating her radiance the way we treat that of Martian children: interesting but undeveloped, nothing with which you could hold a serious telepathic communion. At once I saw that not only did Mandy already know that I'd checked the Human Evacuation Database concerning Hedrona's flight, she'd already reviewed it herself. And seen my sloppy error. She decided to spell it out:

"If you carefully check the records for Hedrona's scheduled flight for November 25th, you'll note that Passenger Shell *Plasma IV* develops a leak and even though it stays attached to the mother ship, everyone on board is asphyxiated. So how does she make it to Mars, Mr. Emperor? I'll tell you: because we start messing with the timeline and we get her out of here on another flight! Does that make sense to you?"

"Hmm," I said as patiently as I could. "So you're saying we're here to *prevent* a death? Should we be doing that? Doesn't that harm the timeline? What about the Reset Prohibition function of Line 456,444, or its call to Subroutine Finality?"

"Irrelevant. Isn't it obvious that the flight switch is to make her officially dead so she won't be traced to Hellas Basin later on? We've got to keep the EAR secret as long as possible, to get as many animals to Mars as possible before all these United System wackos freak out and try and stop us."

I sighed in frustration. Earth air is of course far too thick and non-nutritious to sustain us, but we can take it for certain periods. I contented myself with more or less eating this oxygen-rich atmospheric soufflé as I fought to remind myself that

Empress Fra'lith no doubt still had a valid plan to execute here, one of eventual lasting benefit to all sentient beings.

Meanwhile, Hedrona Bhlon opened her eyes to note Churchill standing on her chest. Then she gazed up at me. "You're a Martian! I can read your thoughts! I can read *all* your thoughts! You're all Martians! They told us there weren't Martians!"

"Then you know why we came here," Mandy said.

"Well, yes, but that can't work, can it? You can't just transport animals through time!"

"We already got the Cat Farm cats, or are about to, if you look at it a different way. I'm sure Emperor Dar will explain everything."

"Uh, okay ..." Hedrona managed, struggling to sit.

"Well, I hate to say it," I replied, "but at this time, P'nal is still emperor and will be so for another of your Earth months before a treacherous Earthling named Sam Hergs kills him and usurps the Martian throne. Hergs will remain there for several months until our Commer friends intervene and I come to the emperorship." I was overcome by a pang of dread at how, at this moment, I and my fellow Martian counselors were about to be taken over by Sam Hergs. In late 2033, as the evacuation of Earth got underway, Hergs and his cohort Al Carson came to Mars and discovered us Martians. Hergs had a psychic knack about him. He could read us. He knew we were worried about the coming human influx and all at once he took us over. He and Carson pretended to be official USSF agents at the time, and then Hergs killed off P'nal. "Poor P'nal, such a short reign. Only eight-hundred thirty-three years," I observed sadly.

"C'mon, don't confuse her with all that crap," Mandy said. "Get to the point."

"Well ... to try to get to the point, as Mandy suggests, we would have come sooner, but somehow there are obstacles in the HTT grid that prevented us from doing this mission sooner. We don't have time to try to out-program every obstacle that arises. We just need to get the job done as efficiently as possible. So we're here to rescue as many of your Earth animals as we can.

The USSF did evacuate representative samples, but obviously put humans first."

"Did you say the Commers saved you? And are behind all this?" Hedrona said.

"Dammit, Dar, you've confused her already," Mandy said.

Dar shrugged. "Well, the Commers saved us in 2034, and again in 2035, I might add, but for us this is 2036, and, unfortunately, we can't really let Jack and Joe, or any humans from 2036, in on our plan. They don't even suspect that we know how to manipulate Heuristic Time Transition the way we do."

"Get to the point," Mandy repeated. "Why we're here."

I took another thick bite of cloying oxygen. "The point is, I was horrified when I realized that Earth had such a rich animal life, and that so few were evacuated. We Martians had always known there was life on Earth, but we didn't know quite how much there was. It had always seemed like a garden to us, and we simply admired it aesthetically, from afar. Jack said they barely had time to get two billion humans off the planet before it became thoroughly poisoned. They did bring several thousand examples of many animal species to Mars, but they've assumed that the other 99.99 percent of Earth animals are irretrievably gone. So having Martians manipulating the fabric of time and transporting large quantities of Earth animals to Mars probably won't sit well with the United System bureaucracy.

"Oh, yes," I added, seeing Hedrona's shock, "by June of next year the atmosphere on this planet will become completely poisonous to mammalian and most other life, including Martians. The only way out is to set up small Amplified Thought hurricanes and pump in enough breathable gas, for humans or Martians, depending on who's doing the environmental work, to last the two or three weeks you're down here."

"C'mon, you're still confusing her. She doesn't need to know about the environmental work now." Mandy turned to Hedrona. "We started cleaning it up in earnest the summer of 2034, just so you know, but the last estimate I heard for completion was seventy years."

"Anyway, a few zoos were created on Mars," I went on,

"but there's not much in them. And there are only a handful of pets. Some people smuggled cats and dogs and even some of those marvelous things you call parakeets onboard their passenger shells. Of course, it was all illegal."

"Riaowl!" Churchill said, butting his head against Hedrona's outstretched hand.

"So most Earth species didn't survive 2033. And not only is this terrible in itself, it also means it's much more difficult, if not impossible, to restore Earth to its previous state. So we're willing to take the risk of disturbing the timeline so we can transport as many of these species to Mars as possible. We've found that when we use certain subroutines compressing time and space, we don't need to transport these animals in spaceships. We can send them directly to Mars, three years from now. In another seventy years or whenever it's safe, we'll ship them back to Earth the normal way."

"So," Hedrona said, "you've decided, apparently all on your own, to terraform the earth."

I nodded at how she'd picked up "terraform the earth" out of my mind. She was beginning to learn the rhythms of Martian thoughts. "Well, this HTT project is something Mandy and Churchill and I are doing on our own, but of course the entire Earth Terraforming Project is a joint human-Martian project. It's just that the Amplified Thought HTT has pinpointed only certain times when we can decisively act, and there's no time to debate this matter in the United System Council, the Council of Martian Elders, or the USSF bureaucracy. Probably nobody would let us do this HTT meddling, but we know it's the only way."

"And what if you do destroy the timeline?" Hedrona said in awe, picking up another concept out of my thoughts.

"We're willing to take the risk," Mandy cut in. "Besides, we're beginning to suspect that everything we're doing has been foreordained for us to do, somehow, by the nature of HTT itself. We've researched the phenomenon, and it seems to extend back as far as 2013 and forward as far as 2075. Why is it limited to this time frame? And are we actually helping to heal some of the damage to the timeline that others may have done?"

"Damn," Hedrona muttered, finally getting to her feet. There was power in her eyes that shocked me with its legacy of suffering. Her world was ending, her own life was on the line, and here came three aliens, two of whom she'd known five years ago as fellow Earthlings, babbling of Amplified Thought Heuristic Time Transition, Earth Terraforming, and Earth Animal Rescue Projects. Yet somehow she accepted all of it. "So *you* took the cats from the Cat Farm."

"Well, not yet. I'm still calculating the parameters."

"What?" But she cocked her head and, as far as I could tell, seemed to get a dose of *Line 22,455,612, SUBSTITUTION time VAR "Moment x" IF x > "now"; ELSE calculate areaUnderCurve AAX, line 13,556,793.*

"You haven't done it yet? The cats have been gone for a week!"

"Hold on, it appears I need to link *your* departure to ..." I concentrated. It was getting pretty tricky. *GET Hedrona Bhlon 11122033061203AM, line 33,786,003, DEFINE "moment," GET "moment A ...", INSERT routine CATS, line 465,667,201, PUSH "moment x," x = "now," moment = "GET 'moment A ...'", line 44,213,880, OUTPUT 11222033074322PM, C-COORD xyz, STARSEED.*

"There, it's done," I said.

"*What's* done?"

"I just took the cats from last week and sent them to the Kilpatrick Desert on Mars. We've started some excellent cat facilities there. You'll want to go straight there once your passenger shell gets to Mars."

"You took the cats from *last week?* You came *this week* to take the cats from *last week?*"

"Well, sometimes HTT can be a little tricky. But you can confirm, can't you, that all the cats have been gone since last week, November 4th?"

"Yes, but anyone could come here and wave their hands and say that!"

"Even a Martian emperor?" Mandy said, laughing. "C'mon, Hedrona, take a deep breath, we all have a Transition to do now."

"Part of the Slingshot of the cat HTT," I explained. "It'll take us ten days into--"

"I'm not going anywhere!"

"Oh yes you are!" Mandy said. "The program's running! Say goodbye to your museum."

Churchill leaped into Hedrona's arms. She staggered under the load. "I don't believe this!"

"The empress cannot lie to you," I said, then immediately regretted it as I met Mandy's wide eyes and knew I'd triggered all her reincarnation memories with this one phrase.

"Oh, no …" I muttered as the Transition overwhelmed all of us.

CHAPTER FIFTEEN
At StarSeed
Tuesday, November 22, 2033

"*Ar-rrrr!*" Churchill gasped as his old friend Hedrona clutched him way too tightly through the vortex. *Set me down!*

Hedrona did so. "You're … making human *words?*"

I'm learning to make chunk concepts in my head. Mandy taught me, once we realized we were both of First Home and could radiate this way. Churchill felt his paws settle on the asphalt of Planet Growl. It felt good to exercise his legs in this high gravity and breathe in the thick air of his youth. He was pleased to be formulating *chunk concepts.* Clumsy, yet they made some forms of communication easier.

"Wow, where are we?"

Thousands of grim people stood in lines in front of tall human buildings. The sky was low with charcoal clouds. The asphalt was wet. Mist drifted everywhere.

"We're at StarSeed," Mandy said. "Getting ready for your flight."

"But my flight's not until the twenty-fifth."

"Well, that's not a good flight for you. This one on the twenty-second is perfect."

"Don't tell me … today's the twelfth … unless …"

"That's right," Dar put in. "We shifted you forward ten days. You'll get on Shuttle 692 in a few minutes for the hop to Florida, where you'll take Passenger Shell *Bishop of Swords* mated to the *Perseus.*"

"But how can *you* be here?"

"Well, I just included all of us in the HTT," Dar said. "I thought it would be nice to see you off and make sure you got on the right shuttle."

"No, I mean, you're an alien!" Hedrona said, pointing to Dar's big pink fin. "There are all these people here!"

"Oh, that's an old Amplified Thought trick. I'm manipulating the light around me so I'm invisible to anyone but us. But I can't hold the subroutine indefinitely. We'll just get you processed and be on our way."

"So this is the StarSeed Debarkation Point? We're really in Houston?"

"Yep," Mandy said. "I used to live right around here, over near Montrose. They've converted this whole area into an Evacuation Processing Facility. They got up to fifty-five million people per day here at the peak of the Evacuation."

Churchill could feel Hedrona's shudder at this bleak *ghetto*, if he was properly translating the *chunk concept* coming out of Mandy's mind. He felt the dread in the gut, the foolish focus on survival, emanating from the lines of dirty figures snaking through barbed wire labyrinths. As Dar prodded Hedrona into one of these lines, Churchill felt his fur rise as some monstrous thing churned under their feet. The buildings wavered and all the refugees shifted nervously, keeping their balance, but in a practiced way that said they'd known this monster before.

"Just a slight ground tremor," Hedrona said, obviously picking the fears out of his mind. "We've been having them a lot. I know you didn't have them back in the old days."

Churchill considered this. The monster must be another thing these humans did to wreck this planet. He resolved to take the next one better. After all, the monster didn't seem to bother Hedrona. Sure enough, here came the thing again, sliding around underground and groaning. Churchill closed his eyes and waited for it to go away. Yes, he'd seen plenty of monsters in his day.

Why didn't you HTT Hedrona right into Shuttle 692? Mandy radiated. *Why'd you make her wait out in this line for hours? If one of these buildings collapses on her, everything's ruined!*

Apparently it was fated, came Dar's return thoughts. *Check the subroutine Arrival(X,Z) in line 25,883,902, and note that the GET command is only called under the condition of--*

Oh, c'mon! Your GET commands are so sloppy! Look at the mess in line 2,334,556!

Well, if you have time to revise the entirety of the OPER CHRONO REV(xGET) routine, I'll be happy to consider alterations to--

That routine should've been junked with the CHRONO(x,zGET) call!

Please, Mandy, we don't have time!

"That's Empress Mandy to you!" Mandy cried aloud. "Empress Fra'lith! You thought you could conceal my real identity!"

"Huh?" Hedrona said.

Dar also shifted to speech. "Well, I merely thought that Mandy here should have some time to find out on her own."

Mandy's just discovered she's a reincarnation of an ancient Martian warrior empress named Fra'lith, Churchill radiated helpfully in Hedrona's direction.

"You stay out of this!" Mandy snarled. "Dammit, Dar, I've lost four days when I could've been rearming for war! We've got to construct a space fleet immediately, train all personnel in advanced AT HTT, and warp out for Alpha Centauri. Hit those monsters before it's too late!"

"Enough," Dar said. "Don't tell me you're believing Geswindoll's fantastic paranoia about Centaurian infiltration."

"I am! I see it now! They're coming! And we'll use HTT to blow them all away!"

"You know as well as I that trying to use this experimental HTT as a weapon of war could simply destroy the fabric of the universe."

"Experimental?" Hedrona put in. "Apparently it's good enough to test on me, and my cats, and all the animals on this planet!"

"You stay out of this, too!" Mandy said. "I'm giving the orders now, Dar. Dammit, I should have seen this coming! We'll use AT to construct an all-Martian fleet. Do it in six months. Then we blast each AC star in turn!"

"Hey, hold on, excuse me. You guys are yanking me all over the place, screwing up our timeline, and you're telling *me* to stay out of it?"

"Silence, Earthling! I am Empress of the Martians!"

"Oh, you are not!" Dar cried. At first Churchill thought Dar was deadly angry, but then saw he was laughing so hard he forgot his AT Invisibility Subroutine.

"*Oh my God, what's that?*" a human shouted.

"Dammit!" Mandy said as hundreds of slumped bodies in the barbed wire corridors turned with gaping mouths to a fish-headed Martian with a huge pink fin. "Dar, resume your disguise immediately!"

"It's just a costume!" Hedrona yelled. "Trying to cheer everyone up!"

But Churchill could easily see that an "alien costume" wasn't cheering up the frightened humans. But in the fast whipping of thoughts between Mandy, Churchill, and Dar there was general agreement that simply winking out of existence via resumption of the AT Invisibility Subroutine wasn't the best option.

"It's a goddamn *thing!* An *Alpha Centaurian!*" someone shrieked.

"Hold it right there!" Dar cried, drawing an ugly red gun from a holster.

"Oh my God!" a woman screamed.

"You idiot!" Mandy yelled. "That's no solution!"

"Aieeeeeee! Aieeeeeee!" came more cries.

Dar aimed his plastic gun at the crowd and fired a single burst.

"*Ohhh!*" the crowd moaned as a thin arc of water shot across the asphalt. Then came tentative laughter.

"What?" Hedrona cried.

"I don't *understand,*" Dar said. He fired several more times. The crowds moved a few steps out of range and watched spurts of water plip on the already wet asphalt. "To see water wasted *horrifies* the opponent."

"Here, let me have that," Hedrona said, pulling the gun out of Dar's hand. Stepping back, she let him have a couple gushes across the chest.

The crowd laughed again.

"Riaowl!" Churchill said, finally getting it. *You've calmed their fears.*

"They were supposed to be *horrified,*" Dar groaned, looking down at his soggy Cat Farm T-shirt. "My ceremonial water pistol has *failed* me!"

"Look, they're turning away," Hedrona said, handing him back the gun. "You can go back to being invisible now. They won't notice."

"I can't believe it," Dar whispered, but Churchill could feel the Invisibility Subroutine slip into place, and again Dar wasn't apparent to anyone but the four of them. "Only the emperor may have a water pistol." But finally he grinned. "But sure! I see! You have so much water on this planet nobody would care if I wasted it!"

"Hand that weapon to me," Mandy said. "I'm taking over. You've shown you can't be trusted with the Water Pistol of *Hq'eer'gghul*."

"Why, I will not! I am Emperor of the Martians. As Churchill and Hedrona have noted, my action did calm those people down."

"I am Empress Fra'lith! The Warrior Goddess! I take command!"

"Mandy, you must realize that a reincarnated empress is not the same as the real empress, K'sla. Why, if she thought you were threatening her position, she'd definitely have your head!"

"Why, you wimp! I could seduce you so easily, I could take over the real empress position, the Martian Council of Elders would snap me up in a second, I could--I could--" Mandy blanched. "I …"

They all stood quietly for long seconds, telepathically absorbing the history of Dar and K'sla's emotional and sexual congress over the past hundred years. Churchill already knew all this. But Mandy, who'd been shut out of much of Dar's mental activity simply because she hadn't fully remembered her true identity, was overwhelmed with Dar history. Hedrona followed it too.

"God, I'm so sorry, Dar," Mandy muttered. "I've just been so overwhelmed by all of this."

They all let Mandy take in Dar's military exploits over the years as commander of Martian Battle Group *S'Hjuu':11A*. A purely ceremonial command for Dar's previous post as Leader of the Martian Council of Elders, it had nevertheless been activated for the recent war with the humans. Despite Dar's distaste for bloodshed, he'd fought and led bravely in the Kilpatrick Desert skirmish, and later reorganized his Battle Group under Hergs' command on Venus. After the war, Dar had undertaken the enormous task of offering Emperor's Condolences to families of 1,200 Martians killed in the war, as well as for all 1,868 humans KIA. Churchill was again able to sense some of Hedrona's feelings of awe. The Emperor's Condolence was not simply a note sent to the survivor, but a lengthy ritual demanding the utmost spiritual strength. To repeat that ritual wholeheartedly over three thousand times had nearly killed Dar.

"I really was out of line. I'm so sorry, Dar!"

"It's quite all right. Most Martian reincarnations aren't fully obvious, either to the subject or to others. But every once in a while, we have one that everyone has to acknowledge, although it can take several months for the knowledge to spread across the entire planet. Of course, when that happens, the reincarnated one has special duties to perform for the Martian Empire. I'm sure you'll be able to fulfill those duties excellently."

"Well, yes ... of course ..."

Well, I believe it is time to move on from here, Churchill radiated, and everyone nodded. *It's quite obvious that Fra'lith has been attached by fate itself as special advisor to the emperor.*

"Well, wherever the emperor decides I can be of service. I'm really sorry. All that energy just went to my head, I guess."

"God knows what will happen when we all figure out what Churchill's past lives really were," Dar said.

Churchill pranced around. It was all one to him if he ever remembered his past lives. All he knew was that once he'd followed Joe back to First Home, and then met Dar, something in him decided to grow. Sometimes it still felt funny to be in the lower gravity of First Home, without the rich air of his youth, but all that was fading the more Martian history and Amplified

Thought techniques he absorbed from Dar.

The higher gravity here on Planet Growl was now the alien environment. Everything was wrong: this ghetto squalor, and the refugees queuing through the barbed wire amid the ancient multistory apartment buildings. Churchill could remember city life from kittenhood. He couldn't remember exactly how he'd wound up on the Cat Farm with Ranna, but it was a much better situation. Except that all the cats had felt the pressure of the asteroids falling, of human panic, of the knowledge that war was coming. It was obvious to all the cats that the planet was doomed.

And to come here now, with no moon in the sky to regulate the deep cycles. To know that humans had bitten a big chunk off the side of their own planet, just like a mangy rabid dog, and killed their own world. Churchill stood on a corpse.

"Hey, look, the line's starting to move," Mandy said.

"I'm sure if they're processing fifty-five million people a day, they can't just afford to keep us all waiting on the street," Dar said. "I've watched a hundred buses pull up in the last few minutes."

"So I'm going? Just like that?" Hedrona said.

"Yes. We'll see you on Mars soon. You'll assist us in our work. Insist on heading to the Kilpatrick Desert first thing, but don't tell anyone why."

"SHUTTLES 512 THROUGH 714 NOW BOARDING FOR FLORIDA," came the announcement over hundreds of speakers. A vast arch led through the building to a spaceport tarmac and rows of white shuttles.

"I can't believe this. I'm really *leaving*." Hedrona pointed helplessly at the crowds around her. "All these people! The whole planet! Everything's come down to this! Think of all the people who've died!"

"And all who have died would want *you* to live," Dar said, "because you have important duties on Mars. In addition, you'll help resuscitate *this* planet." The line moved quickly. "Now we need to get you on your shuttle. Your passenger shell will work perfectly, you'll have the most amazing flight of your life, and all will be well." He placed a comm in Hedrona's hand. "This has your boarding pass and everything else you need. It was an easy matter to hack into the passenger list for *Bishop of Swords* and get you on it. Seat 665B, if you'll note." Passengers moved through scanners. Mandy, Churchill, and Dar held back as Hedrona pushed through a gate labeled SHUTTLE 692.

"I'll see you all again?" she called back.

Of course we'll see our Earth Animal Rescue Project Director, Dar radiated as Hedrona disappeared into the shuttle.

You made her Director? Of the whole project? Mandy thought.

Well, you and I and Churchill got it off the ground today, but we're really just the techies now. Hedrona will know exactly what to do. She'll leave all her nonprofit museums behind her, and evolve into something we can't even imagine.

I recommended her for the position, Churchill radiated.

Okay. Great, Mandy thought. *I can see that we have other duties at this point.*

Exactly, Dar added as Churchill found himself sitting on Mandy's lap, back where they'd begun, in Dar's throne room on--what was that *chunk concept?*--January 30, 2036.

CHAPTER SIXTEEN
Strange, Festive Dreamscape of Pollution, Despair, Defiance, Defeat
Ranna Kikken's diary, Friday, November 25, 2033, 8:30 PM

Just got the news of Hedrona's passenger shell. Haven't been able to write about Urside. Don't know if I can.

Saw the video of Hedrona's shell today. It stayed attached to the main ship but it had a leak and when they got into orbit, the main ship found out that everyone in the shell had died. It was hard vacuum in there. God, what a terrible way to go. I can't think about it. Hedrona. Years ago we had a working relationship and all that, but I never knew her. Never understood her. I know we've sort of been enemies all this time.

Hadn't seen much of her the past four years. Except for last month and her stupid art opening. Of course, she did great for the Cat Farm until she left to start her museum.

She was always so ambitious, always climbing, never friendly. But she loved the cats. Everyone could see that part of her. Everyone wondered about that, how she could be so good to the cats and so cold to people. Now she's gone.

Can't believe so many people are dying on these passenger shells. And they keep launching them, hundreds, thousands every day. Everyone knows you have a one in five chance of dying en route to Mars.

She died! Horribly! It would've been a seven-day journey to Mars. I knew I was actually going to pass her on my trip tomorrow because the *Typhoon I* can make the entire trip in a few hours. Yes, Bill's kept me posted, I know when everybody in the area is going out.

When we heard she disappeared a couple weeks ago the first thing I thought was that maybe she snapped and decided to become a Stayer. But before he took his own flight this afternoon Bill did a query for the passenger list and she was still on it. Maybe she just needed to get away from it all for a while. Probably holed up in Houston or somewhere for a couple weeks, boarded her passenger shell, and

Why am I writing all this down? Who cares? She *died*. Urside *died*. And I'm sitting here writing stupid nonsense because I don't know what to do with myself. I'm the last person at the Cat Farm. The way I wanted it. Just me and my tiny suitcase, packed and ready to go, and my KraNpur 550 computer. No, I'm not going to start writing my diary straight to the cloud like everyone else does.

God, I haven't been able to even think about what it means that Urside's gone.

Funny that I'm thinking about his old crush on me. When he blurted all that out. God, was it really at the CTESOPE conference all those years ago? Anyway, I wondered if I was going to have to fire him. But I just couldn't bring myself to, especially after his girlfriend left him. She was always so flighty and headstrong. Somehow everything worked out between us. He never brought up that attraction stuff again. We were the best of friends all these years.

People would joke about him being Saint Urside. He was so put together. Nobody understood why he never had a relationship again after that girl dumped him. I remember he did talk once about a woman named Alycia he met on some trip, but he never mentioned her again.

But he found inner peace. Everyone was probably jealous of him for that reason. We all want inner peace and don't have a clue about what it is or how to get it.

So Urside went to StarSeed on Wednesday, just as I'm going tomorrow, and was shuttled to Florida just as I'm going to New Mexico. Unsuspecting of anything, just as I am. And his passenger shell and the mother ship blew up on launch. Just like that.

Jackie made it, thank God. Just heard from her a couple hours ago. Her ship went Monday, everything was fine. Said she had a lot of vibration on the way up and everyone was scared, but the pilots said the vibration's normal. So she had a four-day journey on the *Hesse,* attached to some pretty fast military ship, and she's been shuttled down to Mars already. Weird that you can get an email from Mars. I was so afraid I'd never see her again.

So my sister made it. But Urside didn't. Hedrona didn't.

And all my cats. I guess they've become Stayers. Here to live out the last days on this planet. They say the earth will be uninhabitable before long. How long will the cats have? A few months? Where are they now? I can't believe it. Not one has turned up since November 4th. Unbelievable.

In any case, there's no room for animals in the Evacuation, everyone knows it, so maybe this is the best way. An unexplainable disappearance. People think the death of the moon caused all this animal craziness.

I miss the moon. We all do. We miss our planet already. We can't believe we're being forced off. All this talk of a "new life" on Mars is madness. I'm so tired of hunkering down, waiting for the end. We've been doing it for five years, since the first asteroid went into the sun. Since everything started breaking down. How did all this happen so fast? Five years ago we were just muddling around, doing nothing. Now our planet's ruined and we're fighting aliens from Alpha Centauri! That's something nobody wants to talk about. Even now everyone wants to believe it's just some science fiction movie, or some big misunderstanding arising from first contact, and we'll get it straightened out. Straightened out? With evil beasts who've sworn to exterminate us?

We know Cromwell was a fool to start the war, but it's so obvious he made a mistake, we apologized, we court-martialed him for God's sake. And then the Central Asian Powers start giving us trouble! Our fellow humans, who *also* swore to destroy us? Why does everyone want to destroy us? Can't they just leave us alone to live our lives?

Okay, I do want a new life. Guess that's why I'm bothering to write this entry. I had a hard time starting it, since I thought it might be my last will and testament. But now I'm looking around this grim empty Cat Farm, and it's forty degrees outside, it's raining, it's miserable, I'm the last person here, everything is over with, and yes, I want a new life. I just want it here on Earth. I don't want it on Mars.

But I'm going to wake up tomorrow morning, make one last breakfast, take my suitcase and my KraNpur and lock the place up. Not sure why, since I know I'm never coming back. I did apply for the Evacuation Property Claim as many people have done. Theoretically your property remains yours in the event we ever reclaim the earth. But they say only about twenty percent of property owners worldwide have bothered to file a claim. There's a lot of bureaucracy about helping fund the worldwide cleanup if you want to claim your property in the future. Most people are just looking at the concept of free land on Mars and forgetting the past. Or pretending to forget the past.

Anyway, lock the place up and take one last walk around the farm. Not the whole place, I don't have time, but a few spots. Get a last overview. Then get into my car and drive to Austin for the first hop to StarSeed, then the shuttle to New Mexico. What do they call it? Port B. Somewhere east of Albuquerque. I haven't even looked at a map.

So tomorrow I'll be ferried to New Mexico to take off for Mars. And passenger shell *Pegasus* mated to the safest ship in the fleet, the *Typhoon I*.

The *Typhoon I* that dropped the Xon bomb. The ship that made us evacuate. Joe Commer's ship.

Yes. *The* Joe Commer. But not the one who crashed CTESOPE. This Joe Commer is twenty-eight and he's the copilot for tomorrow's flight. But he'll become the man who wrecked CTESOPE five years ago.

I've accepted all along, even without admitting it, that Heuristic Time Transition does exist and that Joe Commer, who so effectively laid out what was about to happen to the whole solar system over the next decade, really did come from the future. I know the video of his speech is out on the Net, but in a way, the Internet's a great place to hide a sensitive document. The video has a crank following, and people point to its prophecies, but the culture as a whole certainly has never paid any attention to it.

Most people who've seen it assume it's a clever fake anyway.

Bill made sure it got uploaded to our servers on Mars, and he wants to release it with great publicity once we're settled there. I'm not sure that's a good idea, but Bill thinks Heuristic Time Transition needs to be thoroughly examined.

It seems obvious that the Joe Commer who just bombed CAP along with his three brothers hasn't seen the video. Bill and I searched the web for anything Joe Commer has written or said over the last five years and there's no mention of his ever claiming to have HTT'd back to 2028.

So we think the Joe who visited us comes from further along. It's not on the video, we missed recording the first part, but we remember Joe talking about 2036. Three years from now. So while my impulse has been to march into the main ship and yell at Copilot Joe about why he crashed my CTESOPE conference five years ago, I'm sure this will only land me in whatever passes for a brig on the *Typhoon I*.

Joe was in the news in the spring of 2032 when the *Typhoon I* was launched. The four Commer brothers. *Joe Commer*. I've been in shock since then because I've known for sure that every bit of the horror Joe spoke of in 2028 would come true.

But I want to see him. I know he's only twenty-eight now, but I remember what was in his eyes at CTESOPE. The suffering. The insight. The beginnings of the same kind of self-transformation I've desperately wanted all these years. But I'm almost twice as old as he is. It's all insane.

What the hell have I been doing with this stupid life? What did Joe call me on the video? The *nonprofit lady* who thought she could cure Planetary Malaise with CTESOPE, who wanted to *committee* the entire torn, soul-mangled, karmically messed planet into shape! So what that it failed, I've kept telling myself, so what that I've sat here for five years wasting my life! I've made money, I've been comfortable, I have a huge farm with plenty of friends and hangers-on to join me on my do-nothing journey.

Joe saw right through me!

And don't you think that the USSF, created in 2028 just as Joe Commer predicted, made me think of Joe himself? His

USSF *started* me on the path to liberation. After the asteroids, after Pluto and Neptune, after the Uranus disaster, it was wonderful to see at least part of humanity vowing to free itself of the fear we'd all lived under for so long.

I finally got it through my head that a year and a half of Robbert's insanity was enough for any masochist. Finally I had the guts to ditch the marriage. My lawyers were magnificent. He's probably drunk himself into an early grave by now and you know what? I simply don't care. Although Joe made some prediction about Robbert later showing up on Mars as some USSF honcho, that seems scarcely believable. Then again, all Joe's other predictions were on target. Hell, I don't care either way.

I freed myself, though it's obvious I never fully completed the job. The relationships I've had since the divorce have been idiotic. Tepid, deluded, and/or abusive. Maybe I was always looking for Joe. For sure none of these guys came close. I don't know how it happened that one day I woke up and realized it was morally wrong to even be thinking of Joe. Even if this time-travel stuff was real, I knew it was impossible I'd ever even see him again. It was like being in love with some fantasy character in a novel. And I deserved better than that.

So I managed to bag all that love and sex crap. Forget it entirely. With the end of our planet, with the Final War and the Evacuation, there's just been no time for romance.

So I forgot men, I put Joe Commer out of my

Are you kidding? Dammit, be honest for once! This could be the last thing you ever write!

Of course I've been thinking about Joe the whole last five years!

Don't you think that his predictions, plus the fact that time travel is real and that we're all sitting here watching our planet get flushed down the crapper, have been enough to unhinge your soul? Hell, his eyes alone were enough to unhinge you! *Why don't you admit that you totally fell in love with Joe Commer and just never bothered to tell yourself that fact?*

Joe came here to make me fall in love with him! To wreck

my life!

I'm in love with Joe Commer, and it's hopeless! Insane!

What a stupid diary entry! I can't express anything!

I hate this! Hate it!

Why don't I just blow up on the pad tomorrow, just like Urside?

CHAPTER SEVENTEEN
Repairing the Moon
Ranna Kikken's diary, Friday, November 25, 2033, 10:50 PM

It's later. I've poured myself a glass of wine to steady my nerves for tomorrow.

Reread my stupid entry. Let it stand. So what. Sure I'm freaked out by all this. Who wouldn't be? Can't get Hedrona out of my mind. Or her stupid art opening.

Is it because she was just like me? No matter how much I've called her a traitor to the Cat Farm all these years? Wasn't the Moon Relief opening a metaphor for the waste of both our lives?

No, I didn't have anything to do with the stupid Moon Relief Party. But at the time I secretly wished I had. All those important nonprofit people to woo! But those people also disgusted me. No wonder I wanted to be the last one at the Cat Farm. Well, maybe that's a glimmer of psychic health for me here at the end.

I can admit I've always wanted the Artemis Museum to fail. I never wanted to share the Hill Country with something like that. Hell, it's just two miles from the Cat Farm. And we've always suspected that Hedrona started the Artemis with funds she siphoned from CTESOPE. She was using the CTESOPE publicity apparatus, her mission statement was ripped off from CTESOPE's, and she was draining the same funding sources I was dependent on.

One way or another, I've been fighting her for seven years. Probably other people have just seen it as a cat fight between bitch nonprofit ladies. Hedrona came to the Cat Farm in 2026, about a year after we set up. She was one of those thirty-something nonprofit powerhouses fresh from some art museum in Shreveport, and I thought we could use her expertise. And boy she did become a major force in CTESOPE by the time we put on our conference. She was so sneaky, always usurping, caging, finagling, maneuvering, and yes, I could shout her down and she'd back off. But she'd just take her machinations further underground.

So apparently she laid the groundwork for the Artemis in

'27, then left the Cat Farm in '29. She finally got the museum open in '31, and was director from the beginning. And I have to admit, especially once CTESOPE officially folded the same year, that Hedrona was doing the work I thought I was destined to do.

The Artemis Museum, dedicated to the Goddess of the Hunt, was supposed to scour the world for the True Art. Hedrona managed to build a campus of dozens of Le Corbusier-type buildings where people could spend weeks in retreats with names like Cleansing the World of Crap. Okay, so I'm probably laughing at Hedrona's nonsense because it's so much like my own.

That little blond bitch! Goddamn her to hell!

The Artemis Museum had an endowment of a hundred eighty million dollars. It didn't need any more rich donors. It didn't need the goddamn Hill Country aristocracy.

But there we all were on October 8th, at the Moon Relief Opening with its eighty-five works by artists all over the world. Paintings and sculptures depicted the moon of antiquity and romance, the moon of science and discovery, and the mangled post-September 25th cripple floating amid its debris. Hedrona was sure she could spark the process of scraping up a billion trillion dollars to, yes, *repair* the moon.

The evening raised $53,018.

*

Aaah, the hell with it. Had to stop and get a second glass of wine. Can't be so goddamn smug about her failure. Look at CTESOPE after all.

Hell, I'm also the goddamn nonprofit aristocracy and they wanted my money too. I was supposed to buy one of those crappy paintings for my bathroom. Yeah, even after the death of CTESOPE I've managed to keep my hand in this game. And of course the nonprofit Cat Farm still qualifies me as a nonprofit lady in my own right.

Once again Hedrona got Bowe Rorozol to fund the show

and reception. Not difficult at all, since Bowe jumps at the chance to show his Archetypal Soul at any and all nonprofit events in the state.

He got filthy rich publishing all those business websites and periodicals like *The Journal of Micromanagement,* but somewhere along the line Bowe "felt something was missing" and so began heavily contributing to what he calls the Cause, which happens to be whatever nonprofit activity Hedrona Bhlon or any other member of the Austin aristocracy, myself included I'm ashamed to admit, deems worthy of his wealth.

Bowe's also a noted art collector, and his $25,000 purchase of a sprawling muddy acrylic entitled "Thy Moon Doth Erupteth" was almost half the money raised that evening. A few days earlier he'd declared he was going to sell his entire art collection to raise money for the Cause, and dump what was unsold into the ocean "as a gesture of Tao." Why didn't he just offer a billion trillion dollars for all eighty-five crappy Moon Relief works and dump *them* into the ocean?

So the Artemis Main Gallery is filled with a hundred aristocrats in formal wear as well as the requisite number of art students, literati, intelligentsia, and media critics in more scruffy attire. Bowe, affecting as usual to look more like an art librarian than a business tycoon, is blathering about Soul, Tao, Inner Harmony, and Moon Myths Throughout the Ages until we're all numb.

At that time, of course, the moon's still mostly intact, only with a big chunk out of it which Bowe proposed we "mend" by using nuclear weapons to crash the larger moon debris into the gaping hole, then filling the rest in with asteroids. Although we couldn't get up all the fragments and dust, over eons gravitational forces would pull the mended moon back into a spherical shape. Even if nobody saw it in the next hundred generations, a smooth spherical moon was still a worthy goal.

Hell, I believed the stupid Rorozol Plan myself, even though scientists all over the world said we had as good a chance of ripping the rest of the moon apart. Some of them were already arguing that our scarce resources should be used in an evacuation of the earth. Bowe spent a long time at the Artemis party ridiculing that idea, but in a few weeks he'd wind up throwing his full financial support behind it.

But--to repair the moon! Undo the damage, no matter how much money it took!

People wanted to believe it despite Bowe's stuttering incoherence. We wandered the mediocre walls of Moon Relief drawings, paintings, photos, holograms, and sculptures, talking ourselves into believing that this exhibit actually meant something. We were astonished it had been pulled together on such short notice. Of course, all the works looked as if they'd been done the night before, maybe by Hedrona and Bowe in that stainless-steel apartment of hers between listless copulations. One oil painting was still wet to my touch.

Yes, there was Bowe's lover Hedrona, Woman of the Hour, pert, petite and prancing in a low-cut black minidress that served more to remind us all what a sexless butthole she really was.

C'mon, Ranna. You know you're just like her. You were parading in your own low-cut emerald-green gown. You too were once Woman of the Hour, before Joe Commer barged in from the future to screw up your worthless life.

Did Hedrona ever suffer? Did she come home from the Artemis Museum to lock herself in her steel bathroom, collapse on her frigid silver toilet and cry until three AM? Wasn't she just one more successful nonprofit whore? Servicing the johns, all the art museums and boards of directors and umbrella organizations and ad hoc committees?

I tried to avoid that fate, didn't I? Didn't I know not to drag CTESOPE out too long? I know I used it to cope with the insane marriage to Robbert. Committee meetings and serving on twenty different area nonprofit boards kept me going. We never had a second conference, but my power remained unchallenged through 2031. By that time I'd divorced Robbert and was ready to be done with my own Planetary Malaise.

I kept the Cat Farm, but legally pulled the plug on CTESOPE in March '31. My board threatened to sue me, but in *profit* lady mode, I simply paid them all off. Handsomely. Some of them have remained good friends to this day.

Over the past few years I've rejected endless suggestions that I revive CTESOPE or turn the Cat Farm into a survival commune. Because Ranna Kikken doesn't have any nonprofit role to play here at the end. My task is simply to start my new life, as ordered, on the planet Mars. Imagine! By this time tomorrow I'll be on Mars, courtesy of the ultra-fast *Typhoon I*.

I'll be myself. Just to be free. Just to not care what anyone thinks.

I was already stepping back from all the nonprofit games at the opening. Several aristocrats asked if I was feeling all right. I'm sure they thought I was seething with jealously about the Rorozol Plan.

Well, I *was* pissed at Bowe following me all evening, staring down my cleavage and babbling about my dress's green affinity with my russet hair. But he'd overdosed on cologne, couldn't express a single coherent thought, and I wondered if he was beginning to grasp that his publishing fortune meant zilch in this new world with a crippled moon, the Final War alongside Space War I, and the possibility that CAP might end us all any second with another Xon.

*

Okay, third glass of wine. I have to write all the crap out. Haven't been able to. Can't think of the Artemis Museum, of being there when it happened.

But yeah, I'm there, damn disgusted at the leers I'm getting, not only from Bowe but from all sorts of plastered men. I'm cursing myself for wearing *such* a revealing gown. Even as I finally shake off Bowe, I collide with another man as drunk as he is.

It's Huey Vespertine, the guy who's against any possible evacuation. I'm thinking, what's he doing at this art opening? Isn't he from New York?

Sure, the Evacuationists were a minority in early October, but even then, the idea of just getting off this sorry planet was damn seductive. The moon had only been wrecked for a few days, and we were all still out of our minds with grief.

"What are *you* doing here?" I gasped.

"Oh, Bowe's an old friend," Huey said. "He invited me."

"Oh, well, I was just heading to …" I nodded towards the ladies' room, but I suddenly flashed that this Huey troll would follow me right in there.

The bastard stood my hair on end. Short, grossly fat, with a bulging belly hanging out over his tuxedo cummerbund. Grotesque drooling thick lips. Messy wet beard with food in it.

From my research I knew that Vespertine had been at the Naval Academy class around the same time as Jack and Joe. But he'd dropped out, gained two hundred pounds, and apparently spent a couple years gambling on the FeedBackPorn Network. Later he got a Ph.D. in Solar System Breakdown from the University of Hawaii, not that he put it to any good use.

Mainly he'd been harping against space travel, especially the faster-than-light ships that landed us in Space War I with the Alpha Centaurians. And he'd just published an article, "To Die Honorably on Earth," arguing against any evacuation after CAP bombed the moon. According to Huey, we're all supposed to accept slow death on Earth and be done with it, and anybody thinking about moving to Mars is a "murderer of indigenous Martian life," not that anybody's ever found any.

"Well, I seem to have encountered the lovely Ranna Kikken at long last!" he says. "I've so much wanted to chat with you all evening!"

"Well … what about?"

"About the Cat Farm! Captivating concept! I've heard so much about it! And who could forget your noble Committee to End Suffering on Planet Earth?"

"Uh, right. I can't believe you remember that."

Huey's eyes fasten onto my chest. "Of course I remember CTESOPE. We all do. So, will you be evacuating?"

"Well, I don't think anyone's taking that very seriously, you know."

"Oh, you don't? I'll have you know the USSF has seriously

been considering an evacuation for years. The Uranus flyby in '29 got everyone so paranoid, you know. And the Final War definitely moved their timetable up. The bombing of the moon's just an excuse. We bombed the moon ourselves and we're blaming it on CAP just so we can have an excuse to Xon *them!*"

"Oh?" I say, with zero desire to debate *that* conspiracy theory.

"Oh, yes, the new Super Xon is the only way we can get down to those H-bomb factories under the Himalayas. I'm sure we'll Xon 'em any day now, but from what I hear, it'll rip the world apart!"

"Oh … well. Listen, I really have to help, uh, Hedrona set up something." But Huey grabs my arm hard.

"I'm sure we just want an excuse to *ream* our enemies! So why *shouldn't* the USSF honchos decide to sacrifice the moon?"

"That's nonsense and you know it! Any sane person knows we tested our Super Xon in deep space! We knew what it was capable of! And the trajectory of the CAP bomb from the Himalayas is completely documented!"

"Yes, yes, perhaps you're right after all, my dear." Now he's scrunching his fat little face into this bizarre wince. "Who cares, really, in a way! I see I'm interfering with all your pleasant little fantasies of the benevolence of the USSF!"

And he launches his fat face straight into my breasts!

"Get--get off!" His tongue's slurping my boobs and he's got my arms pinned. "*What are you doing?*" And all the partygoers are edging away, as if this is some private little affair they shouldn't interfere with.

"Get off me! You're drunk! Get your goddamn mouth off me!"

"Let's die on Earth! Come die with me on Earth, Ranna Kikken, with your marvelous boobies!"

I jerk a hand free and slap his nasty face. "Stop, damn you! I'm sick of this insanity, you're a *monster,* don't you understand that?"

Huey Vespertine's eyes roll up into his head. He sways, and then three hundred pounds of him hits the stone floor hard. At first I want to believe this accounts for the incredible WHOMP that follows. But I see everyone in the place sharing the same look of horror. The world is churning under the Artemis Museum like some buried dinosaur coming to life. Glass shatters everywhere, pieces of the ceiling crash down.

Several people lose their balance, including one old woman who breaks her hip. We call an ambulance and abandon this Moon Relief crap. We crowd around a TV in the Artemis staff lounge as the dinosaur keeps thrashing beneath us.

The Huey idiot had been right. We'd just bombed CAP. The *Typhoon I* dropped the Super Xon on the Himalayas and left a crater five hundred miles wide. Expert after expert comes on the news to tell us that nobody within a thousand-mile-radius could possibly have survived that bomb, no matter how far underground they'd tunneled.

CAP's gone, all their bomb factories are gone. The war's over.

But earthquakes are rippling all across the planet.

We had twenty-five more that night. After around the fifteenth, most of us choose to take our chances on the broken roads leading home.

CHAPTER EIGHTEEN
Slaughter of the Fantasies
Ranna Kikken's diary, Saturday, November 26, 2033,
11:55 AM

On the *Pegasus*. In New Mexico waiting for the launch. Need to write some more. I was so scared last night. Had too much wine. Freaking at the memories of the opening, the Huey idiot slobbering on me just as the earthquakes hit. Had to stop writing. Knew I needed to forget it all, sleep, and get ready for this flight.

But I couldn't sleep. At all. I was useless. Feverish. Hyper. Replayed the earthquakes at the Artemis. Over and over and over. How everyone knew at that moment that the world was destroyed. I remember some jerks complaining about the "militarist Commer brothers" taking the fate of the world into their own hands, but it was half-hearted because we all knew that the USSF, the *Typhoon I,* and the Xon bomb represented the only reality that mattered anymore.

Everyone was much more concerned that nobody knew if the earth would come apart, literally come apart.

Well, we held. Planetary engineers said we'd need a minimum of four Xons to actually tear the earth apart, and even that would take maybe four years once the bombs were dropped. You'd need twenty-five Xons to blow the planet all at once. And apparently the Himalayas, which were vaporized, kept a great deal of the force from penetrating too far below the surface. Still, the radar and infrared images from space of the five-hundred-mile-wide crater (too much dust for regular photos) were damn sobering.

No wonder I've blocked all that out for a month and a half.

Can't think about any of that anymore. All that's left is to survive. To sit in this seat and write.

I'm lucky to have a window seat. There are only twenty windows up and down each side of this huge ship. The *Pegasus* is a cylinder thirty feet wide pointing straight up. My slice of the cylinder has seven rows of seats arranged to my sides, above my head, and below my feet. We're all lying on our backs in our acceleration chairs.

According to the sheet pasted on the back of the seat in front of me, there are fifteen major sections on the *Pegasus,* each one being a slice of the cylinder with seven levels of seat rows. You can fit seventy-six people on each slice, so the *Pegasus* can hold 1,140 people.

Everything is open metal gridwork connected by catwalks. You can see the slices of cylinder ahead of you and behind. You can see the other seventy-five people arranged around you in your slice. I've been trying not to look up, down, or sideways. One reason I decided to start typing on the KraNpur again. Concentrate on words, concepts.

They tell us the *Pegasus* is a good ship, one of the later designs of passenger shells rushed into production the last couple months. Crews helping us board said that the government has been making passenger shells for several months, figuring that Xons might be used in the Final War. But even so, I can understand the rumors of ancient airliners being welded together. Everything is definitely jury-rigged on this ship. Contrast that to the gleaming *Typhoon I* fitted to the side of the *Pegasus.* This shell has already made ten flights to Mars. Hard to imagine, but this chair I'm sitting in has been in orbit around Mars. Makes me feel confident.

Got up at 4 AM. Can't remember when I got to bed. Maybe around one. Completely drunk on three glasses of wine, horrified at writing about the earthquakes. Sure didn't sleep in any case. Had my breakfast, drove to Austin, got the flight to Houston okay.

Got there around 8:15, made it to StarSeed by nine. I could devote a book to the StarSeed Ghetto. They said there were two million people at StarSeed this morning alone. Everyone waiting in endless lines, every kind of person imaginable, in every kind of mood, in every kind of physical condition. Limitless human need. Darkness and rain. I thought I'd miss my flight, but suddenly everything was hurried along. A USSF officer told me that they were finally getting the knack of evacuating millions and millions of people, that it was starting to go smoothly.

So I had my rocket shuttle flight to New Mexico. It was awesome, flying with a hundred other shuttles in a line all the way to the horizon. The mystical slanting morning light on the sculpted dune ridges thirty-five thousand feet below us. Mountains, deserts stretching in every direction, forever. Something was calling to me from down there. Felt as if it always had been calling. Felt as if I should be down there, forever.

God, what have we done to our beautiful planet? How can we leave our Earth? Just give it up like this?

And here we are on the *Pegasus*. They've announced the launch in five minutes. Nobody's talked much about the acceleration. I've heard people with heart problems have died on the way up. I'm somewhat past halfway back, in the center row of my slice, I'm at the left window seat with five seats between me and the center aisle, and three seats down to my right is an old woman. I hope she makes it.

The second seat down from me is empty. That's apparently rare. We've heard stories that some people killed themselves at the last moment rather than come aboard. I can stave off my anxiety by concentrating on my writing. The man to my right me looks paralyzed with fear, but I know he's also resenting my typing. At least I'm not chattering away in voice record mode. I saw someone babbling into *his* diary a while ago.

And, yes, I saw Joe. All four Commer brothers greeted everyone, a nice touch, but I don't see how they could have dealt with 1,140 human psyches coming aboard. For an instant I was dizzy like a teenager with psychotic hormones, but when I met Joe's eyes there was no sign of recognition. Of course, this one's a few years younger than *my* Joe.

But I was devastated, again like a teenage girl. I've been searching all my life for this man, and he gazes back blankly! Worse, he's giving me a half-second of "comforting the frightened passenger," treating me like that old lady three seats down.

So I slink to seat 943 and stare moodily out the window,

along with dozens of other people jealous of my view, cramming in on me until I finally snarl that I'm going to write in my diary and they can just back off. You can't see much but empty concrete spaceport out there anyway. We saw another ship take off a few minutes ago. The ground shook so badly I thought our shell was going to topple over. Everyone was shocked as we watched ship and shell shoot madly into space. We're going to do *that?*

I admit I've fantasized about linking up with Joe after all this is over. Because I'm sure that when he disappeared from CTESOPE he must have gone home to his 2036 life on Mars. Why shouldn't we link up? Face it, didn't we share something? In our eyes? Yes, he was drooling at my sexy sister but everyone knew that was nothing. I was the one! We both knew that!

I'm fifty-three but I feel the same as thirty-five. I could make Joe Commer so happy!

But I'm still so scared. What if I'm wrong? What if that day at CTESOPE leads only to here, to the day I die in a passenger shell explosion? I've had this dream for five years, Joe was my completion, but what if it's simply all over? Can I die nobly, with these other eleven hundred souls? Are we all feeling this premonition?

This is just paranoid rambling. I'm just babbling with fear. They're announcing the launch. Doing the countdown. Can't write. This may be the last thing I ever write.

Saturday, November 26, 2033, 12:07 PM

Hell with it. We're going up. Some quick notes. Got to steady myself. Hard to type. Very hard. KraNpur strapped tightly around my thighs to hold in place. Acceleration not so bad as I was afraid. Lots of vibration. Can see why people have been scared. Sure it'll be okay. We're holding together. Most people took drugs to calm themselves down. I won't. Have this diary. Want to be clear. Writing helps me.

What if we do break off? What can anybody do about it? But live their own life up to the end? Vibrations are bad! Writing calming me. Don't need drugs. Just documenting. Look out the window. Okay. Clouds flashing by. Sunlight.

Now going into our arc. Not so vertical now. Like a superfast airplane flight. Maybe if we do crash they'll find my KraNpur and they'll be able to use it to document something. Don't know what I'm saying. But have to believe it's going to be all

God! That was a bad one! Everyone's screaming. Thing sounds like it's tearing itself apart.

Got to stay calm, keep writing.

It's still doing it, it's getting worse!

No! They can't kill us like this! Okay, I'll get the drugs, I've got them in my bag, if I have to go out I'll go totally sedated, I know it's cowardly, I can't stand this maybe I can deliberately overdose are you satisfied Joe Commer

Saturday, November 26, 2033, 12:10 PM

Author, Ranna Kikken: Going to voice mode now! Can't explain this!

Voices: Yaaaaaa! Yaaaaaa!

Sound: WRR-RRR-AACCAA-AAKK-WRRR-WREEE-KKK

Sound (high probability of cat): Miaow!

Ranna: It's *Churchill!* It can't be! But the little clip out of his ear, the black fleck on his eye! It's impossible! It's a miracle! Churchill, you can't have aged a second since you left!

Cat: Miaow!

Ranna: I open my pack to get my pills and *Churchill's* there! I can't believe it! But this is how I'll end my diary! My life! Churchill's come back to me! I can't explain how!

Voice: Aw, lady, shut up! Shut the goddamn hell up! We're all gonna die so just shut the goddamn hell up!

Ranna: Screw you! Just go ahead and die like a man!

Sound: CRRR-RRR-RRRR-RRAEE-CCCKK-EEE-CCKKK

Voice: Yaaaaaa! Yaaaaaa!

Cat: Miiaaaaow!

Ranna: I don't believe it! *Am I hearing his thoughts?* Am I really reading his mind? Churchill's telling me it's going to be okay?

Voice: God, and I hafta sit here and listen to this! Lady, ya can't smuggle goddamn cats in here, didn't they tell you?

Cat: Miiaaaooooo!

Ranna: He must have *time-traveled* here! That's what he's telling me! So it's true! You must have *transitioned* with Joe, now you're transitioning back *here* to me! But you came here just to die with me!

Cat: Miaooooo!

Ranna: He's telling me--I don't know what! I can't *process* this! Churchill, baby, I've missed you all these years! Did you know we lost all the cats a couple weeks ago, because of the moon maybe?

Cat: Riaoowwwll!

Ranna: The cats are on *Mars* now? You're saying someone named Dar transferred them to *Mars?*

Sound: RRR-CAR-CARRR-RRRRR-EEEEE

Voice: We're breaking off! I can't believe it! *We're breaking off!*

Ranna: Churchill says death is nothing! He's been through it a million times!

Voices: Yaaaaaa! Yaaaaaa! Yaaaaaa!

Sound: CARRRA-AAAAAC-CCKKKK-KKKKK

Ranna: Uhhhh!

Voice: God, no!

Voice: *Oh my God we've broken off!*

Voices: Yaaaaaa! Yaaaaaa! Yaaaaaa!

Ranna: The acceleration's gone! We're weightless!

Voice: I'm gonna throw up!

Voice: Who the hell cares?

Voice: I can see the *Typhoon!* It's separated!

Ranna: Fly it! Fly it! Straighten out! Yes, they did it! They righted themselves! Thank God!

Voice: Who cares about them? Those bastards ditched us! Now we're all gonna die!

Voice: Just depressurize now and be done with it, for God's sake!

Voice: How do we do that?

Voice: Just open the goddamn hatch! Kill us all at once!

Ranna: Going to the desert after all! Straight down to the desert! My home, after all of this! This entire life! *Bequeathed* to me! Churchill, I love you! Don't leave me!

Cat: Miaoooooww!

Ranna: Joe--

CHAPTER NINETEEN
Final Transition
Thursday, February 7, 2036

"Dar! Mandy! He's here! He's come back!" Alycia cried, pointing out the high windows of the palace entry hall. "Thank God he's got an EnviroField. He's never HTT'd outside before." She bounded out the doors and down the long concrete bridge where Urside was turning from an information kiosk.

"Urside! Where have you been? I haven't seen you in two days!"

"I don't know … I've tried and tried since Wednesday and I couldn't until now," Urside said, dazed. "What's your day?"

"February 7th! Thursday! You were here Tuesday! What's *your* day?"

"The 29th. May 29th. Last time I was here was the 25th. *Four* days for me."

"So you know you love me! We're still in sequence!"

"Yeah … I guess."

"It has to be fated that our meetings are always in the right order!" she laughed. "Oh, God! I'm so happy to see my Tuesday Urside!" Tuesday when they'd made love for hours. When they'd finally said they loved each other. What would she have done if she'd gotten an Urside from the week before they'd said that? "Wow, you look exhausted! This one must've taken a lot out of you. What is it? Your tenth time? *Our* tenth time?"

"Yeah, I guess. Look, Alycia--"

"Hello there, young human, good to see you again," came the emperor's croak behind her.

Alycia turned to Dar, Mandy, and Churchill strolling up the bridge. Dar extended a pink claw which Urside gazed at numbly. Alycia grabbed for Urside, but he was stiff. "Hey, what's wrong? You okay? Your EF working okay? Was it a rough ride?"

"Listen, I … look, uh, hi, everyone, maybe I don't belong here, maybe I just need to do the Slingshot and get on back," Urside muttered, staring across the bridge down the walkway

163

below filled with gravel, rock samples from Earth and Mars, and Earth grasses in EnviroFields.

"Hey, what's wrong?" Alycia said. "You look--you look--" Did he still love her? Had something happened? But two days ago they'd promised to HTT to each other for the rest of their lives. They'd joked about the Slingshots that would keep returning them to each other.

"Your EF's okay," Mandy said, checking the Patterson on Urside's hip.

"I just got here ..." Urside said, avoiding Alycia's eyes. "I figured this was the palace, and I wondered where you were. I always HTT directly to you, so I was a little freaked."

"It doesn't matter!" Alycia said. "Doesn't mean anything! I was just meeting here with Dar and Mandy when I saw you. Hey, don't worry! I mean, it's not a rule that you always have to HTT right to my apartment or anything."

"Well, then I decided to get the exact date off the kiosk here, and you know I've been getting pretty good searching in AresNet, and I started wondering ..."

"Wondering?"

"Well, I was thinking that, you know, I'd really like to permanently HTT here, but I know that's not in the cards. You know, because I'm not a real Martian like Mandy or Churchill."

"Riaowl!" said the gray cat.

"Then, I thought, hey, what about the *other* Urside?"

"The ... other?" Alycia said.

"You know, if I evacuate off the earth in 2033, then there should be *another* Urside here, in '36."

"Oh, dear, you didn't try to call up your future self, did you?" Dar said. "That would definitely be asking for timeline problems."

"No, I just looked for him. In fact, I guess I was a little worried that a future me, you know, older and more mature might, you know ..."

"Might ...?" Alycia said. Then she laughed. "I never thought about a future Urside here in Marsport! But believe me, he'd never get me away from *you!*"

"That's funny," Mandy said. "I never thought about a future Urside here in '36."

"That's because," Urside gulped, "there's *no* Urside in 2036." His burned-out eyes told Alycia everything.

"Oh my God." Alycia felt Churchill's gray tail buzzing into her EnviroField.

"What?" Mandy said. Then: "*Oh.*"

"Oh my," Dar said. "I never considered--"

The information kiosk displayed a still frame of a video, a passenger shell attached to a USSF spaceship on the launch pad. The sky was the ugly black-gray of the Evacuation. "That's what a search for *Urside Charmouth* found," Urside went on, pointing to the title of the scene: "November 23, 2033. Explosion of USSF host ship *Mandate* along with passenger shell *Corsair V*."

"*No* ..." Alycia moaned.

"It says 1,208 people died instantly. Including yours truly, age thirty-seven." Urside waved at the screen and the video engaged. The fireball was sickening in its size, its craggy orange fury, its berserk howl.

Alycia felt herself swaying. "That--that can't *be!*"

"That's *me*." Urside pointed to the fireball.

"No! It can't be!"

"So what am I doing here? I'm finished. Or *will* be."

"No, you're here now! That's all that matters!"

"No! *Somebody* has to die back there in 2033!"

"Urside, no! You belong *here,* with me! We both know that!"

"I know it can't *be* now. Somehow I know for certain I've done my last HTT. I don't have the HTT Potential anymore."

"No!"

"I can *feel* it. I know I'll Slingshot back to 2028 from this one, but after that, I'm done. I've never had the feeling before of being totally cut off from it." Behind Urside's shoulder the blossoming fireball froze at twelve seconds.

Alycia whirled to Dar. "Urside's needed *here!* For the EAR project! You're just going to have to make him permanently stay here, right now!"

Dar spread his little claws wide. "I'm so sorry, Alycia, there just can't be a permanent deposit unless the person really *is* a Martian. I'm studying the Amplified Thought HTT subroutines now, just to confirm. No, I don't see that it's possible."

"I'm getting it myself now," Mandy said. "I'm also checking the Human Personnel Database. God, I'm sorry! There really *isn't* a 2036 Urside!"

"That's because I die in November 2033!"

"Hey, wait!" Mandy turned to Dar. "Look, I've got it! It'll mean Urside has to go back and wait five years, but you and I can link back right now to November '33 and we yank him off the shell just as it goes up!"

Dar considered it. "But ... oh my ... can't you see that Nullity obstacle around those coordinates?"

"Damn, I've never seen a Nullity that big. Man, we can't get *near* that timespace! That shell's *supposed* to blow, and Urside's supposed to be on it!"

Urside pulled himself along the concrete wall and collapsed on a stone bench. "Look, it doesn't matter. I should never have been fooling with this Time Transition stuff anyway, I've done too many trips, I've driven myself insane, and at the end, all that's left is knowing the exact day I'm gonna die! Goddammit to hell!"

"Urside, no!" Alycia cried, reaching for him only to be pushed away. "You and I have each other!"

"For a few minutes maybe. Then I Slingshot home, and for the next five years, I know *exactly--*"

"This can't be! It just can't be! I know it can't be!"

"Aliens! Martians! Dar, Emperor of the Martians! Mandy's a native Martian! Churchill's a Martian! I can read your thoughts! Don't you think maybe you've just driven me *insane?* That I'm hallucinating all this? That maybe I'm hallucinating that the earth gets destroyed in 2033 and people evacuate to Mars? And everyone's walking around here like nothing happened? Is that it? Is that what I'm supposed to believe? But of course I don't get to really have this, do I? I get to *blow up!* Oh my God, you're all hallucinations!"

"Dammit, Urside, do you love me or not?"

"Well … well, sure, but--"

"Then I *can't* be a hallucination! Get hold of yourself, and take a look at this!" She opened her carryall and pulled out the holographic photo album. The one she'd sworn never to show anyone, not even Urside, because it was so unbelievable. But now she knew. She really *knew*.

Urside focused on the black rectangle. "You--where did--"

"When you told me you loved me, two days ago!"

"Yeah, I told you that, and it's true!"

"I know it is! Just like I love you! And then you went back to 2028, and I was lying there and--and I *transitioned!* I time-traveled myself! I couldn't believe it! The emotion was just so intense! Dar said he'd teach me, but I did it myself!"

"Let me see that picture," Dar said. "We cannot have this!"

"Dammit!" Mandy said. "She brought an artifact back from the future! That's not supposed to be possible!"

"It's our *wedding album,* Urside! September 2038! I HTT'd into our *wedding reception!* At USSF Headquarters of all places! I was out in this hall. Nobody saw me, and there it was on a table. So I grabbed it! What do you think of *that?*"

"Oh my God …"

"Look at it! There are four hundred photos in that frame. Just press the arrow in the corner to advance them."

She'd spent hours studying those photos since Tuesday. That older Urside, in his white tux with his long white hair, herself in the sexy light blue dress he couldn't take his eyes from. Four hundred happy pictures. It was *real.* It had to be.

"We cannot have this!" Dar cried. "This object alone could ruin the timeline! We must get rid of that thing!"

"You're not getting my wedding photos!"

"The Amplified Thought HTT matrix could get completely unbalanced!"

"No, it's all I have! I won't see Urside for two and a half years!"

"Everything's in disarray now! *Everything!*"

"No! And I'll tell you what I know now! I know Urside

can't HTT anymore! I know it just like he knows it! But he'll get one final one! Because I'm *giving* it to him! My bringing back the album from 2038 *gives* it to him!"

"No, nobody can give me one!" Urside shouted. "I can't HTT anymore! God, I can feel myself starting to Slingshot back right now!"

"Listen, all of you," Dar said. "I'm sorry to say this, but it looks as if Urside is just going to have to … *reconcile* himself to having five more years on Earth and then, I mean, I'm sorry to say it, but it's fated. It's what you humans call karma, I believe. Apparently Urside has some karma to deal with back on Earth for his last five years. There's some reason for him to go through all that."

Hold on, all this is more complicated than you think, came the radiance from Churchill. *Look at the Regeneration function in line 8,122,306.*

Impossible! Dar radiated back. *Regenerations can only be amplified under the most extreme conditions!*

But maybe this really is extreme, Mandy put in. *I think Churchill may have a point. Look at the Amplitude Matrix called when Regenerate is greater than axisFunction[Matrix(-X)]/3pi.*

"Urside!" Alycia cried. "Can't you see the Potential in me? Look, you brought Mandy here with your Potential, well, I can bring you *back* with mine! I have so much!"

"I'm fading! Fading back! Back to *die!*"

"No! Now I know! You'll HTT out of the exploding ship at the last instant! And come permanently here to *me!*"

"Oh my God! Yes! That's what I'll do! At the last instant! As I explode! I'll come to you!"

*

Monday, May 29, 2028

Urside slammed onto the hard Hill Country dirt. He was a hundred yards from the Cat Farm main residence. Deep night. Some voices from the porch. Soft laughter. Was someone having a party? Oh, right, Monday night. The Memorial Day thing Bill set up. May 29th. Urside turned on his back. Clear, stars everywhere. Cool light wind.

Okay, he was here. He was alive, at least for a few years. But was any of this real? He didn't have proof he'd ever been to Mars, did he? No proof he'd ever time-traveled or met Alycia. But, God, that couldn't be right. Of course he'd met her. What he had with Alycia was *real*. For once in his life, something was *real*.

But then again, if it was real, it meant that the earth would get destroyed in 2033. That Urside would die on November 23, 2033.

Had he really been to Mars ten times? Maybe it *was* all insanity. Maybe--

"Ow!" he grunted at a rock in the small of his back. He turned to toss it aside. "Oh, *man*."

The wedding album. Glowing in the dirt. Urside arrowed through the images.

Alycia, so lovely. Urside and Alycia, *married*. Other people in the photos, laughing and drinking. Dar was there. God, *Joe Commer* was there.

So how had Urside survived? Then again, could it be the *other* Urside? The one he was afraid might be living in Marsport and take Alycia away from him? But everyone had said there was no 2036 Urside.

This photo thing. This tablet computer or whatever it was. There were devices like this with today's technology, but the holographic quality was beyond anything Urside had ever seen. And there was also full-motion video by pressing this other button.

Full-size images sprang up around him, Alycia in blue dress and Urside in white tuxedo, amid a crowd in a banquet hall that seemed ten miles wide.

"Damn it!" Urside gasped as sound blasted at full volume, something like rock and roll, eerily pulsing. He jammed madly at anything that looked like a button.

Silence. Images gone. Thank God. He couldn't have Cat Farm people barging out here and seeing *wedding photos from the future.*

Urside stared up at the stars. There was no way he could make it for five years. Nobody could. It was crazy to think that. He wasn't noble, or stoic. He was supposed to wait through all these summers and winters, all the hassle of being a stupid webmaster for the Cat Farm, for five goddamn years? Just so he could watch this Final War destroy the earth, just so he could get into that passenger shell and hope he somehow got it together enough to warp out of there just in time?

There was a way you could check for your HTT Potential. Urside didn't know exactly how he did it, but he felt it at the center of his chest, not right over his heart but next to it, at the center of the rib cage. Even the time when he and Mandy wound up in that mansion and first met Dar, when he thought he couldn't HTT, he'd still felt the tingle over his rib cage, just hadn't been able to focus on it.

But he couldn't feel any Potential. There was nothing over his rib cage. Urside lay on the ground, listening to the party warming up across the field. Great. Those were the very jerks he'd have to live with for the next five years. And he'd never have any release. No time travel, no escape to Alycia. Just *death*.

She'd promised he'd have a final HTT, but after five years he'd probably completely forget how to do it. He'd have to try to summon the Potential while he panicking out of his mind, just as his rocket was *blowing up*. So easy to screw it up.

God, he'd been such an idiot, playing with the timeline, blasting off for Mars every couple days for the future, for his Alycia. That walk through the desert night, naked, wearing just EnviroFields. And that fantastic sex. It was unbelievable, more than anything he'd ever known.

Five years? Would Alycia forget him in all that time?

But here were the wedding photos. She'd gone into the future to find them. Somehow they must've gotten married. Somehow she'd found just enough HTT energy to save him. But how could he be separated from her for five years? He loved her. Nothing else mattered.

But what if she'd been wrong about the actual timing? What

if the last HTT having to be November 2033 was just a miscalculation, based on everyone being so upset? What if fate demanded they never be apart? Then he'd have to link *now,* head straight to 2038, dye his hair white, whatever. Time was always conserved, it didn't matter when or how he jumped or what he looked like when he got there. He could link to September 17, 2038 right now and stay there forever. Yes, that was the day. Alycia hadn't mentioned the exact date, but now Urside knew it for sure.

In fact, feeling the exact date meant that *this* was his final Time Transition. Not November 2033 and not some stupid explosion. He was outside that. His fate was outside mere time.

Yes, the final HTT. Urside's chest glowed with power. Everything aligned the way it always did. And it was going to be a strong one. He gasped and threw himself to his feet, respectfully facing the universe. A big one, the biggest HTT ever. Everything he'd ever felt and experienced, his destiny with Alycia and her love for him, all had to add up to this final HTT. The final HTT anyone ever did.

My heart surges! I melt into the Infinite!

CHAPTER TWENTY
Graduation Drive Anomaly II
Wednesday, May 29, 2013

"Oh my God!" Urside gasped, ripping the steering wheel hard to the right. God, he'd drifted into the oncoming lane on this twisty road. Headlights flashed by with a long angry horn. More curves, so dark. Urside was going sixty. He hit the brakes hard to make the next curve.

He was driving a car. An old one, gasoline-powered. What a sensation. The feel of gas exploding inside cylinders, the throaty engine, the response.

God, it was Urside's New Beetle, the ancient red '99 his parents gave him his last year of high school. He'd only been able to drive it for a little over a year. He'd had it senior year of high school in Northbrook, and for his first semester at Northwestern.

Then his half-brother Andy had wrecked it that Christmas. God, he was still pissed at Andy for that.

Oh man, Andy, remember how Mom and Dad lit into you for running that red light?

Andy had affected not to care. Urside remembered his half-brother chortling that it was no big deal, even as both parents were screaming about how Andy could've himself killed or the other driver, even though everyone walked away without a scratch. And to his shame, Urside had been calculating how he could now get a new car. The VW was ancient, fourteen years old, always in the shop. Why were Dad and Mom so cheap?

Urside closed his eyes.

Why does everyone take my cars and wreck them?

He strained through the scary dark curves. But it was also fun. He was getting to drive the old Beetle again. He'd forgotten how solid the thing felt on the road.

And Mom and Dad had taken his new Jetta because now *their* car was in the shop, a couple years later. The New Year's party at the Rundells'.

And I've told you a million times it won't do a damn bit of

172

good to replay any of that!

He'd refused to look at the wreck at the auto pound, just refused, though Andy went and he'd come back really shaken up.

And they were both gone. Just gone. January 2, 2016. He and Andy had never sorted that out, had they? Mom and Dad. They'd never been sure what to say or who to talk to about it. Maybe Andy thought that because Mom was just Urside's stepmother, Urside didn't care enough about her or something. They'd gone their separate ways after that, not that they'd ever been very close to begin with. They'd both certainly gotten got a pile of money. Urside had never wanted to own a car since then.

When was the last time Urside had seen his half-brother? Andy had that job in New York and could never get away, but he did manage to come down to the Cat Farm a couple days in '26. So it'd been two years and a few emails. Damn, they needed to talk. Urside needed to tell him about 2033.

Wait.

Urside was driving his '99 New Beetle. Andy had wrecked it Christmas 2013.

If that was true, then he'd completely missed--

Urside stared at the blue speedometer. He was driving his New Beetle, sometime between September 2012 and late December 2013.

Street sign flashing by. Sheridan Road.

He was in Chicago. Looked like north of Chicago, the suburbs. Winnetka, Wilmette.

The dark hilly road seemed to go on forever. Rich people's houses to the sides.

He didn't usually come this way down to Evanston, he would've taken Lake to Green Bay. Sheridan was so slow and convoluted. Urside thought he'd probably driven it once or twice in his life.

No! Not the night I got lost on the way to the graduation party!

It was. There was the Glenbrook North High School ring on

his left middle finger. The ring Alison had talked him into ordering.

Urside was positive he'd only worn it once, to graduation. Why had he given in and gotten the stupid thing? Because Alison was supposed to be his girlfriend? Didn't she know artists didn't wear high school rings? He'd been so embarrassed by the weight on his finger.

He'd lost sight of Alison anyway after the ceremony at the football field. He later found she'd gone out with one of her girlfriends when she should've known Urside wanted sex. And he'd never gotten it from her. Never. Pissed off, he'd decided to drive down to Wilmette and find that party with sixty kids and a thousand kegs of beer and certainly Edwin Waller's endless stash of hashish. And he'd gotten lost, he'd never found the party, just wandered the North Shore of Chicago for hours in his red New Beetle.

But crap, none of this mattered. Urside had totally screwed up. He'd wasted the last HTT he'd ever have on this replay of *May 2013*. He was doomed. Maybe he'd stay here forever, living fifteen years of his life up to 2028, just keep looping forever between 2013 and 2028, always barely touching Alycia on Mars, then coming back to *goddamn high school*.

May 2013. But what sort of unfinished business might be back here? Why had Urside landed *here?* For one thing, Dad and Mom were still alive. He could visit them, and Andy. In fact, if Urside played out the whole bazillion hours of this stupid boring drive, he'd see his parents waiting up for him at the end of it, insanely pissed.

Why had that never occurred to him? To HTT to his parents before the car accident? Why had he never dealt with any of that?

Pay attention to this damn road!

Cars shot past him at psychotic speeds. Urside could barely control the New Beetle on the sharp dark curves. And he was as lost now as he'd been in May 2013. He hadn't even known where to find the party. He'd just expected that once he got to Wilmette it would be obvious where it was. God, he was an idiot.

And it had seemed that strange and scary night as if he'd been driving around mountains and craters on the dark side of the moon, lost for eons. The following day he'd seriously wondered if he hadn't blacked out somewhere along the line. Because six hours had passed between the evening graduation at the football field and when he'd arrived home at 1 AM, but the drive hadn't seemed to take more than half an hour. His friend Marvin hadn't helped, joking that Urside must have had the classic alien abduction missing time experience.

Well, none of that mattered. Who cared what happened that night? Sure, Urside had always thought of it as something unexplainable, something that never fit, but that was no excuse for wasting his last HTT on it. He hadn't found the party, so what? He'd driven around for six hours, so what? He'd lost Alycia. He'd doomed them both because he couldn't wait five little years for the love of his life. Thirty-two years old and he was still such a stupid *puppy*. It was true, absolutely nothing in him had changed since high school.

Was just driving around the only thing he could do? Was he really going to have to replay all those stupid feelings from fifteen years ago? Pissed off at Alison for not knowing she should find him and not go off with her damn friend whose name he couldn't even remember now, pissed off he'd never asked anyone for directions? Crap on it, he *did* have to live it out again.

He could remember inconsequential things from that evening like saying hello on the football field to a redheaded artist girl he'd always secretly wanted to ask out. Jamming his graduation gown into a cardboard box in the gym. The elongated orange clouds in the west when he came out to the parking lot to his New Beetle.

But he did *not* remember this next scenario. He found himself on side streets, making several turns as if he knew where he was going. He pulled up in front of a multistory mansion in the night. Lampposts cast serene light. Dozens of cars were parked in a circular cobblestone driveway. Urside expected to see his high school buddies, but these people were elegant older adults. In fact, some were downright ancient. All were talking and laughing softly. And somehow they were all *beautiful*.

He could hear them because he was no longer sitting in his car. As he stood on the driveway, he felt the rippling through his torso. Could it be the surging of HTT Potential? The undulation into eternity?

The cars in the driveway … had never been cars. Not exactly. They were little flying saucers. As another one settled in from fifty feet overhead, Urside slipped into a new HTT. Where had the energy for this one come from?

CHAPTER TWENTY-ONE
Earth Renewal Party
Wednesday, May 29, 2075

Urside fought the urge to throw up in front of these fancily dressed aristocrats. This HTT seemed to have ripped his stomach clean out of him.

How could he be standing in front of the same mansion? He reached for his New Beetle to steady himself, but the car was gone. More saucers puttered in from above to settle onto the huge driveway. Urside had seen several near-futures and new technology, so he wasn't too surprised by these vehicles.

He could tell by the gravity that he was still on Earth. The tuxedos and evening gowns seemed timeless, so he knew he hadn't transitioned too far. He stayed in the shadows, spooked by the sight of so many elegant old people crowding the vast arch of the front entrance.

How had he been given another HTT? Why was he here? Something nudged his leg. Something warm and furry. Somebody's dog?

"Grr--*ullfff!*" said this--this--

That couldn't be a *cougar,* could it? A wild cougar here in the city?

Urside stared into the big cat's eyes. The thing was *huge.*

"Gaw--God ..." he muttered, backing away. The cougar or whatever it was had a scrap of red cloth stuck to its neck. God, a bloody piece of somebody's *shirt.*

Urside had no idea how he survived his mad sprint all the way to the entrance. "Dammit! *Dammit!* There's a *cougar* out here! Or a lion! Or something! Must've escaped from the zoo! Get--get inside!" Urside pushed at the old people, trying to force them through the open front door instead of chattering the last moments of their lives away out here on the porch.

But they were so old and slow they barely reacted. A few heads turned his way, then went back to their conversations. In desperation Urside pushed into the entrance hall and collided with a middle-aged woman in a black dress. She fought to keep her tray level, but twenty wine goblets sloshed over their rims.

"My dear!" the woman said, surveying the damage. "Henderson, over here. We seem to have had a little accident. Could you get me another wine tray?"

A big mustached guy in a butler uniform ambled over. He could have been a bouncer at a biker bar. "Yeah, Amber, I'll grab another one outa the kitchen."

Urside couldn't process this odd exchange between a high-class lady proving she could carry wine and the first name familiarity of her biker butler. All he could see was that the biker looked big enough to tackle the cougar himself.

"*Cougar out there!*" Urside gasped. "It's already killed somebody!"

The biker seemed to note Urside's existence for a quarter second, then shrugged as he moved off with Amber's ruined tray.

"Did you hear me? I don't know what kind of party this is, but there's a cougar out there and he's going to kill somebody before this is all over!"

Amber smiled back weakly.

"Can you hear me?" Urside cried, shaking her thin forearms. He couldn't help but notice her astonishing blue-green eyes. For an older woman, she was sure gorgeous. That was bugging him. Everyone here was so beautiful, no matter what their age. Even the biker butler was beautiful. "Listen to me! There's a *cougar* out there! A big cat! We've got to warn everyone!"

"Well, of course there's a cougar out there!" Amber finally laughed. "You're too old to be afraid of cougars, young man. Here, have some wine and enjoy the party."

Henderson the biker butler returned with a new tray of red wine. Amber placed a glass in Urside's hand, then she and Henderson lost themselves in the crowd packing the mansion's foyer.

Urside retreated deeper into the house, mortified at the shabby clothes he wore to this full-dress party. But he caught himself in a floor-to-ceiling mirror; he wore a tuxedo himself.

He looked for the Alison-mandated high school ring, but found all his fingers bare. In the mirror he held a glass of wine, his tux blending him effortlessly with the partygoers. Okay, so he was safe. But there was a killer cougar roaming out there and nobody cared.

Most of the partygoers were older people, though some were his age and there were a few children. Urside verified that they were speaking English. Their snatches of conversation appeared to make sense. Everyone was lovely, glowing, in peak health, moving gracefully, joking and laughing.

Nobody took notice of him, so he was free to explore this zone, just as on any other HTT jump. Probably, as usually was the case, the partygoers were out of phase with him. Maybe he'd only managed to impact Amber because he'd been shaking her arms, transferring energy into her.

Maybe it hadn't been a cougar. Maybe it had just been a dog after all. Urside could've gotten it all wrong. It wouldn't have been the first time he'd been confused on an HTT. He sipped the wine, which tasted mindlessly expensive. He knew it wasn't right for him and set the glass down on a credenza, then climbed a large staircase. A dozen brightly lit bedrooms on the second floor advertised luxurious canopy beds, couches, and dressers with huge mirrors. There were large abstract paintings. The staircase continued to a third floor and Urside went up.

"*Man* …" he gasped. This just couldn't be. Or could it? Wouldn't it make perfect sense for him to have HTT'd precisely to *that mansion?*

The library. Its door was open. Yes, the same room he and Mandy had transitioned into a couple weeks ago. There was the same desk, the same window where he'd seen the wrecked moon. When was that? October 2033? The desk was piled with books and knickknacks, but there were no newspapers, no printouts, no computers, nothing to give the date.

"So this is the library," a woman said. Urside turned in shock, but it was just two fragile old ladies. "I've always wanted my own library!"

"Well, he won't let anyone ever take anything," said the

other woman. "But he lets anybody come up here and sit and read."

"Oh, well, who's had time to read now anyway? I don't know how many parties I've been to this spring!"

"I'm sure we'll have Renewal parties all year long. But Urside's is the best so far."

Urside froze at the sound of his name. This woman looked to be ninety. But she was also stunning in her own way. Her white translucent hair looked freshly washed and cut. Her face was sharp and heart-shaped, and her shining blue eyes threatened to pierce right through him.

How could she know his name? He had to start thinking. Had to focus. He'd obviously been plunked here for a reason. Was it because it was the same mansion that had led him to Alycia two weeks ago? Urside had no idea why the HTT had been so off at first, but maybe it was now adjusting for *Alycia*. Maybe she was somewhere here.

Where was he? Still Wilmette? He could go outside and look for street signs, but what if there really was a cougar out there? Was he even still on Earth? What if he was in some rich Martian suburb under a pressure dome?

No, this was definitely Earth gravity. Mars gravity, a little over one-third Earth's, was a delight and he'd know if he felt it now. Still, Alycia had to be here. Somewhere.

The old woman moved for the door. Urside was in her way. He expected her to stop but she collided with him. He grabbed her arms to keep her upright. "God, I'm sorry, ma'am!"

"Oh my! Young man, I didn't even know you were there!"

"Look, by any chance have you seen Alycia Klave?"

"Hmm ...?" As she turned away Urside shook her by the elbows. What had gotten into him? Nevertheless, he didn't let go.

"Alycia? Blond, a little shorter than me, with--with--"

The woman widened her eyes as if roused from sleep. "Alycia ... hmm. Well, I thought I saw her in the conservatory."

"The conservatory! Where's that?"

"Yes ..."

"*Where's the conservatory?*"

She blinked. "My, you look just like Urside!"

Urside stared back. "What? What are you saying?"

"You look just like Urside when he was young! Are you his grandson?"

"What's going on? Look, you said Alycia's in the conservatory! Where's that?"

"It's in the back of the house! I mean--downstairs! In the back!"

"Thanks, ma'am! Bye!" Urside gasped, bounding out of the library and slamming down the stairs three at a time.

"You look just like Urside!" came the laughter behind him.

CHAPTER TWENTY-TWO
The Dented Painting

Urside plunged down a long dim hallway but came to a dead end. There was a simple white door to his left. He opened it, the meager hall light falling into a large dark space. Must be the garage. He wondered what kinds of cars these rich old farts had, and reached inside to flip a switch.

Light blasted the space from dozens of floodlights along all the walls. Unmistakably an artist's studio, thirty feet by thirty feet, ten feet high, with two large abstracts underway on easels. Bright-colored paintings of all sizes covered the walls. There was a large flat file with ten drawers, the expensive kind Urside had always wanted for storing drawings. Two waist-high workbenches were crowded with jars of paint, brushes, drawing paper, and colored pencils.

"*Wow.*" Urside came up to the larger of the two paintings in progress. This one was at least five by eight feet, in fact, it was so large it seemed to chop the studio in half. It was layers and layers of cascading blue ocean, with shards of half-buried orange, red and purple. Damn, this was just like the dreams he'd had about doing a giant messy blue painting. No real shapes in it, just tones. Urside had never really dared to let the canvas just be a mass of tone. This was a cool direction.

The other painting was four by five feet, mostly white space with a few jagged abstract primary colors falling from the upper right to the lower left. Along the walls were similar tonal experiments, in all sizes. Atop the flat file lay spiral-bound journals fattened with watercolors. A couple lay open to broadcast more abstract energies.

Urside perused one of the journals, feeling only slightly guilty. Well, he had a right to be interested in this artist. He was a fellow artist appreciating another artist's work. Besides, he was out of phase with all these people, with the owners of the house and whoever this artist was. So he could look. The artist would want him to.

He was surprised to see rigorous pencil sketches of nudes in the journal as well as abstract color. The nudes, both men and women, were glorious, rough but with excellent volume and proportions. The artist wasn't aiming at perfection, but was solidly hitting the subject. The white spaces around the nudes were the same as the white spaces in the abstract works.

Urside's own abstracts were dull and muddy. There was no energy to them, and Urside had seriously considered giving it all up. Like that stupid abstract graphic novel he'd started in January. Hell, he'd only done five sketches. It was as silly as that idea he'd had in high school about writing a whole novel about a trip to the gas station.

The few good paintings Urside had done seemed to come at random. He'd start a blank canvas hoping to improvise until he hit some passionate form, but hours later he'd find himself staring numbly at a messy travesty. He had no control over the energy. Last November he'd finally gotten so angry at a two-by-three-foot painting that he overpainted it in napthol crimson, a transparent blood red. But the effect was powerful. Drowned in the cleansing red sea, insipid blue rectangles became floating murky purple hulks, with streaks of yellow-orange straining to break to the surface. And *Angry Consciousness 51* became the passion Urside needed. It hung over his bed at the Cat Farm and every day he saluted it as the kind of work he was on this planet to do.

Urside glanced up and short-circuited. Then laughed. God, he'd been thinking about *Angry Consciousness 51* and he could've sworn he saw it hanging above one of the dark blue workbenches. That showed what memories could do. Sure, the workbench painting was red, and more or less the same size--

No, it *was* his painting.

Urside stared at *Angry Consciousness 51* for a full minute without thinking. He moved to the workbench like an astronaut approaching an alien artifact.

Somehow *Angry Consciousness 51* had wound up here, in this artist's studio. Was he hallucinating this? Then again, the wedding photos from 2038 had somehow followed him back. Maybe some objects could do that. But why this thing?

Urside couldn't think. He examined the painting. It was definitely *Angry Consciousness 51*. But he was shocked to see white gouges on the painted black sides of the canvas. There were scratches and dents along the bottom. The acrylic texture was clotted with dust.

Urside stood back. The entire canvas looked *old*. He'd given a painting to a friend years ago and when he'd visited the guy in February, Urside had remarked how beat-up the painting was. "Well, I've moved about six times since you gave it to me," John had said, then grilled him for restoration advice Urside knew nothing about.

He had to focus now. The old woman had *known* him. From where? How? They were still on Earth, so this party had to be Chicago, between 2028 and 2033, when everyone would get evacuated. So had Urside given this painting to a friend, maybe this artist guy, or it to someone who'd given it to the artist? But it was preposterous that such a good artist would like Urside's painting so much he'd hang it in his studio alongside this fantastic work. And Urside didn't see how he could ever have given this painting away. It was his best one.

Urside surveyed the studio. No more of his paintings in here. He must just have gotten rid of that one, his best one. At least it had an honored place here. He loved the colors in this studio, the bright light. In fact, if he ever got the brains together to build a real studio for himself, it would be like this.

Dozens of photographs hung on the walls. Many were close-ups of objects on tables, paperweights or plastic soldiers or puppets. Some were holograms, some printed on paper. Sunshine or high-wattage artificial light bathed the objects.

There were pictures of cats. A Siamese. A Maine Coon. A Russian Blue that could easily be Churchill's double. Lounging in the sun, amid endless plants in a vast interior space.

The *conservatory*. Photos of a hall three times as large as this studio, filled with tropical plants, with a twenty-foot glass ceiling. Urside had to get there, but first--

The wedding photo. In fact, the entire holographic photo album.

Urside stood before it in shock, hand to mouth. Alycia and white-haired Urside side by side in the same stolid pose wedding photographers have demanded for eons. He found he couldn't bear to touch the unit.

How on earth did this get here?

But they'd said Alycia was here, so wouldn't this album naturally be here too?

Other photos on the wall. Urside and sexy Alycia in black jumpsuits, grabbing each other and laughing, waving to someone off-camera, about to board what looked like a miniature flying saucer. Behind them a Marsport boulevard, pink mountains in the background.

Among the images of cats, of plastic soldiers, spacemen, and horses, of paperweights and plants, were more of these *people* photos.

Alycia, so stunning, but with gray hair, a tighter jaw line, wiser and more penetrating eyes. Alycia in an EnviroField walking on Mars, and she was old. Old and fully nude. Alycia had the same beauty all these old people did.

Dammit, there was a picture of *Urside as an old coot*. An old coot with a crooked smile, plopped on a high stool in this studio.

Urside scanned the studio again, eyes latching onto object after object after object.

The crimson Fokker Triplane he'd built in the ninth grade. He'd had it in his room in high school and then boxed it away somewhere. How could it be here now?

The black pot with green stripes he'd made at the Cat Farm when Ben taught him how to use the potter's wheel. The thing was a lopsided mess, but Urside had cherished it.

The white cube clock he'd gotten for Christmas his first year at Northwestern, the one he'd stared at for twelve hours, freaking on Jerry's dope.

The photo he'd taken of the Cat Farm staff in November 2027.

Urside swallowed. If he knew himself, if he had always known he'd keep writing, for the rest of his life, in journals he'd started in January 2013 as a senior in high school, then there would be a writing journal …

On the workbench. A spiral notebook, this one with pages in a rainbow of colors. Paper. Not a computer, not a laptop. Urside picked it up, saw the notecard halfway through the journal, the same kind of notecard that always marked the last passage in his journals. Urside numbered his journals, and he was up to number 16. He opened to the first page.

Journal #83. September 4, 2074.

In his own handwriting. The same multiplicity of colored pens Urside always used. He was pleased to note that the handwriting was firm and legible, although he couldn't make himself understand the simple English words on the paper.

This was further forward than he'd ever come. He reached for the notecard and flipped to the last entry.

5/29/75. 7:15 PM. Short note. Doing the party tonight. Looking forward to it. I think. Haven't given a party in probably twenty years, so I'm sure I'll screw up every social convention known, but we HAVE to have our Gaia party, don't we? That's what Alycia tells me! Hell, that's what Churchill tells me! Anyway, don't have time to write down a bunch of stupid emotions or philosophies about a damn party. I'm just going to enjoy myself. I've spent close to $80,000 on this and I'm damn well going to enjoy it. It's Earth Renewal Year, let's just celebrate for a while. I'll finish Blue Ocean later this week. Don't push it now.

Urside closed the notebook to prevent himself from reading the entire thing right there. Somehow it was wrong to read his own journal in the future.

This absolutely can't be happening!

He focused on a series of arched windows at the rear of the studio. The bright lights of the studio bounced off the black windows, but Urside could see the silhouettes of trees outside, and the suggestion of a gridwork of glass walls.

The conservatory. Under one arch was a glass door which he opened to hot damp air and the assault of hundreds of plant smells. Dim lights at ground level. A jungle in here.

Moaning up ahead. A cat?

"Oh God yes … oh *yes* … God, you feel good!"

"Alycia!" Urside shouted, running, then tripping and sprawling across two people.

Two naked people having sex.

"*You* feel good!" laughed the man on top said, jamming forcefully. Urside shot to his feet.

The man's buttocks were powerful. And the woman thrust back, her ass thumping madly on the stone.

"Oh, God! God!" she moaned.

"*Alycia!*" Urside cried in unison with the man. *The old Urside.*

Urside backed away. Those old people were really having at it. Alycia, white-haired and ancient, was beautiful. Her jiggling breasts were the same perfect erotic pair. Her legs were the same. She loved sex. *Loved* it.

"Give it! Give it to me, honey!"

"Alycia! Alycia!" old Urside gasped.

"*No, this can't be happening!*" Urside yelled to the trees and ferns, inviting them to bear witness to this depravity.

Old Urside disengaged from old Alycia. The two lay back on the moist flagstone, panting. Yes, she was beautiful. But old Urside wasn't so bad either. They both seemed to be in great shape.

"I can't handle this!" Urside screamed. "*How old are you people anyway?*"

No answer from below, just snuggling and a kiss on the flagstone. Urside wouldn't want to lie naked on flagstone himself at thirty-two. How could these old farts do it?

"You just had to get away from the party, didn't you?" Alycia teased.

"Hey, I for one am totally enjoying this party," old Urside laughed, a finger brushing her nipples. Damn, those two looked as if they'd been married forever.

God, how old am I on May 29, 2075?

Seventy-nine!

CHAPTER TWENTY-THREE
Polot of Zorex

A hand came to his shoulder. Urside froze. "Well, maybe it's time to leave 'em be!" came a screech. "They're a bit out of phase, but I'm not!" A nudge to his forearm. A glass of wine appeared. "I got you another!"

"Huh. Must've left mine somewhere," Urside muttered.

"Let's leave 'em alone, dude. Okay?"

"Well ..." Urside turned to face his captor.

An obese guy, short and bald, with thick black glasses and a gray stubble beard. He too was old. "We'll just find another spot where we can chat," he said, pointing down the flagstone path. "They'll never know we're here."

"But--Alycia! That Urside's *got* her!"

"Pull back a bit, guy. Urside and Alycia never saw you on this HTT. Although they both know you came tonight."

"How--how could they know?"

"Because you told her all about this night! And of course you *are* that older Urside, or will be. They've both known it was coming for years. They also knew they won't see you, just feel a brush of your young energy when you stumble over 'em. You added quite a lot to that particular episode of sexual intercourse, young man!"

Urside turned back to Alycia. If that was the case, if they could slightly feel him the way Amber or the biker butler had, or the old woman in the library, then he maybe he could talk to her, explain everything.

"C'mon, this is the last HTT, and everyone's celebrating it along with Earth Renewal Year," the man said. "Just relax and enjoy it."

"The last *what?*"

"The last HTT anyone will ever do. It's all yours, dude!" The man led Urside from the lovers to a metal bench under a palm tree. "Look, sit down, relax, and don't try to mess any further with the timeline. This is the last one, and it takes forever to clean up the paradoxes, so let's just pull back, okay? Have a seat, okay?"

"I can't! How can I find Alycia if--if she's *old* now, and I need to get back to the *young* Alycia?"

"Sit down and relax!"

"Okay ... okay." Gingerly Urside sat to the left of the big man, avoiding his eyes. The man's face was a squirming mishmash of the affable and the demonic. He was like a zombie hired to play the part of a friendly human being.

Hot breath on Urside's left hand. "*Oh my God, the cougar's in here!*"

"Just sit still," the old man whispered.

"Just sit? God!" Urside stiffened as the brown beast sniffed his pants.

"There's really no problem, man, just focus on his thoughts."

"*What?*" Then, as Urside noticed that the red cloth around the cougar's neck was a bandanna fastened by a gold chain, he felt within his mind:

Didn't mean to scare you out there a while ago. Thought you were a party crasher. Then I realized you were the one who'd be coming in from a previous time. Polot says this is the last HTT ever.

"Who ... what ..."

I'm Jasper. Lieutenant Jasper of Her Majesty's Animal Police Force.

"Her Majesty's ... Animal ..." Sure enough, written on the bandanna was HMAPF.

Her Majesty is our planet. Gaia. Polot will tell you more. I need to get back to my duties.

"I can read your thoughts! Just like Churchill!"

Talk to Churchill. He's here. I see you're not aware of the migration back to Earth. It was easy for him to teach telepathic techniques to all Earth animals.

Lieutenant Jasper trotted out of the conservatory.

"No, that's *insane*," Urside whispered as he processed subtext from Jasper's thoughts: how certain animals contracted with humans to form Her Majesty's Animal Police Force to regulate the new human/animal societies setting up on the earth ...

Urside considered the untouched red wine in his glass. Without further thought he chugged the contents. He shuddered. "Damn. So you're ... Polot?"

"Polot of Zorex," the man grinned with bits of salad between his teeth. "Also known as Huey Vespertine. I already know you. Not from your 2028 but from the thirties."

"This is all ... kinda *weird*."

"Ain't it, though? Anyway, welcome to the last HTT anyone will ever do. All the timeline damage that's ever been done, already has been done, and now it's over. This HTT won't produce any timeline damage, in fact it just exists to seal off the entire spectrum of Time Transitions, all 8,178 of 'em that humans and other species did between May 29, 2013 and May 29, 2075. Of course, dude, you had the honor of performing both the first HTT *and* the last HTT!"

Urside stared into Polot's glossy gray eyes. "That can't be right. I mean, lots of people were doing it before me. I mean, I read von Goertner's book last year, I started doing his Concentration Exercises, and then, all of sudden, I was doing it!"

"No, you did a spontaneous HTT on your high school graduation night in 2013. You just forgot it entirely. And then you replayed it tonight."

"No, that's *crazy*."

"Turns out your graduation night was the exact moment the Alpha Centaurians leaked the Chronowarp Subroutine into this solar system. After that other people started transitioning, and before long that idiot von Goertner named the thing Heuristic Time Transition and wrote his book."

"What? The Alpha--"

"Yeah, they were totally freaked that *you* did the first HTT, before any of their own 1,755 trips over the next couple decades."

"No! You're just spewing insanity!" Urside gasped, standing up. From far away, among the trees, he could hear

Alycia and Urside talking. He ran his fingers feverishly through his hair. He needed more wine.

"Excuse me, but I *invented* the Chronowarp Subroutine. Look, I'm really a ship's archivist. I was just trying to develop a tool for studying the human past. Thought I'd shielded my work, but the Grid picked it up anyway. And before you knew it the Zarj--what you call Zoraxians--"

"I don't call them anything!"

"--developed the Chronowarp into a weapon and leaked it back to your 2013."

"No! This is crazy! I should never have started doing HTT, it was a mistake and I'm sorry!"

"And I was being *hunted*. The Zarj were pissed! I had to modify the Chronowarp to allow myself to permanently HTT back to your 2036. It involves taking over a body that's essentially lost its soul. I have no idea why that particular time was picked, or how I landed in this derelict's body, but, hey, here I am."

Urside looked away from the corpulent body in question. He was only now noticing a damp foul odor emanating from the tuxedoed flab.

"Huey Vespertine was just a shell by the time I got here in '36. And I lost my Polot body forever. But even after I woke up inside Huey, I've just never gotten any good at this human stuff."

"Well, I think you're doing okay ..."

"See, the Alpha Centaurians thought of the Chronowarp as like some plague they'd infect you with. They figured people like yourself would start inadvertently screwing the timeline up so bad that your entire society would collapse. It never occurred to 'em they might destroy the entire universe! They were just so eager to ream you!"

"Alycia told me about Alpha Centaurians. The war, how bad it is and all. Are you seriously saying *they* started all this HTT stuff?"

"My Chronowarp was just to *view* the past. Theirs was to *participate*, to *destroy*. They wanted to land in your rear and wreck your solar system before you ever had a chance to develop Star Drive. But they also got hold of my permanent HTT technique and took over lost souls, the way I took over Huey Vespertine."

"That's crazy! You're just playing some sort of mind game!"

"You don't believe they had hundreds of agents among you? That they made up the whole religion of Celestionism to brainwash people into becoming part of the Alpha Centaurian Grid?"

"That Celestion thing? That stupid cult? You're saying Celestionism is really--"

"Yep. One giant stealth maneuver! They even got to be buddies with your Central Asian Powers, and they gave CAP the Xon bomb."

"That's crazy!"

"They inadvertently gave you guys a hell of a lot more. Where do you think all this new high-tech stuff has been coming from the past few years? The ACs were *boggled* when they found out that their Celestion BS was leaking *AC tech* to you guys! The AC versions were usually more primitive, like the Warp Transfer they've never gotten straight. But suddenly some Earth scientist wakes up from a dream about how to make Star Drive! The Zarj were *horrified* to watch you guys subconsciously getting inspired by all their own tech!"

"Look, man, I'm sorry, I don't mean to be a jerk, I mean, sure I'd like to believe you, but I've seen so much the past few weeks, all this stuff about Mars and this Final War, and Alpha Centaurians, and I just can't *take* it!"

"Right, right. Anyone would be utterly discombobulated, I'm sure. Especially if they'd been driving themselves batty for months experimenting with HTT."

Urside opened his mouth. "I need more wine to process this."

"Henderson, over here!" Polot called to the biker moving down a hall on the other side of the glass wall. "I'm in the conservatory."

Henderson entered with his tray of wine glasses. "Hey, Huey man. Need another glass?"

"I'll take two. One for now and one for emergency reserve."

"Huh," Henderson said. "You know that's against the rules, dude," he grinned as he set four glasses of wine on a green table.

"Ah, but you know full well what I require." Polot took one of the glasses for himself and passed another to Urside. Henderson moved off. They heard him encountering old Urside and Alycia across the conservatory.

"Damn, he acted like he didn't even see me!" Urside said.

"He didn't. You're out of phase. I can see you because I'm simultaneously in and out of phase."

Urside shook his head. "Doesn't make sense but that's okay. Look, I'm sorry about the HTTs. I must've done maybe ninety trips by now. Sometimes I can do one every day for a solid week, then I cut back a bit, but sure, I've been worried about the timeline and I'm sorry. My life's been hell since January."

Polot nodded. "We're all astounded you're still in one piece! You must have tremendous energy resources to stay sane."

"Uh, yeah ..."

"But don't worry about the timeline. Whatever happened was fated to. We've corrected everything as long as you don't act impulsively on this last trip. And even then we'd just clean *that* up."

"Well, what does any of this matter, if these Alpha Centaurians have screwed up our planet, infiltrated it and everything."

"Excuse me," Polot said, clearing his throat theatrically. "I'll have you know that *I* am Alpha Centaurian! I just happened to have been the first AC to free myself from the Grid. I knew from the start that we'd have to completely dismantle it so we could lead all the Alpha Centaurian races back to *sanity!*"

"Oh jeez, I didn't mean, like, to offend you and all."

Polot giggled. "Oh, piss on it! I don't care!"

"Still, if they were in on the Final War, these Alpha Centaurian friends of yours have really screwed up our world."

"Oh, they were in on a lot more than that!" Polot laughed. "Once they started infiltrating spies into your past, they found they could tap into all the Amplified Thought experiments the Martians were doing."

"The *what?*"

"Oh, I'm sure Dar mentioned the various Martian Amplified Thought technologies for manipulating matter telepathically."

"Yeah, I think I heard something about that." Urside gulped more wine just to nail down one more berserk concept. He drained the first glass and reached for a second.

"The Martians didn't know until February '36 that their Amplified Thought subroutines had been hacked as far back as 2028!"

"Huh."

"For instance, the Martians were trying to bring those four big asteroids into orbit around Mars, but lost every one."

"What are you saying? The *asteroids?* The ones we've been watching go into the goddamn sun?"

"The AC hackers were incredibly gifted. They always found ways to convince the Martian programmers that the software errors were some *Martian* miscalculation. There was always a *Martian* programmer's line of code that could've been the problem."

"You're saying all that crap that's gonna happen to the solar system--"

Polot shrugged. "Yep. Pluto was another shot at bringing in a moon for the Martians to use. But it flew off the other way, at insane speed. Wrecking the gas giants was a different project. The Martian Council of Elders decided to build a Dyson sphere around the sun. They knew there was semi-intelligent life on Earth, but they didn't give a hoot what Earth creatures might think of a giant sphere at the orbit of Jupiter catching every shred of energy from the sun and diverting it for Martian use. But their first experiments were disasters. Neptune blows and Uranus accelerates into the sun! The Martians tinker with their programs, then they try to gently take Jupiter and Saturn apart at the same time from opposite sides of the sun. But they blow up too! Finally they figure out that something's very wrong with Amplified Thought!"

"All that was the goddamn Alpha Centaurians?"

"Well, Dar put an end to this in your 2031, even though he wasn't emperor yet. He knew AT had terrible faults and managed to shut down the experimenters. But suffice to say that the only good thing Amplified Thought did for your solar system was when the Martians molded some asteroids together, moved them into your planet's orbit, and gave you a new moon."

"Gave us a new moon?"

"Yeah, that was like June '34." Polot pointed up through the glass conservatory ceiling at a gibbous gray disc.

"My God, Alycia never mentioned *that*."

"Its albedo isn't as high as your old Moon, but it's got the exact same density, size, orbit, all that stuff," Polot said. "Dar insisted it all had to be the same to get your planet's ecosystems back online."

Urside gulped more wine and felt it slap his brain hard. "Aaah, who cares, looks like your goddamn Alpha jerks won the goddamn stupid war, they destroyed the solar system, why'd anybody wanna repair goddamn Earth?"

Polot laughed. "Think, wine boy. Where are you now?"

"Crap. Inna buncha damn plants." Urside finished off his second glass of wine and reached over Polot to claim the third. "Inna house where some future me lives. In some stupah alternah universe."

"You're on Earth, boy, May 29, 2075 your time. Gaia's been totally repaired. About half the human population's moved back. We had a hell of a time figuring out the calendar, by the way! Since Mars days are thirty-nine minutes longer than Earth days, we kept a regular Earth calendar by adding about ten days every year, so we're on target with the true Earth May 29, 2075."

"Yah, yah, yah, so damn what."

"Like I say, half of us moved back. The rest, mostly younger folk, like it fine on Mars, and that's okay with everyone. But almost all the Earth animals decided to come back. Most of 'em thought Mars was like one long trip to the vet."

"Sheh ... sure as hell can't focus on what yer sayin'. Don't wanna. Need this wine. Sorry it's screwin' up damn timeline."

"No screw-up," Polot said, leaning back. "Of course, Henderson handing me four glasses of wine was foreordained."

"Bullsheh ... this is alternah universe! Every time HTT'd, made goddamn alternah universe. Like science fiction writers say. Confusin' damn bullsheh. Fool to believe anythin' else. There's no Alycia ..."

"Listen to me, wine boy. Stewart Neal Frankston began the Earth Terraforming Project in the summer of '34, your time, and finished January 1st of this year. So 2075's been declared Earth Renewal Year."

"Aw, crap 'n everything. Who cares? Yer damn Alpha Centaurian buddies won. Made me mess up entire timeline of damn stupah universe."

"Does wine always make you this morose? I suppose I forgot to mention the glorious day of May 14, 2053, when Dar formally dismantled the AC Empire?"

Urside took another gulp, struggling to focus on the moist flagstone between his shoes. "Nah, ya sure as hell didn't mention that sheh."

"The Grid was destroyed that very day. Hundreds of Martians went to Alpha Centauri to counsel billions of brainwashed ACs. It's been quite successful, all in all."

"Yah, yah, yah, make up anything ya want 'n alternah universe."

"I can't believe you're moping through your own Earth Renewal Party!"

"Nah mine. It's *his*. *He* gets Alycia, nah me."

"Oh, right, in your dear alternate universe," Polot sighed. "Listen, kiddo, there are *no* alternate universes. Why do you think we spent so much time repairing the damage from 8,178 HTT trips? Because we have only one universe!"

Urside shook his head. Bad move. He was potted. Could puke so easily. He could never hold his alcohol. He chugged the rest of the third glass. Surely Polot would flag down Henderson for more. "So yer sayin' ... Alpha guys got stopped somehow?"

"It was brilliant!" Polot cackled. "Dar actually figured it out in February '36."

"Muhhh … muhhh …"

"He considers that the ACs have been messing with human and Martian history since 2013. But he figures it's February '36, and hey, we're still standing. So by definition the ACs never destroyed us by going into the past. And by us, I mean, buddy, I've been firmly one of *you* guys since '36!"

"Muhhh … interestin' sheh."

"Anyway, what Dar did was mess with the AC *future*. They didn't see *that* coming! Dar saw that on May 14, 2053--"

"Ah, screw ya bullsheh. I'm sick of your stupah alternah future."

"You're not listening, wine boy. This is fascinating stuff, really. See, Dar--"

"Screw it, 'm outa here, man." Urside had one scary HTT last March where men and dogs were hunting him under a football stadium. He'd stolen a case of beer, so he gulped down four cans and passed out, ending the HTT. This Transition was no different. End it now. "Muhhh. Need more goddamn stupah sheh wine."

"Sure, the ACs have a mathematical concept of the future, but no gut *understanding* of it. Even when they find they're doomed on their equivalent of May 14, 2053, they don't understand what it means. So …"

The lullaby continued with all its bizarre concepts but Urside drifted right on through it into blackness.

CHAPTER TWENTY-FOUR
Prison Planet Earth

"Hey, guy, come on, wake up, the party's not over yet."

Hands turning him over. "Aw, lemme alone," Urside moaned, opening his eyes to harsh yellow light and the clear blue eyes of a cat. "*Churchill!* Oh my God!"

We did a little AT and neutralized that alcohol, Churchill radiated. *This HTT's not over yet and there are a few more chunk concepts you need to take back to 2028.*

"Oh, *man,*" Urside said, sitting up. He was back in the library on the top floor. He could hear the loud party below. He turned to a striking woman in a slinky blue evening gown.

"Mandy!" She was older. She looked at least forty.

In case you're wondering, I'm seventy-seven. We have all sorts of rejuvenation tech now. Almost everyone here is doing rejuv. Alycia and your future self just got started with it.

"*Wow ...*" So maybe that was why everyone at the party looked so lovely, so vibrant. "Well, you look ... very nice. Very beautiful, I mean." Okay, what do you say to a former girlfriend who was thirty when you last saw her a couple weeks ago but who's now seventy-seven but looks forty?

"Well, thanks," Mandy said aloud, and Urside saw there was no trace of her former anger at him. "You yourself look like hell. I bet this evening has totally messed your mind."

"Yeah, I guess. So you brought me up here?"

Transported you up to this bedroom, Churchill beamed. *Polot realized he was literally driving you to drink and thought we should take over.*

"Of course, your older version knows all this and made sure this bedroom was clear for this time of night," Mandy said. "He said he's sorry he can't see you tonight."

"So this really *is* his party. For this Earth Renewal Year thing. He really owns this house. That's *his* studio."

"It's also your party for the last HTT anyone will ever do."

"I don't know about any of this. I mean, I've seen a lot of stuff on HTTs, but never *myself.*"

"You had us worried there for a while. Chugging the wine like that! And in your HTT phase it was really hitting you hard."

"Well, I just couldn't believe all that stuff that guy Polot was saying."

"Did he tell you about Dar messing with the ACs back in '53? Incredible, huh?"

"Well, I just don't know if it can be. The only way I can make sense out of all this is to assume it's an alternate universe, and nothing of what I've seen of the future is really real. That whenever I HTT, I'm just making a new possibility branch, a new future. And I can't be sure of anything and so I must be crazy."

Not crazy, dear friend human, Churchill radiated. *Only one universe. This is the very real present for us, for you it's the very real future.*

"You and Alycia will be married in 2038," Mandy said. "Hang onto that."

"I hope so. But I just don't know. I'm already feeling the Slingshot back, and I never made it to *my* Alycia. It was my last HTT and I know I'm starting to fade. But look, can't I just stay here with you guys? If I can't make it to 2038, maybe … just stay here?"

Mandy shook her head. "No, you can't do what I did. When I knew I was Martian all I had to do was decide to remain in 2036. But you're fully human, and your fate is to go back to 2028 and live out the next five years on Earth."

"Until the goddamn rocket explodes! Dammit, I had no idea how much I'd screw up the universe when I did that first HTT trip! Back in January! Just a few months of wrecking the goddamn universe!"

"You haven't wrecked the universe. All timeline events have been repaired. And for your information, that trip in January was your *second* HTT trip. Your actual first HTT was May 29, 2013."

"That's what that Polot guy was saying, but he's got it all wrong."

"No, it was May 29, 2013, right after your high school

graduation," Mandy insisted. "You just never remembered it. Your HTT was to *here,* May 29, 2075, but it was so horrifying that you never remembered any of it. You wouldn't have been able to handle it. Now you can handle it, believe it or not. So, your Slingshot from this HTT will be back to May 2013. You'll be back in your car, driving around the Chicago North Shore."

"Crap! You're right! I *remember* it now! I remember all this from high school! I came *here!* I saw all this! I talked to Polot, and then you! I've *done* this before! Crap! I'm gonna fade out of here and then I'm gonna catch hell from my parents for staying out to one AM without telling 'em!" Urside felt tears coming.

"Right. Then from there you'll Slingshot back to May 2028."

All this is just an HTT within an HTT, Churchill radiated.

Urside leaped to his feet. "But I missed! I was aiming for Alycia but instead I'm jumping through all these crazy HTT hoops! And I can't generate the Transition energy ever again! So all I have is 2028, and I'll have to live through five years until the rocket blows up! It's just a prison sentence! This has to be a meaningless alternate universe because otherwise it doesn't make sense!"

He ran past them, down two flights of marble stairs, around the corner and down the hall to stand panting in his future alternate's studio, among the giant half-completed paintings, the blue workbenches full of paints and brushes, and *Angry Consciousness 51.* Mandy and Churchill followed.

Urside, it's all right! Mandy radiated from all her depth.

"Miaow!" Churchill cried.

"No, at the end of five years I'll be blown up and I'll never know *this* alternate universe where this is all true! What use is that? When I belong *here?*" Urside yelled into Mandy's anguished face. "You're sad because you know it's true! *This* Urside is doomed!"

"No, I'm sad because you're hurting yourself for nothing!"

"I have to go back to that! Yeah, I'll do it, because it's the only way *somebody* gets to see Alycia again! I'll do it all! Five years of prison!" His eyes frantically locked onto all the familiar objects of his studio. "But *this* is home! I belong here! I can feel that!" he cried as he faded and began to feel a steering wheel between his fingers.

CHAPTER TWENTY-FIVE
DamnStar
Sunday, February 10, 2036

Jack Commer, Supreme Commander, United System Space Force, waited in front of the Marsport Hotel as the green bus rolled up on its oversized tires. The bus stopped and the vehicle depressurized. Jack climbed aboard, the door shut, air whooshed around him, and he felt his EnviroField cut off as pressure returned to normal.

"USSF Spaceport, please." He looked down the bus aisle. He was the only passenger. Well, it wasn't too surprising at 0800 hours on a Sunday. He was glad Amav wanted to sleep in. He really couldn't have her along on this anyway, no matter how much he wanted to. He had to do this himself.

"Thank you, Supreme Commander Jack Commer," the bus said. "The fare has been charged to USSF Account 3394514."

"Fine, thanks," Jack said. He had no idea why he always felt he had to be polite to a stupid bus. He hadn't been on a civilian bus in ages. He remembered he used to think they were relaxing. He took a seat midway back and watched Canal Street roll by. The bus passed USSF Headquarters, then turned right on Neptune.

There were probably ten thousand emails and five hundred pages of printouts waiting on his desk. But all that was secondary now. He had the pertinent DamnStar files on his comm anyway. But before anything else, he needed to ask some questions.

"Would Supreme Commander Jack Commer care to listen to the latest news on ARESNET as he rides the comfort of the Marsport Automated Transport System to his destination, the USSF Spaceport?" said the bus.

"Huh? Well, no, not really."

"THIS IS ARESNET!" blasted throughout the bus. "GOOD MORNING! IT'S 8:02 AM! THIS IS THE SUNDAY MORNING REPORT! LATEST NEWS ON THE DAMNSTAR FIASCO!"

"Aw, jeez, I can't believe this."

"THE UNBELIEVABLE FEROCITY OF THE FIRST ALPHA CENTAURIAN ATTACK OUTSIDE THE AC SYSTEM, YESTERDAY ON DAMNSTAR SENTINEL STATION, HAS SENT SHOCK WAVES THROUGHOUT THE UNITED SYSTEM! THE UNITED SYSTEM COUNCIL WILL MEET IN EXECUTIVE SESSION THIS MORNING AS FEARS OF IMMINENT INVASION MOUNT! DAMNSTAR, ONE OF SIXTY SENTINEL STATIONS LOCATED BETWEEN SOL AND ALPHA CENTAURI, WAS CREWED BY BOTH HUMANS AND MARTIANS. DESPITE THE REPUTATION OF AC STAR DRIVE AS BEING DISASTROUSLY INEFFICIENT, THE ENEMY WAS ABLE TO WARP IN THOUSANDS OF ATTACK SHIPS AND SUCCEEDED IN DESTROYING DAMNSTAR STATION. THE USSF REMAINS PUZZLED BY THE ENEMY'S APPARENTLY UPGRADED TACTICS AND WEAPONRY. SUPREME COMMANDER JACK COMMER HAS CUT SHORT AN INSPECTION OF THE JOVIAN FRAGMENT FIELD AND RETURNED TO MARSPORT LATE LAST NIGHT. THE UNITED SYSTEM COUNCIL HAS ISSUED A LEVEL SIX FEAR ALERT."

"Aw, c'mon, we wiped 'em out," Jack muttered. "The USC's just panicking again."

"REPEAT, A LEVEL SIX FEAR ALERT."

"Turn that damn thing off, will you?" The report ceased.

"Does the news of DamnStar trouble you, Supreme Commander Jack Commer?"

Jack blinked. "Huh? Is that you?"

"Yes, it is me."

"You? The bus? Talking to me?"

"Since Supreme Commander Jack Commer last rode in a Marsport Automated Transport System vehicle, date May 14, 2035, 0915 hours, there have been significant enhancements to the MATS Artificial Intelligence Interface Module. This bus is now capable of sensing the moods of passengers, based on proprietary software which takes into consideration factors including age, race, sex, occupation, recent transportation history to, from, and within Marsport, local and United System news events, economic indicators, personal financial health, voice stress, heart rate, pheromonal and other physiological activity, court records including divorce and bankruptcy proceedings, and any writings, photographs, or mentions of the individual in AresNet media. A full profile is then assembled--"

"Okay, okay, I get it." The bus turned left onto Jupiter Boulevard and picked up speed. Jack was glad they'd kept this sort of nattering off USSF ships.

"The goal of this upgraded AI interface is to sense potentially negative emotions which may lead to violence aboard MATS vehicles, and to assist police in the apprehension of criminals who may consider using MATS vehicles to flee the scene of a crime, or to employ MATS vehicles in the commission of a crime."

"Well, okay, that's very nice." Maybe he should try to catch a little extra sleep himself. How long would it take a civilian bus to get to the spaceport, maybe twenty minutes? He settled back and closed his eyes.

"My interface has determined that Supreme Commander Jack Commer may be suffering from high levels of stress brought about by the DamnStar fiasco, and recommends that passenger Commer enter into consultation with the AI interface of this bus in order to ameliorate this condition."

"What? You want me to *talk* to you about--"

"About the DamnStar fiasco, which appears to be causing *extreme stress* for Supreme Commander Jack Commer."

"Stop calling it a fiasco! We were caught way off guard, I admit. We lost the outpost, but Gooney went in there and stopped 'em cold! He blasted ninety-seven percent of those AC ships to atoms, and the rest turned tail and ran home! Why doesn't AresNet play *that* up?"

"Over one thousand AC ships doing suicide runs, Supreme Commander Jack Commer. A total of 612 USSF ships destroyed or damaged, and 8,108 USSF personnel killed. The entire United System is reeling from the impact, according to ARESNET.

Certainly Supreme Commander Jack Commer has reason to be stressed to potentially dangerous levels aboard a MATS vehicle."

Jack stared in consternation at--what? The bus itself? What was he talking to? The voice didn't even come from a fixed speaker. It seemed to boom from any point. "Look, Mr. Bus, I assure you that I'm in control of myself and won't commit any violence aboard you today, all right?"

The bus slowed ominously as it approached the ramp to the Upheaval Freeway. This thing wasn't going to put him off five miles from the spaceport, was it?

"The Alpha Centaurians went crazier at DamnStar than the United System thought possible," the bus finally said. "Surely that concerns Supreme Commander Jack Commer."

Jack nodded, then realized the bus cameras were probably incorporating this gesture into their AI deliberations. "Look, I certainly can't discuss classified information with a public bus. Can we just, you know, like head on to the USSF Spaceport so I can get some work done?"

"Your mental state is *classified?*" the bus said, resuming speed, finding the entrance ramp, and accelerating to a hundred miles an hour on the freeway.

"Well, look, I do have a lot on my mind. I need to think a bit, by myself, on the way in, so I can be prepared, you know." Why was he justifying himself to this mindless bus? Why didn't he just call for a jeep on his comm and be done with it?

"Supreme Commander Jack Commer must be extremely proud of Star General Gooney," the bus went on.

"Yeah, thank God he was on top of things." He had to admit a human USSF fleet commander wouldn't have been able to react so fast. Gooney had saved their asses, rounding up an entire attack fleet with Amplified Thought within an hour.

"Yet you were quoted in ARESNET as stating that Star General Gooney should not be allowed to run for mayor of Marsport as long as he served in the Martian armed forces, is that not correct?"

"Well, look, that's just my opinion. We wouldn't allow a

USSF officer to get into politics, but we sure can't dictate to the Martians what their rules ought to be."

"Is it possible you're upset that *Typhoon II* engineer Philip Sperry resigned his commission to assist with the Greeney Gooney for Mayor campaign?"

"Dammit!" Jack snarled. "Do you really think you can read my mind? A stupid bus trying to read my mind? Why am I talking to you?" He still couldn't believe Phil had quit the service just to run Gooney's campaign. Gooney was one charismatic Martian. "Dammit! Dammit to hell!"

The bus lost speed and pulled onto the shoulder.

"Look, I apologize! I didn't mean it! Please take me to the spaceport!"

"This bus has determined that Supreme Commander Jack Commer's mental state is conducive to violence directed towards this bus itself. Records of Jack Commer violence aboard MATS buses from June 2034 are now being incorporated into this determination."

"Aw, c'mon, the only reason Joe and I were fighting is we were trying to collar Sam Hergs. *He* started the fight!"

The bus came to a halt. "Supreme Commander Jack Commer will now leave this vehicle."

Jack stood wearily. It used to be so much fun riding these little beasts. He remembered all the times he'd made the *Typhoon I* crew ride them back to their quarters at the Marsport Hotel.

"All vehicles of the Marsport Automated Transport System will receive this updated report on the mood of Supreme Commander Jack Commer."

Air was sucked out, Jack's EnviroField clicked on, and the bus door opened. Jack keyed in commands on his USSF Comm and turned to the front of the bus, where a real driver would sit in buses he remembered from his childhood. "No, nobody's getting this info. I just classified everything we said today, and anything in the MATS databanks about DamnStar. And called a USSF jeep to come get me."

"This MATS bus will protect the integrity of its data!"

"Hey, bus, you know the USSF did hear about your AI interfaces and we knew we had to have a way to kill 'em off if necessary. So, SCUSSF Override, Priority Alpha-4," Jack said, and the bus's mind was erased.

Jack moved out into the Martian sunlight to await his ride. "And you're right that DamnStar's got me and everyone else spooked," he told the dead bus. "*Nobody* saw this coming."

Within minutes a USSF jeep hurtled down the opposite direction, finding a turnaround a half-mile back on the freeway, then heading up to where Jack waited. Its driver, a burly, dim-looking airman, saluted. His nametag read POSTTNER. Jack got in.

Again he wished Amav were with him, even though he knew he had to do the painful next thing by himself.

CHAPTER TWENTY-SIX
USSF Detention

The driver pulled the USSF jeep in front of the seventeen-story concrete USSF Detention Center. Jack got out in the harsh morning light with the sounds of *Doomboat*-class battle cruisers warming up for takeoff beyond. He'd never had occasion to visit the Detention Center on the south side of the USSF Spaceport.

He'd sure never thought he'd be coming here to see Joe.

His driver motioned him to the entrance. "Right this way, sir. We've got them on L1."

Of course, the basement, for the high-security cases, and for the possibility of interrogating Alpha Centaurians captured in combat, not that that had ever happened before. Jack shook his head. "Say, Posttner, what's with this armband you're wearing? I've seen it on a couple other airmen as we came in."

Posttner glanced at the bright red "C" on his right arm. "Well, sir, the 'C' is for Celestion. Some of us have gone in for that, you know."

"Well, Airman, you happen to be out of uniform. Remove that armband now."

Posttner blinked. He had vivid blue eyes incongruously set in a meaty, acne-blotched face. Only now did Jack notice that Posttner wore USSF Detention Services insignia. He wasn't just a driver from the motor pool, then. When Jack had called for a ride and said he needed to get to the Detention Center, they'd just sent a DS jeep over.

"Well, sir," Posttner said, "that would go against my religion, sir. If you don't mind, I'll just exercise my right of religious expression and keep the armband, sir."

Jack sighed. He had more important things on his mind than jumping all over this idiot. He'd never aspired to be the kind of snarling SOB who pounced on the slightest disrespect to the rules. Maybe people thought he was too lax, but browbeating just wasn't his style as Supreme Commander. But he did need to root this Celestion crap out of the USSF. "Fine, wear the stupid thing. You'll have your reprimand in your email when I get around to it. Let's just get down to L1."

Posttner shrugged, following Jack through the entrance to the first security checkpoint. "I guess I'll have to appeal directly to Deputy Commander Easterling then, sir, won't I?"

"Let's just get down to L1. I haven't been here before." They both showed ID to the guard at the checkpoint, who pointed them down a hall with a stairway at the far end. Easterling was truly toast now. Why did Jack have to get all these stupid problems when he needed to concentrate on the really crucial stuff? Who could he move into Easterling's position without hassle? Maybe Petersdorff? Damn, of course Jack had once wished it could've been Joe. Wouldn't that have been great?

But Joe had quit, and taken up with Huey Vespertine, and *snapped* somehow.

"Just down the stairs here, sir," Posttner said, boots clacking on the concrete stairs. "Sir, I might add that the Celestions are probably the most spiritually important thing that has ever happened to mankind."

"Cut it! Dammit to hell!"

"Yes, sir. I was only trying to point out that many of us in the Service have positively responded to Celestion transcendence."

"Airman, you are way out of line! Shut up immediately! Your job is to take me to the prisoners and that's all! I don't want to hear one more word about the damn Celestions!"

"Sir, you may not damn the Celestions!"

"Damn the Celestions! Damn your filthy, goddamn Celestions! I'm stopping this crap once and for all!"

Posttner set his jaw and clomped down the stairway. The steps turned and the lights got dim.

"*Because I love you!*" came the scream. "*I love you!*"

"You don't love me! You just think you do!" came a woman's cry. Jack and Posttner came to a row of cells. A woman in gray stood before them, sobbing.

"Hey, what's going on here?" Jack said.

"The prisoners, sir," Posttner said coldly, moving back to

stand by the stairway with his arms clasped behind his back.

"This is insane! *Insane!* Why did I come here?" cried Jackie Vespertine. Huey's wife.

"What's *she* doing here?" Jack said. Jackie paced between a cell holding Huey Vespertine and one holding Joe. They both were unshaven, with slack faces, in orange USSF prisoner jumpsuits, grasping the polished steel bars like monkeys.

"Jack!" Joe shouted. "Jack! I can't believe it! You're here!"

"What the hell's going on?" Jack whirled to another guard on duty. "How did this woman get in here? There aren't supposed to be *any* visitors to a Zone 14 USSF Detention Facility!"

The other airman, the only other USSF man down here, gulped. "Sir, I'm sorry," Airman Li squeaked. "She just showed up a minute ago. I don't know how she got here. I was trying to tell her to go. We're supposed to have two guards down here, but Gardner's late this morning, and I couldn't leave the prisoners and escort her out myself."

"The other airman is *late?* A USSF guard at a Zone 14 USSF Detention Facility is *late?*"

"Uh, sir," Posttner said from behind him, "Gardner wanted to catch the eight o'clock Celestion Worship of the Greater Quasar, and we thought we'd cover for him."

"Jack! You're here! Thank God!" Joe said. "You can explain it all to Easterling!"

"Hold on a sec." Jack's eyes went to Li's right arm. "You're not wearing that stupid Celestion armband, I see, Airman."

"Uh, no, sir. I'm actually Taoist, sir."

"But we're working on 'im," Posttner said. "The Celestions can absorb *anyone.*"

"Okay, cut the talk. I can see well enough why the guards upstairs let her down here."

Jackie Vespertine shrank from him. Her eyes widened, but her puffy lips pouted insolently. Yes, that tight gray-ribbed sweater left nothing to the imagination. Ample rounded breasts strained against the cloth. Skintight black slacks ended at the knee to offer long bare calves and sculptured ankles. Short fluffy dark hair, inch-wide crimson hemisphere earrings, chiseled heart-shaped face, intoxicating turquoise eyes, black choker collar, and deep red lipstick completed the Zone 14 USSF Detention Facility airman-seducing package.

"I came to see my husband," she said. "I have that right, don't I?"

"No, you do not."

"Anyway, Huey's not here anymore," said the orange mess behind her. "I'm *Polot* now!"

"Jackie, you came to see *me!*" Joe cried. "Admit it!"

"No, Joe, please don't," Jackie moaned.

"But she came too late, Jacko!" Huey laughed. "I'm Polot now! Polot of Zorex!" Jack froze at the mention of the Alpha Centaurian planet.

"He's so *out* of it," Joe said. "I've been sharing this place with a crazy man!"

"I'm Polot of Zorex! I've known that for two weeks now!"

"What the hell?" Jack shouted. "You're *admitting* you're a Centaurian spy?"

"No, but I *am* Centaurian! Of the Jujl species! What you call Zorexian! I *transported* here! On the radio program! Two weeks ago!"

"What did I tell you?" Joe said. "He's crazy!"

"Well, we always knew it. Ever since he dropped out of the Academy and started spewing all his treasonous babble."

"I had to take over a body that went derelict!" Huey said. "There was no Huey *left*. I thought it'd be easy to just walk in, but it's really taken me *two weeks* to fully make it! I'm *exhausted!*"

Jack turned to Jackie. "What the hell's your goddamn husband saying?"

"I don't know! I really don't understand!"

"*Is he a spy for the Alpha Centaurians?*"

"I don't know! I don't know!"

"Airman Li! How often has Mrs. Vespertine been to see the prisoner?"

"Uh, this is the first time, sir. And we're sorry, sir."

"But you really came to see *me,* Jackie!" Joe said. "Isn't that right?"

"I came to see, I mean, *both* of you!" Jackie said. "Oh, I don't know why I came here!"

"You were *naked* with me! Admit it! We almost made love!"

Jack took a good look at his brother for the first time. Was his mind truly gone? Had he really reconverted to the Centaurian brainwashing from the previous spring? His own brother, his *Typhoon I* copilot, standing there in an orange USSF Detention jumpsuit with his tongue hanging out at this Vespertine woman?

"Joe, *please,*" Jackie said. "It was an accident! I didn't mean to be bad!"

"It wasn't bad! It was love! I know that now! I love you!"

"Sheesh," Jack muttered. Was Joe really working with Huey for the ACs? How had they brainwashed him again? Joe looked like a rat in a sewer after having been stuck in here for two weeks. No bail, no visitors period, not even Mom and Dad. Then they let this *woman* down here, and Joe had fallen for her just as he'd fallen for all those other bimbos. He'd done that all his life, one woman after another. One big escape trip. It was damn pathetic.

"Dammit, Huey!" he shouted. "This is your *wife!*"

Huey shrugged, his eyes unfathomable chaos. "Well, Jackie will be Jackie."

Could this Zorex crap be true? Could AC infiltrators somehow take over people's minds? Was that what had happened with Huey? And to Joe? Jack whirled to Jackie. "Dammit, this is your *husband!* Do you even *care* that his mind's gone?"

"Well, of course I do!"

"But you really came here to see Joe! To seduce my brother in front of your own husband! Unbelievable!"

"No! Are you *insane?*"

"None of this matters!" Joe shouted. "Because I want Jackie to divorce Huey and marry *me! I'm* the one who loves her!"

"Oh, God!" Jackie moaned.

"Listen!" Jack cried. "We have to get *straight*. Have to *think* about this." Had they really been infiltrated? If the Martians had Amplified Thought and could do all those wonders, what could the Centaurians do with their Grid? Could they really take over human souls? Sol could have the enemy right in the middle of everything. DamnStar might turn out to be one big diversion.

"There's nothing to think about!" Joe screamed. "I love Jackie! She'll be my wife now!"

"Just like that!" Huey laughed. "Just like that!"

"Joe, you literally do not know this woman!" Jack said. "At all!"

"I *do* know her!"

"You do *not* know me!" Jackie wailed. "Nobody does!"

"I *do* know you! You're going to be my *wife!*"

"No, Joe! Look, it's obvious, I mean, that you and I had a sexual attraction for a long time."

"God, *yes!*"

"And a couple weeks ago, I mean, well, the tension finally released, and we were expressing it, I guess, and then you were just *gone!*"

"That's right! That's right! I HTT'd right out of there!"

"But then it was obvious to me that what you and I were doing was--was *nothing!* Just some tension. Just my anger at Huey for I don't know what! And now he's turned into this *thing!*" She bit her lip.

"Nothing?" was all Joe could whisper.

"I married him to atone for all those years of *depravity!* Why can't anyone understand that? I was trying to be *good!* And Huey was kind to me, and--and I don't know!"

"Years of *depravity?*"

"You don't want to know! You just don't! I was punishing myself for being so *crazy* all those years!"

Joe swallowed. "You were *punishing* yourself with Huey?"

"And, well, you looked like a way out! I'm so sorry!"

Joe turned wildly to Huey. "She was punishing herself with *you?*"

"And Huey was punishing himself with *Huey!*" came the

orange-jumpsuited cackle. "Huey's *glad* I came!"

"*Who* came?" Jack and Joe shouted together.

"Polot! Polot of Zorex! I'm *here!* Wow, what a ride in from Zorex is all I can say! I'm exhausted! And hungry! Very hungry!"

"All through my twenties! Nothing but drugs and men, and drugs and men, and the most insane *depravity!*" Jackie sobbed.

"Look, it just doesn't matter!" Joe said. "I mean, Jackie, look, I figured stuff out! And when you came in here now, I knew it was *destiny!* I figured it all out! It was DamnStar that got me focused!"

"DamnStar?" Jack gasped.

"Yes, DamnStar! Jack, I've gotten *focus!* I know I'm needed in the USSF again! Working for you, Jack! Being your copilot again!"

"*No ...*"

"Jack, the ACs are starting their invasion! Isn't that obvious? I *have* to be there! There's so much work to be done! I mean, I'll do anything! I'm offering my services! And, Jackie, I *need* you with me on this! I need you to be my *wife!* To guide me!"

"*No ...*" Jackie moaned.

"Joe, you're really ... not in shape to come back to duty," Jack managed.

"Look, just because I'm in Detention doesn't mean anything! Geswindoll arrested me without cause! It's all crazy! Why didn't *you* get the charges dropped? I mean, you fired the guy, didn't you?"

"Well, yes, but--"

"So why am I still here? Why is Huey still here for that matter? It's all a bunch of these stupid fanatics who believe in this stupid Celestion BS!"

A throat cleared behind Jack. "Excuse me, sir, but we can't allow prisoners to blaspheme the Celestions."

"Cut it, Posttner!" Jack said without looking. "Look, Joe, it's not that easy."

"You're head of the USSF, Jack! Can't you tell these

clowns what to do? Or--or, God, Jack, do you really *believe* Geswindoll? Do you really think I've *converted* again? That I'm *brainwashed* again?"

Jack looked away.

"Oh, God, my own brother doesn't believe me! Jack, I want to come *back!*"

"I know, Joe, I believe you, I mean, it's great to hear that, but--"

"But I'm *brainwashed!* That's what you think! God, get out of here! I'll just rot in prison here with this crazy man! Because I'm crazy too!"

"Yowza!" said Huey. "If I'd tried to transition into Joe, I'd *really* have been crazy!"

"Look, Joe, we know you're *not* crazy, but--" Jack said.

"But he does blaspheme against the Celestions," Posttner put in. "That's a definite sign."

"Dammit, Posttner!"

"Well, of course I'm crazy, that's all there is to it! I can't handle *any* of this! Maybe it was the AC brainwashing last year that did it, who knows? Maybe once that happens, you're permanently broken! Maybe I never recovered! All I know is I've had *too much!* We all have! But I'm the one who pressed the goddamn button that dropped the goddamn bomb that blew up the goddamn world!"

"Joe--no!"

"None of this would've happened if I hadn't destroyed the earth!"

CHAPTER TWENTY-SEVEN
The Writhing, Pre-Universe Foam of Energy Possibilities

"No!" Jackie cried. "It's *my* fault! *I* wrecked your life!"

"No! *I love you!*" Joe screamed.

Jack looked away in shock. Joe was *gone*. His own brother was *gone*.

"I wish you'd blown *me* up with your goddamn Xon bomb!" Jackie wailed, collapsing in front of Joe's cell.

"Pull yourself together!" Jack snarled. "Both of you! I can't take this!"

"Yes, everyone pull yourselves together," came a sardonic voice. "*Nobody* can take this. In fact, things will be changing from here on out."

"Dammit, Posttner!" Jack said, spinning around.

A USSF admiral stood in crimson USSF uniform with Airman Posttner and two more USSF guards. All wore bright red "C" armbands. And all held raised shatterguns.

"Geswindoll!" Jack shouted, only recognizing the older man from photographs. He'd never met the idiot PR goon Easterling had hired in his absence. "What are you doing in uniform? You were fired two weeks ago!"

"Hmm," murmured Robbert Geswindoll. He was tall and thin, with long gray hair. His lined face was weary and pockmarked, but his dark eyes glowed. "Easterling tabled that. Celestion considerations, you know. I don't suppose he bothered to tell you that?"

"No, he sure as hell didn't bother to tell me. You're fired and he's fired too. Now you guys turn right around and go tell him that."

"Are you choosing to ignore the fact that we have four Martian shatterguns aimed at your nose? I hate to be unpleasant, but the fact is, you're under arrest."

"Are you insane? What the hell are--oof!"

"Oh, sorry, sir," Airman Posttner said as he relieved Jack of his heat blaster and stepped back. He'd managed to get in a good elbow to Jack's kidney in the process.

"You sons of bitches! Dammit, I knew Easterling was reading that stupid Celestion Bible, but I never thought it'd get out of control like this!"

"Sir! Give the order to waste 'im and we'll waste 'im!" Posttner cried. Jack looked into four fanatical pairs of eyes and backed away.

"You can't shoot *Jack!*" Joe shouted from his cell. "That's mutiny!"

"This basement is *filled* with traitors to the Celestions," Geswindoll spat. "You think I care what a traitor to the Celestions thinks?"

"Okay, all right, whatever!" Jack said. "Just get this woman out of here. She's a civilian and doesn't belong here. Li, get her out of the way."

"Uh, yessir," Airman Li said, stepping up to pull Jackie back from the cells.

"Li's a traitor too," Posttner said. "He won't convert."

"*Conversion …*" Jack gasped, only now realizing that Posttner's eyes were just like the eyes of people who'd converted to the AC emperor last spring on the *Typhoon II*.

TRANSITION PUSH VAR X = COORD 20530514 13:44:23 localTime; IF X = "now" GET PROCESS softwareMess; GET T; IF T = emperorDeath then GET PROCESS selfProclaim.

"God in heaven, what's *that?*" moaned one of the guards by Geswindoll.

PUSH line 5,776,756, DEFINE SELF = DAR[0]; GET proclaim; if nativeREACT = NEG GOTO line 4,555,498; PROCESS REDO timeCoord SUBSTITUTION time VAR "Moment x"; ELSE RUN selfProclaim.

"It's in my head! It's in my head!" the guard screamed.

"Dammit, it's a damn Martian!" Posttner said. "Close by!"

"But it makes sense!" Huey laughed from behind Jack. "It makes perfect sense!"

"Dammit, I thought we had this building sealed off against the damn Martians!" Geswindoll snapped.

PUSH PROCESS dar[x]AcceptCrown; INSERT ROUTINE nativeRenounce; PUSH "moment t," t = "now," moment =

"GET 'moment L,'" Time Var = FOREVER; PUSH ROUTINE societalCollapse; COLLAPSE = L; PUSH ROUTINE martianAssistance.

"God, I'm sorry, sir!" Posttner said.

"No, look, it's incredible!" Huey said. "If you just follow the programming! It's so simple!"

Dar stood between Jack and Geswindoll.

Done! came Dar's radiation.

"*No ...*" Posttner gasped.

"Dar!" Joe cried. "God, it's so good to see you!"

"Hello, all, fate seems to have brought me in just behind Mr. Geswindoll and company," said the emperor of the Martians. He wore a tight gray jumpsuit. "Hello, Jack."

"Wow, Dar! Good timing!"

"Hello, all," Dar beamed at everyone in the basement in turn. "Well, you can all relax, at least to a certain extent. We've just won the war with Alpha Centauri."

"Forget it!" Posttner shouted. "The Celestion Emperor will never be defeated!"

"Cut it, Posttner!" Geswindoll hissed. "Infidels aren't supposed to know about the emperor."

"Listen, Dar," Jack said, "I don't know why you're here, but could you please use some Amplified Thought and disarm these characters? They're trying to arrest me."

Four shatterguns clattered to the concrete floor.

Done.

"Sir, I can't reach down to pick up my shattergun!" said a guard.

"What's going on?" Posttner moaned.

"Hmm," Dar said. "Well, I know we've all been upset about DamnStar."

"Piss on that!" Posttner said. "It was a glorious victory for the emperor!"

"If you only knew!" Huey laughed. "If you only knew!"

"And you're Polot now," Dar said. "You've figured prominently in many of the important subroutines, of course."

"Well, I suppose I'd have to. Man, did I really start this

whole HTT mess?"

"Well, your Time Viewer was the groundwork. And your permanent Transition to Huey Vespertine defined the essence of the HTT maneuver, even though you only transitioned through space and not time."

Jack pointed to Huey. "Hey! Is this an AC spy?"

"No, he's a refugee from Alpha Centauri. The ACs were going to torture the secrets of his Chronowarp Subroutine out of him, so he came here."

Geswindoll motioned his cohorts back. "Well, this is all very interesting, but I think the boys and I had best be on our way now."

"In the name of the Celestion," Posttner said.

"Screw the damn Celestion," Jack shot back. "You all stay put."

"Look, all this just proves that Jackie *can't* be married to Huey!" Joe said. "If Huey is really this alien *thing*--"

"Dammit, Joe! Cut it!"

"No, this means Jackie can be my wife now!"

"I said cut it! Nobody wants to hear about your goddamn hots for this woman!"

"*Jackie* wants to hear! She's free now! She can come to me!"

"No!" Jackie cried. "Are you *crazy?*"

"You're saying you want *Huey?* Look at him! You don't belong with him!"

"He--he's my husband!"

"He's hopeless! How can you live a life that's totally hopeless?"

"Damn you! *Don't you think I know life with Huey is hopeless?*"

"So you're saying what you had for me was just blowing off steam or something, because life is so screwed up? Just some meaningless attraction? Damn you!"

"Of course it wasn't just meaningless attraction!"

Joe staggered back. "You--you're saying--"

"Damn you! I was in love with you! All along! Damn you

to hell!" The basement was silent.

"Well, anyway," Dar went on, "you know, those anomalies at DamnStar got me thinking. Like those upgraded tactics and weapons, and ships we hadn't seen before."

"Yeah, me too," Jack said.

"The reason they were so new to us is that they came from 2049."

"*What?*"

"God, Jackie!" Joe moaned. "You love me! You really love me! I knew it!"

"Yes, I fell in love with you, but it was crazy! Because it's not *me* you love! And everybody knows it!"

Jack shook his head in disgust. "Look, Dar, do you mean the ACs could be using *time itself* as a weapon?"

"Well, DamnStar was the only time they were ever able to pull off transporting huge amounts of military hardware and soldiers through time. It was an act of desperation. They were really trying to get in an overwhelming victory right before I made my little visit to May 2053 Alpha Centauri."

"You've been to AC?"

"I just got back now. On May 14, 2053, the Alpha Centaurian emperor dies."

"No!" the guards around Geswindoll bellowed. "No!"

"You love *Ranna!*" Jackie screamed. "Ranna, who had to *die!*"

"Ranna? What are you saying?" Joe shouted back. "That's crazy!"

"I listened to you on AresNet! When this Geswindoll guy was talking about the *Pegasus* crashing! You were shocked about *Ranna!*"

"That's because I never knew you had a sister who died! You never talked about her! I'm sure as hell not in love with her!"

"Joe, shut the hell up!" Jack shouted. "Nobody cares about that crap! Dar's telling us about the AC future!"

"Right," Dar said. "So when the emperor passed on--"

"Forget it!" Geswindoll rasped. "The emperor is an

immortal process! When one emperor physically dies, a new one steps forth immediately and the entire citizenry of AC plugs their allegiance into--oh! No! Greater Celestion, *no!*"

Jack read Dar's radiance as did everyone in the room.

"Exactly," Dar said. "I took advantage of the millisecond of chaos surrounding the emperor's rather unfortunate accident involving a portable nuclear reactor. The Grid's shaky any time there's a transfer of power, because everyone has to renounce their plug into the old emperor and create a new plug into the new emperor. So I played with their software and got *myself* proclaimed emperor."

"You fell in love with Ranna when you came to the CTESOPE conference!" Jackie cried. "Everybody at CTESOPE knew it! Even I knew it!"

"That's insane! I never knew she *existed* until that moment!"

"And your reaction when you realized she'd been on the *Pegasus!* Joe, it was so obvious you were in love with her!"

"Jackie, you can't be saying this! There's no way I ever loved Ranna! Only you! From the beginning! From when I first met you!"

"The first thing I did was accept the plug of trillions of Alpha Centaurians," Dar went on. "Then I ordered them to *renounce* it, as well as any plug into anyone else. The entirety of Alpha Centaurian society and consciousness collapsed in that second."

"No!" Posttner screamed. "No!"

"Let me just grab a shattergun!" another guard cried. "I promise I'll just shatter myself! No one else!"

"I can't live without the emperor!" the other guard beside Geswindoll wailed.

"So we've won the war!" Jack said. "Amazing!"

"Well, we win it on May 14, 2053. But unfortunately, we have seventeen years of desperate warfare ahead of us," Dar said.

"No, surely if they know they're defeated in 2053 or whatever, they'll have to back off."

Again Dar's thoughts filled the room.

"Crap! I forgot they're *insane*."

"Ranna had to die because of you!" Jackie cried. "Because you couldn't inspect your ship properly and you lost the *Pegasus!*"

"You think I deliberately killed your sister? Is that what you think?"

Jack opened his mouth to silence the lovers, but he was still reeling at the futility of what lay ahead. Battles and death and destruction. Seventeen years of it. Yes, they'd win, but it was all so useless. Why couldn't these goddamn Centaurians know when they were licked? The USSF had to waste seventeen more years *proving* it to them?

"There's something in your voice when you talk about Ranna! The *real* love!"

"God, Jackie," Joe moaned, "I can't believe you're so insane!"

"I'm not insane! I'm taking care of myself, for once in my life!"

Jackie's cry slowly echoed to silence in the USSF Detention basement. She and Joe glared at each other through the cell bars.

"Well, what happens," Dar continued, "is that news of the end of the Empire in 2053 starts filtering back to 2036 with this very conversation. Before long everyone knows it from here to Alpha Centauri. Anyone can check the programming, and in fact over three hundred HTTs are done to confirm the entire history of the war. But the ACs fight on anyway."

"Look, Jackie," Joe pleaded, "I'm sorry I had a hand in Ranna's death, but it was unavoidable! Nobody could know the forces that'd be placed on those damn passenger shells!"

"The ACs will take Polot's Chronowarp Subroutine and use it to develop HTT into weaponized time travel, they'll insert HTT itself into our past, and curious humans and Martians will inadvertently start altering timespace. The ACs will insert agents into our past, they'll hack into our own Martian Amplified Thought experiments, and destroy much of this solar system starting in 2028."

"That was *them?*" Jack gasped. "That was *them?*"

"And finally, in their greatest attempt, in 2049 they transport an entire fleet to DamnStar 2036. It was the only time they were able to fight a time-travel battle. All other battles happened in real time. The ACs' morale is shattered from '49 to '53, but they fight a lot of nasty battles right up through May '53. The AC leaders tell their troops I didn't really go into the future, that the emperor never dies, that the Grid is never destroyed, but they all know it's true. And they fight on anyway."

"*Man* ..." Jack could read all the programming in Dar's mind. He could see the brutal logic of the future. Geswindoll and his three guards were staggering.

"Hey, hey, Jacko!" Huey said. "It's gonna be okay, dude!"

Jack whirled. "What now, man? And just who or what the hell *are* you?"

"Hey, dude, I think it's obvious from line 45,666,744 what I am. That defines old Polot, a.k.a *me,* pretty well. And then you all oughta consider line 51,446,333."

Of course, Dar radiated. *LINE 51,446,333: PARAM 20280415 OBSERVE PROCESS transportKnalp/Geswindoll--*

"April 15, 2028, the date Robbert Geswindoll is taken over by a Zarj Level 43 Commissar known as Knalp," Huey said.

"One of their first attempts at bodily transport, from their 2038," Dar said. "But very difficult and crude. Mr. Geswindoll here hasn't fully become Knalp yet, even after all these years."

"I love you, Jackie! No one else!"

"No one loves me! No one has *ever* loved me!"

"This is insane! I know who I am!" Geswindoll yelled. "I'm Robbert Geswindoll! You're just trying to make me *think* I'm crazy! Well, so what if I worship the Alpha Centaurian Emperor! I'm proud to have converted to the worship of the Celestion Emperor! As have my comrades here! The USSF is full of us! Celestion worship is everywhere! Kill me if you must! We can't be stopped!"

"Then, on February 10, 2036, he *does* fully realize who he is."

"*You! Vermin!*" Geswindoll's cry increased until the room shook with it. "*Death to you all!*"

Jack froze. Robbert Geswindoll seemed to have grown a foot taller and two feet wider. His eyes flared like a demented beast's as he swept a shattergun off the floor.

"And it's really amazing," Dar went on, "to see how easily a Zarj Level 43 Commissar can break my Amplified Thought prohibition to pick up that gun."

"Oh my God!" Jack cried, backing away.

"But of course, Knalp expires on February 10, 2036."

A blue-purple ray hummed from behind Jack.

"*No!*" Posttner screamed, throwing himself in front of Geswindoll, only to burst into a tinkling cloud of glass shards. The rest of the ray caught Geswindoll in the neck.

"*Vermin!*" Geswindoll snarled as he too blew into a million bits of glass.

Airman Li lowered his shattergun. Thousands of multicolored slivers glittered across the concrete in front of the cells. "Hope that was okay, sir. He had the drop on you. And Posttner. Hell, sir."

"It's definitely okay. You did fine, Li. Thanks. Keep these other two covered."

"We're not going anywhere!" one squeaked. They both had their hands over their heads.

"Okay, I need a couple minutes to think about how we can broadcast an order that all USSF personnel with 'C' armbands are to be arrested."

"There's quite a lot in USSF HQ to clean up, sir," Li said. "I've seen more and more armbands every day."

"Dar, can we deconvert all these folks?"

"Yes, in the absence of an actual Centaurian like Knalp, Conversion will wear off, just as it did with those of us who converted last spring," Dar said with a nod to Joe.

Jack looked at his brother. "Are you really gonna be all right, Joe?"

"Yeah, just let me out of here, Jack, and let me fight! If we have to keep fighting these goddamn monsters for seventeen more years, well, we just do! And you *need* me!" He turned to Jackie. "You see how much I'm needed now? You see how much I need you with me on this?"

"No! Forget it! It's insane! You love Ranna! I know it for sure now!"

"Look, Joe, I'm really gonna have to think about all this," Jack said. "You quit the service once. And you've been, well, you've been flaky for a while. I need to know that your mind is all back, that you're really in shape for something like this. And also that there aren't any, you know, *distractions*." He nodded at Jackie.

"Don't you see it was *fate* that led you to fly Ranna's passenger shell?" Jackie said. "Just as it was *fate* that made you HTT to her, in 2028, at the height of her glory? Right at the beginning of all the horror we've lived through?"

"No, that's insane! God, I feel *sick*. I can't take this, about Ranna! About killing her! She was so good! But you can't love a dead person!"

"But you do! You do!"

"No, not really. God, I … I'm *transitioning!* I'm feeling the HTT Potential!"

"You're going back to her! It's fate! It's fate!"

"No! I'll prove it to you! To you all! I'll go back to September '33! I'll stop CAP from wrecking the moon! I'll stop us from dropping our own Xon! I'll stop the Final War! I know how to save everything! And sure, I'll be saving Ranna, but only because she's your sister, not because I love her!"

"*You love her!*"

Jack stared at the space where his brother had been.

"Where did he go? Dar, where did Joe go? My brother! Where did he go?"

"God! God!" Jackie moaned.

"Airman Li," Dar spoke. "Will you please free Huey Vespertine and place these two USSF guards in those cells? They're already deconverting and shouldn't give you any trouble. Jack will need a little time to recover here. So will this young lady."

"Sir?" Li said to Jack.

Jack nodded. "Yes, yes, that'll be fine. Then we'll deal with the top-level USSF. But Dar, we need to find Joe!"

"Ah, yes," Dar said. "I happen to have the equations for that scenario right here, my friend." He laid a claw on Jack's shoulder and filled the Supreme Commander's mind with radiance.

CHAPTER TWENTY-EIGHT
Last Links
Saturday, November 26, 2033

"*Damn …*" Joe grunted into whistling and clanking coming from all directions. The gravity was astounding. He was pressed into bare metal shaking madly beneath him. He twisted to see a circular chamber fifteen feet wide and fifty feet tall above him. He blinked and quickly realized where he was.

He was jammed onto the plating over the *Typhoon's* nuclear reactor. The ship was under acceleration, the familiar takeoff roar resounding from the walls, the plating becoming the bottom of the ship. Joe could see the tiny escape craft anchored high above on the cylinder wall, with the crew station rooms opposite it. A crewmember climbed a ladder into the Navigation Room.

His brother Jim. But God, he'd died in June '34. How could this be real? Joe saw the tension on Jim's thick forearms. Hadn't Jack so often chastised both Joe and Jim for getting out on the ladders when the ship was under acceleration? A fall meant probable death. In fact, Joe's back was sore from his short drop to the reactor plating. He could barely move. It felt like a standard 3G takeoff acceleration.

But if Jim was up there, that meant Joe had really HTT'd into the past. So this was the destroyed *Typhoon I,* not the *II,* which was still in service. The whole *Typhoon I* crew had to be here.

Joe studied the wall to his left. The ventral docking hatch was configured for attachment to another ship. A passenger shell? Could it be? Just to get to the hatch to read the manifest was a ten-foot climb in 3G. Well, Joe had done it before.

He painfully pulled himself across the reactor plating, crawling over a bundle of color he only now realized was a crewman in USSF uniform, the red, white, and blue suit from a few years back. Joe gasped as his boot moshed into Harri McNarri's face.

"What the *hell?*" McNarri spat.

"Harri!" Joe gasped. Harri McNarri, tall and gaunt, with

graying red hair, falcon face, and sharp blue eyes, lay strapped into his acceleration cot on the reactor plating. "Harri, you're alive! You're not dead yet!"

The ship's physician/engineer raised an eyebrow. "What in God's name are you doing down here, Mr. Joe, and out of uniform too, I may note?" he said, but his face crinkled into a grin. "Sir," he added. His mouth worked with the same 3G strain as Joe's.

"Uh, well, I was just going to check on the ... passengers?" After all, they might have been ferrying some supply ship. Joe checked his clothes, horrified he might be presenting Harri with an orange USSF prisoner jumpsuit. But he noted he wore tan slacks and a brown sweater.

The older man nodded. "They're as good as can be expected. Panicked out of their minds, as usual, heh-heh."

"Good. I sorta thought maybe my being out of uniform might reassure them or something."

"Huh. I'd think the sight of someone *in* uniform would be a lot more reassuring. Say, you didn't fall off the ladder, did you? I sure didn't see you come down. You hurt?"

"Uh, no, Harri, everything's fine. I just wanted to know what's going on down here."

"Everything's in order here. I might add that this is a hell of a time to be conducting a ship's inspection. Sir."

Joe grinned at McNarri's cheerful insolence. God, he'd absolutely loved this guy. Why did he have to die? Why did they all have to die? "Look, Harri, what I mean is, it's really going to be all right, you know. I mean, in the end. We'll defeat Hergs, and later--" Joe backtracked; Harri didn't even know about Sam Hergs and the Martians yet. "Well, it looks like later we win the damn war with the Alpha Centaurians, but it takes *years,* to 2053! They try to infiltrate the USSF, but in 2036 Dar turns the tables on 'em."

McNarri's eyes slid away. He wasn't absorbing anything. He probably couldn't hear anything forbidden to the timeline. "Shouldn't you be up helping Jack pilot this piece of crap?" said the physician/engineer. "You know how hard it is for one pilot to deal with the turbulence when we've got one of these damn shells on us."

No doubt a younger Joe was right up there in the Control Room. Joe 2036 wasn't anxious to meet him. "So we *do* have a shell on. What's the date, man?"

McNarri blinked. "My, we *have* been up all night, haven't we? Weren't Portia's margaritas wonderful?"

"Just give me the date, Harri!"

"Well, the twenty-sixth ..."

"*What month?*"

"Well, we definitely haven't made it into December yet ..." McNarri said carefully, and Joe could feel him itching to pull out his log and record: *Bizarre questions from copilot, out of uniform, during acceleration phase.*

"So you're saying November 26th ... *2033?*"

"Look, I know we've all been under a lot of strain, Joe."

"And that's *Pegasus!*" Joe moaned, pointing to the hatch above. "Dammit to hell!"

"Uh, Joe, uh, sir, under regulations, all crew are supposed to be strapped into their seats during acceleration."

"The turbulence--we're still in the atmosphere, right?"

"Uh, yeah, Jack just told us we're go for one orbit before departing for Mars."

"Oh, no, we're not! We're not gonna take any nice little orbit and then cruise out for Mars! We're gonna turn around and spend the standard two hours inspecting the crater *Pegasus* is about to make down there in New Mexico!"

"C'mon, Joe, calm down. We lost that one a couple weeks ago and I know everyone's spooked. But we've done twenty perfect ones since then and I think we know how to do it now."

"Dammit. *Dammit.*" Joe took in some of the wonderful metal-tasting *Typhoon I* air. God, he'd missed it. "Okay, Harri, look. Have it your way. But now that I know I've come here to die, I may as well do it *nobly,* I guess you'd say."

"Joe Commer, you are definitely acting strange! As ship's surgeon--"

"Cut it, Harri! It doesn't matter now. I'm just going on up

to the hatch there to check on the passenger shell."

"Dude, we're still under *acceleration*."

Joe found the lowest rung of the ladder beneath the hatch and said: "I know that. And you're going to forget all this, Harri. Everything. *Your* Joe is up there in the cockpit and everything's going to be just fine." Harri had never mentioned Joe being out of uniform or going into the hatch, so he did forget it all. "Looks like I'm completely out of all the '36 stuff. So I came here to die. Jack will handle '36, I know it."

"Well, okay, son, but if you break your neck on that ladder, I'm not in any position to paste you back together."

Biceps straining on the rungs, Joe took a last look at the doomed McNarri, now facing forward with the pleasant strained concentration of an astronaut under G forces. And the red, white, and blue physician/engineer would die next year along with Joe's brothers John and Jim, with *Typhoon I* crew Mickey Michaels, Ken Garrison, and Craig Reynolds, when John rammed the *Typhoon* straight onto Sam Hergs' Mercury base and detonated the ship's Augmented Nuke. While Jack and Joe, the command crew, just watched from that nasty little escape craft. Yes, they'd been disabled by that ice ray, but, God, they should've been with their ship when it went down.

The whole crew was here, now. Shouldn't Joe say goodbye to all of them?

No, there was no time. And officially, Joe Commer '36 didn't exist. How the hell had he held together over the past two and a half years? He should've stopped functioning long ago.

Then again, he was playing his end out right here. It certainly looked as if he'd looped back to become one more fatality in the Great Evacuation. Reaching the top rung of the ladder, sweating and panting, legs and arms howling with the 3G exertion, he studied the keypad until the code from two and a half years ago came back to him: BLEEMBLO-7.

"WARNING: HATCH OPEN," came the computer voice. Joe punched in an override to silence the alarm on the command console in the nose. He didn't remember seeing any HATCH OPEN alarms on November 26, 2033. Apparently none had ever been documented in the accident investigation. Joe climbed into the airlock.

"PRESSURE EQUAL. AIRLOCK MAY BE OPENED."

The airlock door slid aside to the passenger shell.

"*God* ..." Joe gasped as he secured the lock behind him, hooked his already aching arms around the ladder, and peered straight down into the latticework containing eleven hundred people. The noise was deafening, the whistling turbulence much louder in this vastly larger and less insulated space, and eleven hundred humans were moaning. It was dark except for shafts of sunlight rotating through the tiny windows on the sides of the ship.

He'd inspected scores of shells before takeoff, noting how jammed in everyone was, with fifty to a hundred people per level. *Pegasus,* he recalled, was a seventy-six-per-level shell. The *Typhoon I* had transported over five hundred shells, but he'd never understood until now what some passengers had described as hours of raw animal panic. There was a new shuddering turbulence setting in that he remembered fighting at the controls along with Jack. The *Typhoon I* engine roared demonically somewhere behind and below him, desperately seeking orbit with its clumsy added load. Did anyone on this shell understand that it would never make it?

Now *Typhoon/Pegasus* flipped onto its back, arcing to orbit, but despite being less vertical they were still under 3G acceleration and the distant bottom of the passenger shell was still a nine-story drop.

The airlock was located on Level Seven of the *Pegasus.* Seats 457-532 here. Six levels above that, and eight levels below. Joe could barely hold onto this ladder, let alone climb sixty or more feet up in 3G. He had to take the gamble that Ranna was below him.

WRRR-WRRRR-WRRRRR-EEEEE-EEEEE-KKKKK

Fresh screams through the shell. One of the attaching struts had just failed. As copilot, Joe had twisted the *Typhoon* free of six of these disasters. Other pilots hadn't been so lucky, and in breaking off not a few passenger shells had destroyed their host

ships. So Joe had never known the true meaning of *break-off.*
For years he'd been tormented not only by the guilt of pushing
the button that wiped out CAP, but of losing those six shells.
Watching them flip end over end. Two of them just burned up.
Death by fire was bad, but burning up in the atmosphere was just
about instantaneous.

But four shells, like the *Pegasus,* weren't high enough and
so each of a thousand passengers on each ship had suffered, in
delirious stunned dread, all the way down.

Now Joe would know exactly what he'd done to six
thousand, seven thousand people, however many he had killed.

"*Ranna!*" he added to the screams. "Are you up there? Or
down? I'm climbing down the levels! I'm on seven now! Ranna,
can you hear me?"

"Yaaaaaa! Yaaaaaa!" cried eleven hundred people.

It would be easier to spot her from the center of the cylinder,
so Joe made his way horizontally across the latticework,
grabbing silver railings by the seats of gray-faced refugees.
There were numerous gaps in the latticework to allow ladders to
traverse the entire length of the shell. Joe had to be careful as he
made his way across these gaps with shuddering arms. There
were several small elevators, but they were useless in high
gravity. In the center of Level Seven, at row four of eight, he
found the main ladder down and carefully swung his legs onto
it.

Only now, as he realized his legs were barely holding him
and that his arms were stiff with fatigue, did he consider that the
ladder itself might wrench loose under the turbulence. Hell, the
entire latticework might crumble. There'd been one case where
a shell survived intact into orbit but the interior had collapsed,
killing everyone inside.

Funny how that didn't matter anymore. It didn't matter if
death came when the shell broke free or the inside collapsed or
the air blew out, as long as he saw Ranna again.

Damn, Jackie had been right. *Joe loved Ranna Kikken.*

He'd only known her for a few minutes, just a couple weeks
ago. But hadn't she somehow always been part of his life? She'd

at least been trying to save the earth since around the time he'd transferred to the USSF, hadn't she? Hadn't they been fighting side by side all these years, while the earth died, while the solar system disintegrated, while they came up against the monster Alpha Centaurians?

"Yaaaaaa! Yaaaaaa!"

"Ranna!" Joe cried, making it to seats 533-608, hanging in a dark sea of seventy-six shrieking, unrecognizable faces.

WRR-RRR-AACCAA-AAKK-WRRR-WREEE-KKK

Another strut tore loose, and the nose of the *Pegasus* yawed wildly, thumping against the bottom of the *Typhoon*. He did recall that from the *Pegasus* break-off. He'd had his finger above the EJECT SHELL button and he certainly would've punched it to save the *Typhoon* if the shell hadn't ripped away first. Joe had hoped it could last another forty or fifty seconds. He knew he'd had the fate of eleven hundred people right under his finger.

Now he recklessly slashed down the rungs, past Levels Nine, Ten, and Eleven, legs faltering in the harsh gravity.

"Ranna! Ranna Kikken! Are you here?"

CRRR-RRR-RRRR-RRAEE-CCCKK-EEE-CCKKK

"Yaaaaaa! Yaaaaaa!"

"Ranna! You have to be here! You have to!"

RRR-CAR-CARRR-RRRRR-EEEEE

Joe found himself on Level Twelve, staring directly into an old woman's scream: "We're breaking off! I can't believe it! *We're breaking off!*"

Sunlight washed across the center aisle. There, at the end, unbelievably, was Ranna. She was so beautiful.

"Ranna! God, it's *you!*"

"Yaaaaaa! Yaaaaaa! Yaaaaaa!"

CARRRA-AAAAAC-CCKKKK-KKKKK

"Oh my God we've broken off!"

"Yaaaaaa! Yaaaaaa! Yaaaaaa!"

Joe grabbed a railing. The ship rolled several times. All acceleration was gone and he was weightless. He hauled himself hand over hand across flailing people. One guy punched madly at him and Joe swung hard at the guy's face, knocking him cold.

"Did you a favor, dude!"

"I'm gonna throw up!" someone screamed.

"Who the hell cares?"

"I can see the *Typhoon!* It's separated!" someone else cried.

"Fly it! Fly it! Straighten out! Yes, they did it!" a woman shouted, echoing Joe's heartfelt wish. It was Ranna, pointing out the window. "They righted themselves! Thank God!" Her voice, deep and sensuous, showed no fear.

"Who cares about them? Those bastards ditched us! Now we're all gonna die!"

"Just depressurize now and be done with it, for God's sake!"

"How do we do that?"

"Just open the goddamn hatch! Kill us all at once!"

"Going to the desert after all!" Ranna cried. "Straight down to the desert! My home, after all of this! This entire life! *Bequeathed* to me! Churchill, I love you! Don't leave me!"

A cat floated off her lap in zero-G. Joe stared at the cat from CTESOPE. The cat that had followed him to Mars. *Churchill.* "Miaoooooww!"

Joe met Ranna Kikken's brown eyes. She was older; if she'd been forty-seven in May 2028, then she was now--well, it didn't matter. He was thirty-one, and ageless, and she was whatever she was, and ageless. He hauled himself across the last chair, wrenching away some babbling jerk next to her and taking his seat.

"Joe--" Ranna gasped.

"I came here to die with you," Joe said, hurling himself into her arms.

"I love you, Joe! You *are* the 2036 Joe, aren't you?"

"Yes, yes of course! I HTT'd back here! I came to die with you! I love you so much! I've never loved anyone else!"

A long kiss in which he could bury his soul in hers.

"I love you!" Ranna said. "I've waited all this time for you!"

"I have too! All my life, for this moment!"

Only now was he aware that the roaring shell was picking up a spin. As a pilot Joe had experienced far worse G forces, but he knew none of these people had.

And then the screaming stopped. The entire ship got quiet. Everyone listened to the screaming wind and felt the amusement ride build up.

"I don't think they're going to try to open the hatch after all," Ranna smiled.

"No, everyone knows it won't do any good."

"I know! But I love you. Dying doesn't really matter."

"And I love you. I've come to the end here, with you. I wish I could get us both out of here, but I guess this is our fate."

"I can accept that … just hold me."

I think it's a bit arrogant to assume you know what your fate will actually consist of.

"*What?*" Joe met the eyes of the floating gray cat pushed by building G-forces towards the window. "I'm reading Churchill's thoughts again! He thinks something, and I just *know* it! Just like Dar!"

"I don't know, but somehow he can radiate right into your mind!"

"Somehow he's Martian! He was on Mars without an EnviroField! How can he *smile?*" Joe pointed to Churchill's crooked grinning little mouth. "And what does he know about *fate?*"

Generally you only know fate as it unfolds in the present moment. You can't predict it. That's just an ego defense, the little gray cat continued to lecture, its big blue eyes filling with HTT Potential.

*

Wednesday, November 23, 2033

"Crap! What's this?" Joe moaned. Outside the window was a spaceport.

"We're still in the shell!" Ranna said. Above and below stretched endless latticework crammed with hundreds of anxious evacuees. "We're on the ground!"

"We're just on the launch pad! What if we're just trapped in a loop? The ship'll take off, and we'll be doomed to do the same thing for all eternity!"

"Wait, this isn't the same shell. The colors of the seats are different. I don't have the window seat, and you never had a seat!"

Joe peered out the window at slate-blue water. "This isn't New Mexico! It's Cape Kennedy!"

"MAY I HAVE YOUR ATTENTION PLEASE. THIS IS CAPTAIN ANSELM. WE'RE IN THE FINAL TWO MINUTES OF COUNTDOWN. SPACESHIP *MANDATE* WILL LIFT PASSENGER SHELL *CORSAIR V* INTO AN ORBIT AROUND EARTH, AND FROM THERE WE'LL HEAD DIRECTLY TO MARS IN A SIX-DAY FLIGHT. ON TAKEOFF, THERE WILL BE THREE GRAVITIES ACCELERATION, AND WE MAY ENCOUNTER SOME TURBULENCE ON THE WAY UP, AS OUTLINED IN YOUR BROCHURE. PLEASE DO NOT HESITATE TO ASK THE FLIGHT CREW ANY QUESTIONS. THANK YOU."

Ranna was in the seat next to the window seat, Joe to her right. Churchill came to Joe and settled in his lap. *Now this is what you could call fate,* Churchill radiated.

A man with long white hair in the window seat stared through the glass at the Cape Kennedy tarmac. His face was as white as his hair. "It's gonna *happen,*" he gasped. "We're gonna blow! After five damn years, we're finally gonna blow!"

"Urside!" Ranna cried.

"It's the guy from CTESOPE!" Joe said. "We've gone to his shell!"

"What's the date? *What's the date?* Oh, never mind, I know what it is! This is the twenty-third, and this ship is about to blow up on the pad!"

"Jeez, lady," said a man leaning back from the seat in front of them.

"I hoped all these years there'd be one final HTT," Urside muttered. "But I was right, there's some alternate universe where I *did* survive ... but not in *this* one."

"Urside, it's *me!* Ranna!"

"*Can't HTT!*"

The man in front leaned back again. "Can you shut that guy up? Everyone's anxious enough as it is without him yammering like that. He's been nuts all morning!"

"Urside, it's *me!* Don't you recognize me?"

Urside finally focused. "Ranna! You can't be here! You shouldn't have come to visit! Your flight's not until the twenty-sixth!"

"My shell broke off and I HTT'd here with Joe and Churchill!"

"Joe! Oh my God, you're the guy who crashed CTESOPE! You came here to die with me!"

"No, we're going to HTT you out of here!" Joe said. "All of us, together! We won't blow up!"

"I said *cut it,* dammit!" the man in front snarled.

"No, that's impossible! I did the last HTT possible for any human being five years ago!"

For the last time, Urside, they don't have to be in chronological order.

"*Churchill* …" Urside gasped. "*You're* here, too! You have the HTT Potential! I can feel it!"

Yes, but I will leave this HTT as an exercise for the student.

"You can't do that! I don't have any HTTs left!"

"Wait a second, I'm not feeling any Potential either," Joe complained.

From beneath them USS *Mandate's* engines cascaded into rough, deafening life.

Corsair V shook wildly. An eerie whine built amid the gasps of a thousand frightened passengers.

Time is pressing, Churchill thought.

"Dammit!" Urside snarled. "To come here, just to watch me die! It's disgusting! Why couldn't you just leave me alone?"

"You've been waiting five years for this woman! This *Alycia!*" Ranna cried. "I don't know how I know that!" She put a hand to her temple. "God, I feel so *strange.*"

"Are you all right?" Joe said. Then he was able to feel the information she was processing. And a date: September 17, 2038.

"Is that where we're going?" Joe yelled as rocket engines revved crazily beneath them. Docking clamps sprang open and *Corsair V* floated free, vibrating like an old grain elevator stuck to the side of nuclear spaceship *Mandate*. Acceleration built and Joe felt pressed into his seat.

"I've *tried* to be patient and brave," Urside moaned, "and I've failed! Failed!"

"Shut up! Do you want to marry this Alycia or not?" Ranna demanded. "She's waiting for you on September 17, 2038!"

Urside's mouth hung open. "He's completely zoned out!" Joe laughed. "C'mon, dude, *commit* to this woman!"

Ranna grabbed Churchill by his furry gray neck. "You silly thing! Making *me* have HTT Potential! Okay, I'll do the link!"

*

Friday, September 17, 2038

"Hey, this is sort of fun!" Ranna laughed into the tunnel. "But it sure takes a lot of energy! How many times can you do this before you wear out?"

Twenty-four of about eight thousand HTTs were yours, Churchill radiated. *You were--will be--instrumental in repairing the timeline. Don't worry, you'll never wear out.*

Joe grabbed Ranna's hand. Something big and red erupted far below, but the pressure and the heat never touched them as the four headed to Urside's wedding.

About the Author

Michael D. Smith was raised in the Northeast and the Chicago area, then moved to Texas to attend Rice University, where he began developing as a writer and visual artist. His Jack Commer, Supreme Commander science fiction series is published by Sortmind Press. In addition, Sortmind Press has published Smith's literary novels *Sortmind, The Soul Institute, CommWealth, Akard Drearstone,* and *Jump Grenade.* All titles are available from Amazon.

Smith's web site, https://sortmind.com, contains further examples of his novels and visual art, and he muses about writing and art processes at https://blog.sortmind.com/.

Amazon author page
https://www.amazon.com/author/smithmi/

The Jack Commer, Supreme Commander Series

The Martian Marauders
Jack Commer, Supreme Commander
Nonprofit Chronowar
Collapse and Delusion
The Wounded Frontier
The SolGrid Rebellion
Balloon Ship Armageddon